The *Cagliostro* Chronicles 2: Conflagration

By Ralph L. Angelo, Jr.

The Cagliostro Chronicles II: Conflagration
By Ralph L. Angelo Jr.
Cover by Gustav Barta
Edited by Tommy Hancock
Copyright 2014 by Ralph L. Angelo Jr
Published by Cosmic Comet Publishing

Contents

Dedicated in loving memory to my father,
Ralph L. Angelo Sr.
I miss hearing your voice, Dad.
10/2/32-12/15/13

Prologue

Warning! It is highly recommended that your read 'The Cagliostro Chronicles' (Book One in this series) before reading this novel.

What has gone before:

Twenty four months ago Mark Johnson, CEO of Johnson Aerospace as well as a brilliant engineer/scientist/inventor discovered the secret to piercing the light speed barrier, finally after many years of failures giving Earth its first faster than light ship, the *Cagliostro.*

But the *Cagliostro* and its crew were almost immediately attacked by shadowy forces; leading to the discovery of a long standing conspiracy by dark forces across the galaxies who sought to stifle the Earth's expansion and exploration into deep space. This led to the discovery that high ranking government officials around the globe were replaced by shape shifters as well as other monstrous beings specifically put in place to stop Earth's space faring vessels from ever leaving its solar system.

A war ensued with the denizens of the Earth alone against the forces of the Agalum Empire. Earth survived and won the first battles, its mighty space ships battling the Agalum to a standstill until Mark Johnson and the crew of the *Cagliostro* could deliver the final blow, saving the people of the Earth from subjugation and obliteration.

But that was only the first skirmish in what would become a long standing war across the stars themselves, with the very future of humanity at stake.

Chapter 1

The *Cagliostro* listed badly in space; plasma venting from its port tail. Nearby an Agalum ship floated, dead in space, its hull ruptured. Bodies floated through the void nearby it.

"How long until we can limp out of here?" Mark Johnson shouted into the microphone built into his command chair.

"Not as fast as I'd like, that's fer sure," Dan Sledge's voice replied over the comm.

Mark punched the arm of his command chair and cursed.

"Mark, we need you to be the captain now." Ariel O'Connor grasped his arm while speaking to him, driving her point home.

"Don't worry, Ari, I am and will be. I'll get us out of this yet."

James 'Red' Robinski suddenly turned from his console and shouted, "We have incoming. Two ships, both two man fighters on an intercept course with us."

"Eddie, do we have weapons?"

Eddie DiGenovese spun and shook his head negatively, "Not yet, Boss."

"Crap," Mark muttered under his breath. He rose from his chair and headed toward the maglovator door. "I'm going down to help Danny. We'll be out of this in a few minutes. Eddie, do whatever you have to to buy us some time."

Eddie nodded grimly and nervously saluted.

The maglovator door hissed close and Mark commented to himself, "Now I know we're in trouble, Eddie isn't making a wise crack. Great."

Mark exited on the engineering deck and made directly for Dan Sledge.

The two men were almost polar opposites in looks. Mark was six foot two with his longish brown hair wavy, almost to his collar. He walked with an almost feline grace and power to his steps. He was average weight but well-muscled, looking almost like a jet setting playboy instead of a genius inventor and trillionaire CEO.

Dan Sledge, definitely Marks right hand man, was another case altogether. He was six feet tall, but built like a rhinoceros. He was stocky and broad shouldered. His muscles bulged beneath his tight fitting silver and blue tech suit that all of the crew wore. His face was wide and flat, and his close cropped brown hair had an almost military look to it.

Sledge was a genetically enhanced former Jupiter colony member. He was brought up on one of the giant planets floating gas mining stations; just to live there required genetic alteration to survive the crushing gravity. His strength was ridiculously impressive. Two years ago at the start of the war against the Agalum he had hefted a forty ton nuke and carried it to an airlock before tossing it untold miles in airless space toward its destination.

But these two men, as well as the rest of the command crew, were as close as family.

"What's goin' on, Boss? What're you doing down here?" Sledge asked. He was kneeling on the ground in

4

front of an access panel, and had to look up at Mark to speak to him.

Engineers and other personnel hustled about behind the two men, while two other members of the engineering staff joined them at the sub panel. Sparks flew from it, but Sledge ignored them, working in their midst.

"Things are getting a little intense topside, so I figured I'd come down here and hide from it all," Mark replied with a straight face.

"Grab a spanner and those insulated long reach spreader pliers. I need ya ta hold those two sections of the power coupling cable apart while I install a new one."

"All right, Danny," Mark replied.

The ship shook and both men stopped what they were doing and looked up, toward the command deck.

"Uh oh," Sledge muttered.

"Forget it for now." Mark ordered, "Let's get this thing fixed so we can fight back at least."

Again the ship rocked, this time more violently. The two techs with Mark and Dan looked at each other silently and nervously.

"What's goin' on up there, Mark?" Dan worked as sparks flew about, burning his hands. He continued to ignore them. Mark held the power cables apart while Dan quickly and faultlessly worked.

"Oh, just two Agalum two man fast attack ships trying to blow us all straight to hell, that's all."

"The hull holding okay?"

"It's fifty feet thick and armored all around. That doesn't mean it will hold forever. But for now it's good."

"That's comfortin' ta know."

"How are you doing in there?" Mark asked.

"Almost done. Hang on, Boss."

"Okay. I can't see a thing with your big head in the way."

Dan chuckled. "You always say the nicest things ta me."

Again the ship rocked and now sirens blared.

"Uh oh," one of the techs muttered.

Over the intercom Ariel O'Conner's voice announced, "Hull breach on deck ten. Clear deck ten immediately. Repeat, hull breach on deck ten. Clear deck ten immediately."

"That ain't good," Dan announced quietly.

"Can't worry about it now." Mark replied, "The *Cagliostro* has been through hell recently. We have to get back to Earth for refits."

"No kiddin'."

A last blast of coruscating sparks showered over Dan's shoulders. He quickly backed away, turned to Mark and said, "All done! Get us outta here!"

Mark keyed the communicator built into the cuff on the right sleeve of his tech suit and then spoke, "Get us out of here, now!"

Instantly the hyper-warp engines returned to life, their low hum winding up steadily and quickly in a rising crescendo that rang throughout the great ship; then in a burst of light, the *Cagliostro* leaped away from its attackers.

Both men ran toward the maglovator while the two techs finished closing up the panel behind them.

Less than a minute later they were on the command deck and a young pilot named Samuels stood and exited the pilot's station, leaving it to Dan.

Mark took the command chair behind the row of command deck stations.

"Shields?" he asked.

"Fifty five percent and climbing," Red answered.

"Double rear power while the magno discs charge up to full potential." Mark ordered.

Red nodded in agreement. If Dan looked like a rhinoceros, Red looked a lion. He was brawny and solid. He spent two hours every day in a regimented work out. One hour working his muscles, another hour practicing various martial arts. He was a grim faced man who rarely smiled. His close cropped red hair was shorter than Dan's. He stood six feet four inches, and while not as wide as Dan, he was more precisely and perfectly muscled. He looked like a red headed Hercules.

Red was a tough guy who took his business seriously. He liked his job as security officer aboard the *Cagliostro*, and he liked his friends on the ship more. But at the moment, he didn't like what he saw on the sensor array before the ship.

"We've got company." Red Growled.

"What? More of it?" Eddie asked, wide eyed and surprised.

"Yeah," Reed replied, "two medium sized Agalum ships are ahead of us. They're vectoring for a strafing run."

"Shields front," Mark ordered. "Where the hell did they come from?"

Red complied immediately. An instant later glowing balls of energy sparked across the shields, fired from the enemy vessels. The *Cagliostro* rocked with each impact.

"Return fire," Mark commanded, "solar canons at one hundred percent, followed by a brace of star core missiles."

"The two behind us just caught up," Red advised.

"Of course they did," Mark grumbled. "Status?"

"Not good. They're trying to take out our main engines. Shields are holding, but not for much longer, and those engines are beginning to vent plasma to space." Red informed them all.

Mark snapped his fingers. "That's it! Drop out of hyper-warp, now."

"Are you nuts?" Red yelled. "We'll be sitting ducks."

"No, we're about to win. Drop out of hyper-warp and immediately vent all the cooling plasma from magno-disc number one." Mark replied.

"We won't be able to get to full hyper warp on only one disc, you know," Dan offered.

"I know but we're about to be trashed if we don't do this. It's four against one. This is our only way out."

Dan shrugged his mammoth shoulders. "You're the Boss."

He dropped the ship out of hyper-warp and immediately dropped all the plasma from the right side magno disc's storage cell, leaving a sparkling trail, many miles wide behind them in deep space.

"The two in front of us overshot us when we dropped out of hyper-warp," Red announced.

"I thought as much," Mark replied. He leaned forward and held his chin while in deep thought. "Viewer on rear."

Instantly the view on the screen at the head of the command deck changed to the rear of the ship. The ejected trail of plasma floated miles behind them while the four pursuing ships flew through it, seeking to gain on the *Cagliostro*.

Mark grinned, then said, "Okay they're all in and making a bee-line for us, Eddie, fire it up, *now!*"

Eddie did not hesitate, firing the two working rear solar cannons into the cloud of flammable plasma. It exploded instantly. The rear view was immediately a pure white field of destruction, while the *Cagliostro*'s monitors instantly compensated for the brightness of the explosion, dimming the scene.

But the *Cagliostro* shuddered violently, the crew actually thrown from their seats within the command deck.

"What happened?" Ariel asked.

"Dammit!" swore Red, "the burning plasma trail led right back to our fuel tanks. If we didn't have safeties in place the whole ship would've gone up."

"But it didn't Red, just like I knew it wouldn't. I designed this ship, remember?"

Mark paused for a moment and then asked, "Status report?" as the ship finally stopped shaking.

"All four of those ships are disabled at least. I'm measuring life signs, but that's about it," Red replied.

"What about us?" Ariel asked.

"We need engine repairs or we're never going to make it home again," Dan announced stoically.

"Are there any Earth-like planets in this system?" Mark inquired.

"One," Red answered with his usual enthusiasm. "Looks uninhabited too."

Mark nodded slowly. "Make for it. We need repairs."

"I just hope I can get us back into space once we land," Dan grumbled quietly.

"If not we'll just have to start building some log cabins," Eddie replied, smirking.

"You're not really that funny, ya know that, DiGenovese?" Red growled.

Eddie began to answer then closed his mouth, having thought better of it.

The *Cagliostro* limped across the alien solar system they found themselves in, trailing plasma from the damaged engine as well as a trail of particles from the damaged rear cannon.

"How much longer?" Mark asked grimly.

"An hour, maybe two," Dan replied. "Our speed's not exactly constant. The engines heat up, I have to shut 'em down. We coast for a while. Things cool off, I fire 'em up again."

Mark sighed. "All right, Danny. Do what you must. Get us down there safely so we can start repairs."

"Mark," Ariel began, "should I send out an emergency beacon?"

"No, there are too many Agalum ships around this system."

"Are they going to be able to follow our trail?" Eddie questioned.

"Possibly, but it can't be helped. That plasma should dissolve in a few hours. If no ships pass through here we'll be okay. If they do, we may have more trouble. Just get us down there as soon as possible, Dan. Once the engines are fixed we're bee lining it for Earth."

***

An hour and a half later the *Cagliostro* began its descent toward the unknown world below.

"Main stabilizers are at forty percent power, Boss. This is gonna be a rough landin'," said Dan.

Mark gripped his chin pensively.

"Understood." He replied quietly.

The *Cagliostro* began to skim the atmosphere until it slowly dipped beneath it.

"Hull temperature is climbing, but shields are holding, as is hull integrity," Dan announced.

Mark nodded.

The *Cagliostro* shook as it nosed deeper into and began bouncing off of the atmosphere.

"Whoa, what's with the rough ride?" Eddie hung on tight to his chair and console nervously.

"Keep yer yap shut, pipsqueak," Dan growled. "I'm concentratin' on keepin' us in one piece."

Mark leaned forward. "Dan, any spots that you would recommend landing on so far?"

"I see one close to our general vicinity, a few hundred miles off that's accessible and has some cover for the ship."

"Good," Mark nodded. "I want the ship to be hidden. If there are some sort of life forms here, they don't have to know they have visitors."

The *Cagliostro* rocked again, causing breaths to be sharply in taken, and grips to be tightened. The ship began to slow, its skin shunting heat from entering the planet's atmosphere.

Finally mere feet above the planet's surface, the *Cagliostro*'s nose rose up in a stall-like maneuver and the ship hovered above a lush valley of dense growth. In the midst of the valley was a deep ravine with many overhanging trees.

Mark pointed at a spot on his personal holographic view screen on his console. Instantly the image was transferred to the main viewer as well as the smaller personal viewers across the command deck. "Enter there, clear any trees in the center with the solar cannons," Mark ordered.

"What about indigenous life?" Ariel asked.

"I'm not picking up anything close by, Boss," Red replied. "It looks like there may be some bird or serpent-like creatures out there at the edge of the valley, but they're already scurrying away from us."

"Good," Mark commented, "Take those trees down ASAP."

Eddie nodded and fired the forward cannons in one blast, instantly clearing a space almost eight hundred feet wide beneath the immensely tall canopy of trees. "That should work, boss. There're still enough of these trees bent and overhanging the forest floor from above to keep us hidden, even though I turned a lot of 'em to kindling."

"Good job, Eddie." Mark acknowledged. Then he turned toward his pilot and said, "Take us in, Dan,"

The big man nodded, and hovered the ship into place beneath the lush growth that surrounded them. The ship settled down with a gentle thud.

"We have a lot of burning foliage out there, Mark," Red proclaimed.

Mark nodded "Release the flame retardant foam, ten thousand gallons should do it."

"Ten thousand gallons it is, Sir," Red replied.

"I want life scans done immediately. No one leaves the ship until I'm certain it's safe. We may be here a while. I don't want any surprises." Mark turned to Dan. Let's get to work."

The two men left the command deck together.

Chapter 2

Dan and Mark along with a crew of ten men labored nonstop to repair the damage done to the ship in the extended battle they had just come through. Internal systems were being repaired and rerouted by the hard working.

Mark, Dan and their repair crew were huddled together in one of the magno-disc conduits working within the tight confines. After many moments of silence Dan turned to Mark, and wiped sweat from his brow before speaking, "Hey Boss, I know we gotta get off this mud ball, but uh, we should take a break sooner than later ya know? We been at this fer what, fifteen hours now?"

Mark looked at his holographic chrono; a holographic watch of sorts that popped up on his blue and silver tech suit's sleeve and sighed, nodding in agreement. "You're right, Danny. We both need a break. In fact the rest of this crew does too." Mark looked at the rest of the people working with him and Dan, and then continued, "I'm sorry, all of you. I had no idea that much time had passed. But I want this magno-disc repair to continue. Get a second crew on, this Danny, and then go get some shut eye. You are right though; we have been at this far too long. Have the second crew logged in for an eight hour shift. After that we'll replace them again, that is if the repairs aren't completed at that point."

"What about you Mark?"

"I'm going to do the same. Between our narrow escape and our wonderful landing here, well, we're lucky we made it this far."

"Worst part of all of this is we ain't that far from home, at least not in hyper-warp terms," Dan commented.

"I know. We're what? A day at most?"

"Yeah. About that, Boss. Without hyper-warp we might as well be forty years away."

"I know, Danny, I know. We took some bad damage here. How are the repairs on deck nine going?"

"It was deck ten, not nine, an' they're finally nearin' the halfway point. But the crew's gonna have to go outside to finish them up."

"Deck ten, that's right." Mark shook his head in consternation.

"Hey you okay, Boss?" Dan asked quietly so as to not alert those nearby.

"Yes, Danny, I'm okay. Just getting bleary eyed from all of this." He waved his hand about him at the damaged engine components. "What about replacement parts? How's the fabrication lab doing?"

"I'll call 'em, Boss. In fact I'll stop in on deck six before I get some rest just to make sure they're on track."

Mark nodded. "Good. Get that second crew in here, and then go get some rest yourself. I'm getting to the point that I can't think straight."

Mark rose from his crouched position and patted Dan on the shoulder, then limped off toward the maglovator.

Dan watched him disappear into the sliding doors, then turned back to his crew. "Okay I'm going to call in a replacement crew now. You guys go get some rest, you've earned it."

"Thank you, Sir," was muttered over and over again by the bone weary group.

Dan touched the sleeve of his jacket once again, connecting to the communications web aboard the ship. "Sledge to engineering lab, I need a replacement crew on deck seven immediately to continue engine repairs. I'm awaiting their arrival."

***

Mark arrived at his quarters and walked in. The room was empty. *'Where's Ari?'* he thought silently. He tapped his sleeve once more. "Johnson to communications."

A young woman's voice replied, "This is communications, Miss Wallflower speaking." Mark knew who she was and besides her rather comical last name she was the model of efficiency and decorum. She stood five feet five inches tall with long brown hair. She was pretty and she did a good job. "Miss Wallflower, where is Miss O'Connor?"

"Miss O'Connor is outside the ship with the survey team Sir, reconnoitering the area."

He cursed quietly under his breath. "Get me a direct link to her please."

"Will do, Sir," Wallflower replied.

An instant later Wallflower called him again. "Sir, I have Miss O'Connor."

"Very well, Miss Wallflower, thank you." Mark paused a second until he heard a faint beep from his suits sleeve, then he asked, "Ari, what are you doing? I told you to stay on the command deck."

"Mark, everything's fine. I just wanted to get off the ship for a few minutes, that's all. I'm out here breathing the fresh air. There's a science team with me looking over the flora and fauna. I have to say it's surprisingly Earth-like."

"That's not a bad thing," he shrugged. "What about life signs, did we pick any up?"

"No one is sure. They're picking something up, but it's muted or masked."

"What's doing that and is it natural?"

"Unknown, Mark."

Mark paced about his room a second in thought then added, "Okay, how about you getting back up here and joining me while I get Monroe out there to head up the investigation."

"I beat ya to it, tough guy. Monroe is with me already looking into things. She says it's going to be a while before anything concrete is decided."

"All right. I'll call her when I click off with you. Now come back inside, please?"

"Okay party pooper, will do."

"Good. I'll talk to you in a minute."

He clicked his shirt sleeve above his wrist once more and said, "Madison Monroe."

Instantly a rather pleasant female voice replied, "Madison Monroe here."

"Madison, this is Mark Johnson. I want you and your team to stay close to the ship. If you find anything troublesome or in any way dangerous I want you all back inside here pronto, understand?"

"Yes Sir, I got it."

"Good, be careful out there, Madison."

"Will do, Sir," came her curt reply.

Mark disconnected the contact. But almost instantly the comm unit within his shirt sleeve pulsed light softly and buzzed quietly. He tapped it again and saw Ariel's name appear in a hologram above his right arm.

He tapped his sleeve once more. "What is it, Ari? Are you back on board yet?"

"Nope," her voice replied. "I had a better idea. How about you come out and visit me out here? It's kind of nice out here. Serene even."

"Ariel…" he began, instantly annoyed. He had been on edge for days, weeks even, and this was not helping.

"Hey tough guy, how about just coming outside and taking a few deep breaths? The air is safe and clean. We all double checked, and it's kinda nice out here. Relaxing even. Come out for ten minutes, then we can both go back inside. You'll like it out here, I promise."

Mark shook his head angrily, then deflated slightly, his head sinking into his chest. After a moment he finally replied, "All right Ari, I'm on my way. But all I'm giving you is ten minutes, got it?"

"Got it, Boss," she acknowledged mischievously.

***

A few minutes later, Mark exited the *Cagliostro* and found Ariel waiting for him at the boarding ramp.

"Well? What do you think?"

"About what?" he answered.

"This place, what do you think I meant? It's amazing isn't it?"

He glared at her, annoyed, and then began to look around, taking a deep breath cautiously before exhaling and taking a second. He listened closely and heard all manner of winged creatures calling to each other in hoots and whistles, as they flew overhead. The foliage was thick, so thick it almost blocked out the sun.

"This place is a jungle," he announced to no one in particular.

Overhead unseen birds flew past calling to each other somewhere beyond the verdant tree tops.

After a moment he called back to Ariel. "So no one has discovered if there's any intelligent life here yet?"

"Well…" she began, "I think there may be more than meets the eye here, but for some reason my telepathy is not getting a solid feel on anyone, or anything but I sense they are here. It's just as if they are intentionally blocking me."

"That's new."

"Yes it is, and it's a little annoying."

"I believe it." He smiled and put his arm around her, pulling her close. They walked over to the landing gear and sat with their backs against it.

"Not the most comfortable of back rests, but not that terrible either," Mark noted.

"It's better than a rock somewhere." Ariel turned and looked him in the eyes and smiled. "How are the repairs going?"

He felt himself relax immediately.

Mark returned her smile. As he looked into her eyes, he felt himself unwinding like a spring being released after far too long. The tension seemed to drain from him, at least for now.

"Slowly. We took a lot of damage. We got battered."

"But don't forget," she held a finger up and wagged it, "we still won."

"You and I would not be alive to have this conversation right now if we hadn't," Mark nodded grimly, a knowing smile on his face.

Johnson leaned back and looked around, studying the dense foliage that lay just beyond the ship. "So what do you think, Ari? Is whatever's out there intelligent? Or just some animal form of life?"

Almost as if on cue, a team of scientists suddenly broke through the foliage running for the ship, hands in the air and shouting unintelligibly. Mark and Ari were on their feet immediately.

"Whoa, WHOA!" Mark repeated himself holding his arms out to stop the running team of scientists.

"G-get back onboard the ship!" one man stammered as he pushed Mark out of his way, practically frothing at the mouth.

Another shouted as he brushed past, "It's coming! Run!"

Mark turned and shoved Ari behind him, onto the entry ramp. He pulled his blaster in a lightning quick move. "Ari, are you getting anything?"

He knew she was already using her telepathic abilities to search for whatever mind out there was coming this way fast.

"Yes!" She practically shouted, "But it's not human. It's some kind of beast. It's all emotion and rage, and it's very angry right now."

An Earthshaking roar punctuated her sentence as both of them turned their heads toward the sound. They slowly backed up the ramp. Mark tapped the cuff of his right sleeve. "Red, you better get a security team out here quick."

"What's going on?" Red replied instantly.

"The Sci-guys pissed something off, and it sounds like it was something big. It's definitely heading our way!"

Another roar, closer, reverberated about them all.

"On our way, Boss," Red replied.

"Mark," Ari began, "how tall do you reckon those trees are?"

"Well, we're beneath the tree cover and the Cag is two hundred fifty feet tall from bottom hull to top hull. Add another fifteen feet of landing gear..." he trailed off.

The trees shook with each successive roar, until suddenly they split apart, as two tremendous hands reached through them first and then shredded them like kindling to get them out of the way.

A creature pulled itself forth. Standing almost a hundred feet tall, it stared down at them and bellowed its rage once again. Its huge belly sloshed from one side to the other, and its hairy paws crushed trees as if they were toothpicks.

"It's an ape," Ariel muttered in surprise.

Red and his crew of ten men exited the ship at the same time the huge creature appeared, weapons already aimed and ready. Its arms hung to the ground and its face was oddly shaped. Its head was a 'V' shape, with widely set apart eyes. Its most surprising feature was the color of the beast. Its fur was a bright red. It stood up fully and bellowed once again, then began to approach the *Cagliostro*, rage spilling over its countenance with each successive ear-splitting bellow!

Chapter 3

The towering monster roared once more and then heaved itself forward toward the *Cagliostro*. Without hesitation, the ten man security detail along with Mark and Red began firing their blasters at the behemoth.

The monster swung its arms back and forth as if it were trying to clear a pack of mad insects from its body.

"All this firepower, it's like we're just stinging it," Red shouted over the din.

"Yes, I know," Mark answered. He touched his cuff once again. "Eddie! Shields up and prepare the forward solar cannon."

Eddies voice played over everyone's suit comm. "You all better get back in here then and fast. If I fire that cannon-"

"I know all about the distinct possibility of radiation burns and everything else that goes along with it. I designed the damned thing. Just get ready to fire it, and get those shields up now," Mark reiterated.

Mark turned back to the security team that was still firing on the huge brute. "Back inside guys, everyone now, that includes you, Red."

"After you Boss man." Red replied.

'Both of you get inside now!' Ariel's mental voice shouted within the confines of both men's minds, doubling them over.

Mark rose up first and turned toward Ariel. She expected him to be angry but he was just the opposite. He smiled almost giddily and "Do that to that thing over there." He pointed at the brute now pounding on the force shield. Each strike of its fists sent sparks showering across the shield.

Ariel looked at the creature, then at Mark.

"Do it, Ari. Let's see if we can drive it off without hurting it."

She looked at him incredulously, then nodded slowly. "I'll try, but it's a really primitive creature." Ari turned back and stared at the monster hammering relentlessly at the ships invisible shields.

Almost immediately the monster grasped at its head and doubled over in much the same manner Mark and Red had a moment earlier. It took a step backward, then another. Each time it held its head but then released and tried to step back toward the ship. Each time it would act as if it were in deeper pain.

Finally the monster turned and thundered off into the forest, smashing trees aside and leaving a singular path of destruction in its wake with each step.

"You did it, Ari!" Mark turned back to his girlfriend, who suddenly appeared woozy and in danger of falling. Both Mark and Red caught her simultaneously.

"Whoa there, Ari," Red soothed. "We gotcha."

"Th-thanks, boys. I got a little lightheaded there, that's all."

"Don't worry about it, honey. We'll help you in the rest of the way," Mark reassured.

The two men looked at each other, worry etched upon their faces.

"Boys, I'm a telepath, remember? I know what you're both thinking. Just help me inside and let me rest a while. I'll be fine."

"Okay, Ari, here we go," Mark gently replied.

A horrible bellow shook the trees about the *Cagliostro*. Both men turned back toward the path the ape had taken, only to see it thundering back toward them, a tremendous boulder held above its head. It stopped short of the shield and hurled the huge rock, smashing it into the invisible shield. Once more the creature roared its defiance and flung itself at the shields, hammering at them repeatedly.

Both men looked at each other and rushed up the ramp.

"Eddie," Mark shouted, knowing the maglovator's comm system would instantly connect him to the command deck, "Fire at will. We tried to be nice, but this is getting ridiculous."

"You got it, Chief," came DiGenovese's reply.

The instant the doors opened to the command deck Eddie was aiming and firing on the brutish monster, blasting holes in the ground at the thing's feet, knocking it to the ground almost instantly.

The huge red furred ape backed up slowly as Eddie continued to fire. The barrage opened up one crater after another in the ground, forcing the hundred foot tall ape to run away into the forest and disappear.

"Nice shooting, Eddie, but if it comes back again, put a hole in its chest we could fly the *Stargrazer* through," Mark said.

DiGenovese nodded. "You got it, Boss."

Mark turned to his security chief. "Red, take Ari to sick bay."

"What?" She shouted while jumping to her feet, immediately becoming light headed.

"Whoa." Ari held her head and staggered.

"Red," Mark insisted, "take her down there please. I don't care if you have to toss her over a shoulder to do so."

"You got it, Boss," Red replied as he picked up Ari across his burly arms and carried her into the maglovator. She stared angry daggers at Mark. He shrugged in reply, and then thought, *'Sorry, Ari, but I want you checked out. I never saw you hurt that badly after using your powers.'*

She grunted angrily in mental reply, then said nothing more.

"Boss!" shouted Eddie. "We got company."

"What, is King Kong back?" Mark turned toward the view screen to see what Eddie was talking about and froze.

Outside surrounding the ship and trying to punch their way through the defense shields were at least a hundred men, all naked to the waist, war paints covering their faces. They held spears, crude swords and even cruder bows and arrows.

But the most disconcerting thing was the color of their flesh.

"These guys are as red as that ape-thing was," Eddie proclaimed.

"Yes, they are. And I swear that war paint is some sort of glow in the dark thing. Look at the way it kind of shines when they enter the shadow of the ship." Mark commented.

"I'm getting the feeling this is one heck of a weird planet. Giant apes, fire engine red natives. What else can happen here?" Eddie added.

As if in reply the natives suddenly backed away from the ship aiming their crude weapons up and gibbering to each other fearfully.

Red re-entered the command deck from the maglovator.

"Everything okay with Ari?" Mark asked.

"Doc Troiano's looking her over now," Red replied.

Mark nodded. "Red, outside sound on. I want to know what they are afraid of and give me a view above the ship as well."

"You got it, Mark," the burly security man replied.

Instantly the view switched and they saw something descending out of the sky, claws outstretched, reaching for the natives below.

"Is that a-"

"Yes, it's a Pterodactyl, or what would pass for one on this crazy world, Eddie," Mark finished.

The leather skinned avian creature flapped massive wings and dove down toward the natives. The prehistoric seeming beast flew down like a giant bird of prey; it's leathery wings and cruelly shaped mouth with its razor sharp teeth instilled instant fear into the natives. Its bone ridge upon its skull was the first thing to slam into the invisible force shield that surrounded the ship.

The dinosaur-like creature was instantly stunned. It dropped to the ground, dead weight. Without hesitation the natives were upon it tearing into it with their knives and spears.

Everyone watched silently while the natives hacked at, and eventually killed the creature and then stripped its carcass in minutes.

"Something's not right here," Mark commented in a low voice.

"What?" Eddie asked.

"Think about it. They had no fear of us at all. They pounded on our force shields, but withdrew in fear at that thing's coming."

"Well maybe it was because they didn't know what we were?" Eddie offered.

"No. They attacked with a small army. There was a hundred men there. The ship's sensors confirmed that. I have a sneaking suspicion they thought they recognized us." Mark continued.

"That don't sound good. We've never been here before."

"No, Eddie, we haven't. But maybe someone else with a shiny metal ship was."

"Sometimes, Mark," Red commented, "you scare me." He shook his head and stared at the screens on his console.

"What, you disagree?"

"No, it's not that. Your logic is usually flawless and this is no exception. I can't argue with you at all. You're probably right. These guys saw a shiny ship hidden here and attacked it. What do you think made them search us out?"

"What else? The King Kong wannabe. He ran from us. Think about that. They had to know something deadly was down this way, but what would make an ape run like that? It was either something that was an unknown that they wanted to investigate, or something that drove off the ape before."

"Like another ship," Eddie chimed in.

"Yeah, that's about right, Eddie," Mark affirmed.

A familiar voice intruded upon their conversation from the inter-ship comm. "Mark? This is Troiano. I need you in medical immediately."

Mark looked at Eddie and Red, then got up and walked toward the maglovator. "Red, you're in charge here until I get back. If those pests outside start becoming a problem again or if 'Mighty Joe Stupid' returns, let me know."

"Will do, Mark. Go take care of Ari."

Mark nodded without looking back while the maglovator door hummed closed behind him.

He ran down the hall toward the medical bay and tapped his sleeve once again. "Dan, status?" Instantly the communications array forwarded his call to Dan Sledge who was working on the main engines with a crew.

"Still workin' on it, Bossman. Things are coming along but it's slow goin'."

"Are we able to get off the ground if we had to right now?"

"Oh yeah, Mark, that's not a problem, but we'll never be able to make hyper-warp. We're workin' to rectify that situation though."

"Any idea how much longer?"

"Could be hours, could be a week. The machine shop and electronics lab are makin' replacement parts as fast as possible, but if we need any raw materials, we'll have to go out and dig 'em up."

Mark sighed resignedly. "All right, Dan. Let me know what I can do."

"Will do Mark. Sledge out."

Mark turned a corner and entered the medical lab as the conversation ended.

Dr. Troiano, a small attractive woman with long brown hair, stood tapping her foot with her arms crossed as she looked at Ariel, who was lying on a gurney. Troiano was a pretty woman with a sort of impish quality about her when she relaxed and smiled. She was not smiling. She looked down her nose above the glasses she wore and stared at Mark.

"Your girlfriend is not taking this very seriously and her situation is anything *but* not serious."

"Whoa, Ann, what are you talking about? Take a step backward and fill me in."

"Ariel here has bleeding on the brain. If this is not taken care of immediately she could be in big trouble, Captain Johnson."

Mark knew the severity of the situation immediately. Troiano never called him 'Captain Johnson' unless things were deadly serious.

"What does she need? Surgery?"

"No one is cutting my head open!" Ariel shouted.

Mark walked over to Ariel and put his hands on her shoulders. "Relax, Ari. Let Ann talk. Go ahead, Doctor."

"Thank you, Captain Johnson," Ann Troiano replied, "No, she does not need surgery, yet. She has to lay off using her special powers at least for a few days. Whatever she used her telepathy on must have had a much different brain than she did. Not more advanced or more intelligent, but more raw or primitive. She stressed out her brain trying to reach this thing. What was it?"

Mark looked at Ariel, who motioned with her hand that he should go ahead and tell Troiano.

Mark sighed again and screwed the corner of his mouth up. "It was a sort of ape or gorilla. It was about a hundred feet high, and its head had a V-shape to it."

Troiano threw her hands in the air and looked at the ceiling in angry surprise "Are you kidding me? She wanted to talk psychically with this thing? Hey here's an idea, in the future, blow a hole in its chest if it's attacking us." She turned toward Ari. "You better take this seriously. You may have one hell of a gift there, but if you do not watch it and tread carefully from now on, you could end up either dead or without your gift permanently."

Ariel looked at the floor and answered in a voice slightly above a whisper. "I think that happened already."

"What? What are you talking about?" Mark asked anxiously.

Ariel locked eyes with him and continued, "I-I can't hear anyone's thoughts at all. I always had the ability to hear people's thoughts all the time, not really listen in, but I always psychically heard this background noise, a sort of dull murmur that I learned how to tune out. I can't hear it in my head anymore."

"Since when?" Mark asked cautiously.

"It started when I almost fell on the ramp coming back on the ship. I still heard your mental 'voice' on the command deck but everything has gradually gone quiet

33

in my mind. For the first time in my life I can't hear others thoughts. Mark, it was almost an empathic feeling I would get. But now it's all gone. I feel so…alone." She looked up into his eyes, questing for answers.

Mark hugged her and let her rest her head on his shoulder.

"Doctor, I'm leaving her to you. Ariel, you have to listen to Ann. She knows what's best. Doctor, put her in one of the private suites here."

"I already planned that, Mark." The fact that Troiano had not called him 'Captain' once again did not go unnoticed to Mark Johnson. Immediately he relaxed, a little at least.

"This is my fault, you know," Mark spat out. "I ordered Ari to make the ape go. I made her attempt to contact it."

"Well, next time you'll know better, won't you?" Ann Troiano looked at Mark and softened when she saw the pain in his eyes. "Go get some rest, Mark. You look like hell. We need you operating at one hundred percent as much as we need the ship to. Don't worry about, Ari. I've got her under my watchful eye, and I promise you, she'll be all right. Now go get some rest, you big galoot." She gently shoved him out the medical lab's sliding glass doors.

Mark turned back and nodded to both Troiano and Ariel, then turned and headed back toward the maglovator.

Mark walked in silent contemplation. Ariel meant the world to him, though he rarely told her. The past two years had been a hell of another sort, with the constant back and forth fighting between the Earth and its

34

stripling space fleet and the Agalum race and their many galaxy spanning fleet of vessels.

Earth was outgunned, but the saving grace of it all was that the Agalum and their allies had all grown fat and lazy over the centuries, more than content in their power. As far as they were concerned no one, no race on any planet, could stand up to them.

Until they somehow discovered the Earth over a century ago, what they had seen in mankind was a predator that was not to be underestimated. But they did just that. They underestimated mankind and sought to curtail man's hunger for exploration of the depths of space. For many years their plan worked.

For over a century the Agalum conspiracy had worked surreptitiously to undermine Earth's space program. Presidents were replaced with shape shifters who did everything they could to destroy the space program. Ships were destroyed and astronauts died under mysterious circumstances. Finally the space program ended up being farmed out to the private sector over the years, and NASA became nothing more than an organization of space traffic controllers.

The accidents continued to happen even with the private companies taking over the space program, but now there were many companies to watch over by mankind's secretive opponent as opposed to one. Their plan had backfired against them. There were too many corporations with too many different ways of doing business in too many different facilities across the globe to keep track of, and to secretly undermine. Men like Mark Johnson came along and began to make strides.

Space became accessible, but only to what astronauts and explorers would term as 'locally'.

The enemy must have settled for this after a time because things seemed to even out. At least until Mark discovered through countless hours of seemingly eternal testing the way to break down the light speed barrier.

As per usual with Mark Johnson, not only did he break the faster than light barrier, but he did it in such a way that his ship was the fastest ship anywhere.

'They waited too long.' Mark mused silently as he entered the maglovator. *'They should have been more concerned with updating their own star faring vehicles instead of trying to curtail our efforts.'*

A moment later he exited the maglovator and re-entered the command deck, "Status update?" he asked Red Robinski.

"Unchanged, Mark. How's Ari?"

Eddie turned and looked at Mark also, wanting to hear how Ariel was doing himself.

Mark cocked his head sideways and shook it slowly. "Not great. She has bleeding on the brain."

"What?" Eddie asked, his face belying his shock.

"Troiano says she'll be okay, she thinks, but she wants her resting for at least several days. The worst part of this is it seems that Ari has already lost her powers. She claims she hasn't been able to use her abilities since the ape attacked."

He sat down in his command chair and shook his head side to side slowly, biting his lower lip before continuing, "I can't believe I made her attack the ape that way."

"You can't blame yourself Mark. Who could have known?" Red offered.

"I know. You're right, Red. But it's hard not to take the blame for this. It was my blunder, and it may cost her permanently."

A mechanized voice blared over the conference room comm, jarring them all from their conversation. "Intruder alert, Intruder alert."

"What the hell?" Mark jumped from his seat and stared at the view screen. Most of the natives were gone.

"Where'd they go?" Mark questioned.

"Behind that treeline." Red replied, pointing at the viewscreen.

Mark spun toward Red, "And what could they have been doing while out of your sight?"

Red grimaced, his face turning the color of his nickname, "They dug tunnels."

"They tunneled beneath us? Who fell asleep on the job and did not see that?" Mark shouted angrily, "Wake up Robinski. It's your job to watch out for stuff like this."

"Intruder alert, intruder alert," continued to blare annoyingly over the comm.

"Find the intruders now!" Mark snapped.

"Got 'em," replied Red sheepishly.

"Coming up the gangplank into the ship slowly and carefully five of them."

"Lori," Mark turned to a young red head who sat at the comm station where Ariel normally sat, "turn off that damned alert. Red, show these newcomers our hospitality we reserve for invaders."

"You got it, Boss." Red thumbed a button on his virtual console. The image of the walkway leading to the outside on the gangplank filled with gas. Instantly the invaders dropped to the floor unconscious.

"Red, get a security team to take them all to cells on the detention level. Obviously relieve them all of their weapons, and post a team on the ramp outside. If anyone else comes out of those holes shoot them." Mark paused a moment, then added, "But only to stun. Don't kill them, unless it's a life threatening situation. Then do whatever you have to."

Red nodded stoically. "Understood, Mark."

"Good. Let me know when you get them secured. I want to have a talk with our guests when they wake up."

Red nodded, then turned and exited the command deck.

Chapter 4

"What do you people want?" Mark asked. The loincloth clad red skinned aliens looked quizzically at him from the floor of their cell. The five of them sat cross-legged upon the floor and rocked slowly back. They sat in a circle.

Mark turned to Red who stood next to him. "They just sit there rocking. They haven't said a word since they awoke," Red affirmed.

"I assumed as much. Let's leave them for now. When Ariel is better she can talk to them telepathically. If they start actually talking the ships language system can begin to put together a translation. But they have to speak first."

"I know Mark, you don't have to explain it to me." Red replied.

"I figured you would Red, I sometimes just like to think out loud."

"Understood boss." Red quietly answered. He was still feeling guilty about missing the aliens tunneling under the force field, and both men knew it.

Mark turned to the security men who stood on either side of the force field door. "Make sure at least two of you are on duty at all times. If you think you need more men, then get them down here. I don't want any surprises with these uninvited guests."

"Yes Sir," A security officer name Jacoby answered.

"C'mon, Red. Let's go." Mark turned and headed back toward the command deck.

The comm unit built into the sleeve of Marks tech suit lit up and the voice of the comm officer taking Ariel's place, Lori Westin, called to him, "Mark?"

He tapped it and replied, "I'm here, Lori. What can I do for you?"

"Mark, we have what looks like an Agalum G'Kor class battle cruiser entering the system and heading straight for this planet."

Mark and Red exchanged stunned and serious glances. Both men ran down the hall to the maglovator and entered it.

An instant later they barged onto the command deck.

Mark queried, "Update us, Miss Westin." Both men surrounded her console.

"Uh, Mark, or Captain, it, the big ship I mean, just slipped into orbit. I can't get any images but tridar readings indicate it's just parked up there."

"Are they scanning the planet?" Red asked.

"No, they're not." Lori replied.

"Then what are they doing?" Red questioned.

"N-nothing…Sir. They're just sitting there."

Mark stood quietly a moment and then ordered, "Okay I need to see this. Let's send a couple of stealthed probes up there immediately."

Red nodded in agreement, punching a button on his security console. Instantly two magno-disc powered probes shot out of the ship's bow, immediately curving upward and streaking away, disappearing in the sky. Both were no bigger than a softball.

"Are the cameras live yet, Lori?"

"Yes Captain," she replied.

"Lori, it's 'Mark', not 'Captain'. I may have that title officially, but I like things loose and fast on this ship."

"Okay, Mark," she agreed uncomfortably.

Mark and Red exchanged quick glances, then returned to their respective stations.

The instant Mark sat down in the command chair the main view screen sprang to life. The images were split in two, one from each probe. The small ball shaped devices used camouflage technology so they blended in with their backgrounds.

"Now that's curious," Mark commented. "That ship is just sitting there in orbit, and it *is* a G'Kor class."

"We are so screwed," Eddie murmured.

"Not yet we're not, Eddie. Red, engage the camouflage. Let's hide the Cag, just in case." Mark said, "Red, take control of the two probes please. I want them to be hidden. Find floating debris up there they can latch onto or hide behind. I think there were some asteroid pieces in orbit, correct?"

"Yeah that's right, Boss. There are. I can maneuver the probes into hiding behind them. We can keep an eye on our unwanted guests from there." Red replied.

Mark nodded approvingly. "Good, do it." He sat there quietly a moment staring at the view screen image of the almost two mile long battle cruiser on the screen before them.

"What do they want here?" Mark stroked his chin and asked quietly.

"Mark?" Eddie questioned.

"Eddie, I don't think that ship is looking for us."

"So what's it here for then?"

Red turned suddenly and barked, "We're all going to find out. Two ships just launched from that thing heading nearby our position."

"Explain 'nearby'."

"Mark, they look to be heading almost right for us, but not quiet on top of us. We could be in trouble if those guys are scouring the area."

"Great." Mark grunted, "Go to full red alert. Be prepared, everyone. Things could be going bad in a big way."

The crew stared at their displays and awaited Mark's next order.

"Here they come," Red announced.

A dull roaring could be heard overhead and then disappeared in the distance.

"What the hell? What just happened?" Eddie asked.

"Those ships flew right past us and kept on going," Red answered.

"Where are they going to though? That's the question." Mark asked.

Red replied, "I don't know, Mark, but I can bet it's safe to say that these guys are going somewhere they don't want us to know about. I can definitely tell you one thing though; those ships weren't looking for us,"

"So they don't know we're here," Mark surmised.

"But what are *they* here for?" Red asked.

"I don't know, Red. But I think it's safe to say whatever it is, it's something we're not going to like."

"Mark, what do we do?" Eddie asked.

"For now, until the ship is repaired and fully operational, we lay low. The repairs will continue as fast as humanly possible."

"What about those clowns out there?" Red nodded toward the viewer at the red skinned natives. They were now camped out around the ship, actually making fires and cooking over those fires.

"What are they eating?" Lori asked.

"The pterodactyl I think. It's not exactly a lot of food," Eddie replied.

"I have an idea," Mark announced as he turned and exited the command deck.

***

Five minutes later Mark, Eddie and Red along with a small contingent of security people walked down the boarding ramp toward the natives carrying platters of steaming food.

"You really think this is gonna work?" Eddie asked.

"We won't know until we try," Mark replied.

"Sometimes, Boss, I think you're nuts," Red added.

"Why are we doin' this again?" Eddie queried.

Mark shrugged. "The enemy of my enemy is what?"

"In this case it could be someone who wants to eat us," Red offered.

"You know, you are really a glass half full kinda guy," Eddie remarked as he placed a platter of food on the ground at the inside edge of the force field barrier next to the others.

Outside the barrier the natives forgot about the small pieces of the flying creature they had upon their spits and were all pressed up against the invisible shield, ogling both the strange new invaders and the food.

Mark tapped his right cuff and spoke, "Danny, move the field back in five feet."

"You got it, Boss," Dan Sledge's voice replied.

The natives suddenly fell to the ground as the force field barrier they were leaning against disappeared.

They slowly, cautiously approached the metal trays of hot food, looking at Mark, Red and Eddie with furrowed brows and almost animal uncertainty.

Slowly one of the natives crept forward. He reached a tentative hand toward the platter before him and removed a piece of chicken. He was immediately surprised at the heat of it and juggled it between hands, almost dropping it. But after an instant he cautiously moved it to his nose, sniffing it. Then he licked it. Immediately he was intrigued. He bit down and a smile spread over his face. He waved to his compatriots, and they descended upon the awaiting trays of food like ravenous fiends, devouring everything before them at an almost alarmingly fast rate.

"C'mon gentlemen, let's go back inside," Mark ordered.

Eddie and Red exchanged glances and followed Mark up the ramp and back into the *Cagliostro*. The doors hissed shut behind them and locked.

The three men returned to the command deck where Dan was awaiting them at his usual console.

Mark looked at his friend and asked, "What'd they do after we left, Danny?"

"They finished off the food and then looked up the ramp, like they were hoping more would be coming out."

"What are they doing now?" Red asked, his eyes slit.

Everyone watched the monitor as all the natives turned to stare up the path they had taken to get to the *Cagliostro* in the first place. They dropped whatever scraps of food were left and grabbed their crude spears, chattering nervously amongst themselves

"It's coming back," Red announced.

"Of course it is. It smelled the food," Mark agreed.

"Yeah, you said that was gonna happen," Danny rumbled.

"You're up, Mr. Sledge," Mark announced.

Dan Sledge nodded his head. "On my way."

"You sure you don't want one of the armored heavy battle suits?" Eddie called after him.

"Naah, I'm good. This won't take long."

Dan disappeared into the maglovator. Everyone else on the command deck returned their gaze to the view screen.

The trees shook as the natives began to nervously scatter. An instant later the towering red furred ape appeared through the thick trees, bellowing madly.

Chapter 5

The fearsome red ape-like monstrosity with the v-shaped head bellowed its rage again. The natives fearfully pointed their spears at the towering hundred foot tall creature.

"Gangway!" a voice roared from behind the beleaguered natives before they could even throw one crude spear at the lumbering monstrosity.

Within the ship Mark commanded, "Now, drop the shield and bring it right back up after Dan clears it."

As one the natives turned toward where the voice had come from in time to see Dan Sledge take three bounding steps then ~~to~~ leap at the red furred beast, both fists forward. He hurtled through the air as if he was shot from a cannon and impacted the ape directly under the jaw. The creature staggered immediately, as if drunk~~en~~. Sledge dropped to the ground in a crouch and immediately charged the beast, again leaping fifty feet straight up, this time swinging his massive right fist into the beast's chest.

As if Dan were David fighting Goliath the ape went down with an Earth shaking thud. The impact was so great that the natives were all thrown from their feet.

Dan walked up the giant creature's body until he was standing on its chest. He reached his hands up above his head in double clenched fists, prepared to administer the finishing blow.

But the Ape moved like lightning and grabbed Sledge around the waist with both hands.

"Whoa!" Dan barked in surprise.

Aboard the *Cagliostro* everyone on the command deck immediately snapped into action.

"Eddie, do you have a clear shot?"

"Not yet, Mark. I don't wanna vaporize Dan."

"To hell with it! Get out there with a blaster rifle and take that thing out. If the ships guns are too big for something like this we'll do it man to monster."

"Wait, Mark," Red interrupted.

"What?" Mark was now riveted to the view screen.

Dan brought both his hands down on the towering behemoth's own red furred hands, with such shattering force that the creature instantly dropped him. Howling, the monster rubbed its wrists as it backed up.

Dan shouted, "You ain't goin' nowhere, you crazy lookin' ape. Now you've gone and pissed me off."

The ape continued to back pedal but Dan was immediately upon it. This time he grabbed its leg and heaved upward, tossing the creature off its feet, to the astonishment of the natives who were now cheering Dan on.

The great ape brought its hands up and slammed them down toward Dan's head. Dan instantly ducked beneath them and leaped again, balled up both his fists together, and swung for all he was worth from right to left in mid-air. The blow connected with a loud crack to the ape's jaw that reverberated throughout the dense woodland. The ape-thing fell over, poleaxed and unconscious. The ground shook with its fall.

"Watch them now," Mark cautioned to Eddie and Red.

The natives swarmed all over Dan, patting him on the back and cheering.

"Lori, is the translation program getting any of what they are saying? Is it able to latch on yet?"

"Just now, Sir. They're saying…'God-killer'. Yes that's it, 'God-killer' over and over."

"Is that thing really dead?" Eddie queried.

"Naaah, it's out cold, that's it." Red looked at the ships sensor display and confirmed, "According to the sensors its unconscious."

Mark smiled. "Good. Let's go meet our new best friends, but before we do let's bring their companions out to them as a measure of good faith."

"I'll have a security crew bring them up right away Mark," Red announced.

Mark nodded. "Good, have them meet us out there. We'll await their signal that they're on their way."

"You got it, Boss," Red acknowledged.

***

Five minutes later Mark, Red and two security men with hand blasters exited the ship on the entryway ramp with the five natives who had tried to sneak onto the ship in front of them.

The former captives chattered incessantly with their cohorts while Dan walked back up the ramp toward his companions.

"How's it looking, Danny?"

Dan turned back toward the group of natives and spoke. "They seem ta be lovin' me for takin' that thing down. It musta been a grade 'A' pain to them."

"Have they been talking?"

"Yeah, Mark they have, but I got no clue what they're sayin'. Hopefully the translation program can do its job now."

"Let's give it a shot." Mark tapped his sleeve and a hologram image of a control panel sprang up. He tapped the virtual keys and typed a few commands. He finished off with a sequence that collapsed the holographic control panel. An instant later the alien's voices were being translated by the tech suits the crew wore and the ship's powerful computer systems.

"Hhhmmm, we should be able ta communicate with 'em now," Dan announced.

"Should be, Dan. By the way, none the worse for the wear against Kong over there, right?" Mark nodded toward the unconscious ape-like giant.

"Naaah, Mark, I'm fine." Dan smiled and flexed his right bicep.

Red grimaced. "I still don't trust them."

Mark slapped him on the shoulder as he walked down the ramp. "That's what I pay you for, big man."

The group moved back toward the natives who seemed to grow less wary of them with each second.

"Hello," Mark began. "We are travelers from far away. We mean you no harm. We simply need time to repair our ship which was damaged on the way here."

The leader of the pack of natives looked at him quizzically as the suit's tech replayed everything Mark said in his own language.

"Ship?" The native asked. "The great silver bird is a ship? What does 'ship' mean?"

Mark and the others looked back and forth before Mark sighed and began to explain. "I built this vessel or ship. It is like a boat that sails among the stars." He waved his hand at the sky.

The leader or Chieftain nodded in agreement. "We… know of such things. Others have come and now live in the mountain of fire. We thought you were like them. That is why…we attacked you. They have…done us much…harm. They have…taken many of us as workers. Those taken have not…returned."

The crew of the *Cagliostro* looked at one another.

"What did this 'others' look like?"

"Some have purple flesh, others yellow. Some make our minds scream in pain without saying a word."

Dan turned toward Mark. "That's all Agalum."

"I know, Danny," Mark returned his gaze to the chieftain. "Where are your people now? How many are still free?"

"Only small amount left. Perhaps five hundred more than is what is here." The translator program concluded an instant behind what he had said.

"How many were taken?" Red queried.

The chief looked to them and replied slowly, "Thousands."

Chapter 6

"What'd we stumble onto?" Dan asked. The command crew, less Ariel, were seated around the table in the command conference room.

"We'll have to find out. I have to assume it's some kind of forward base in the making at least, if not completed," Mark replied.

"It makes sense," Red offered. "The atmosphere's breathable and the indigenous population is no threat. Hell, a single guy with a rechargeable hand blaster and a force field or an armored suit could conquer this whole planet."

"Yeah, these people ain't exactly a threat to the Agalum," Eddie agreed.

Mark nodded in agreement, "No, but they make great slave labor."

"For whatever they're building here," Red added.

"I guess that answers the question of where those two extra ships came from that joined the attack on us before we crashed here." Eddie added.

"This would be the most forward base the Agalum have built, if it is that," Mark announced.

"Yeah, It's only a day from Earth at full hyper-warp," Danny agreed.

"If this is a base, we have to either shut it down or get word back to EPIC," Red commented.

"The Earth Protectorate Interstellar Command needs to know about this as soon as possible. This is a launching point for another invasion. They could mass ships here and be in and out of our home system in a day. If they rotated ships both ways it could be a never ending assault from here," Mark commented and then continued, "I have both Lori Westin and Miss Wallflower rotating shifts on the comm, scanning all frequencies and all bands."

Dan turned his head slightly and squinted his eyes before asking, "Why d'ya do that?"

"Do what?"

"Why d'ya call Lilly 'Miss Wallflower'?"

"Well, it *is* her last name, and to be honest every time I think of her whole name, well, I have a hard time taking her seriously, and she is very good at what she does."

"Ah Mark sometimes I don't get you."

"What can I say, Danny? I'm quirky. And to be honest, calling a woman 'Lilac Wallflower' or 'Lilly Wallflower' just makes me want to smile."

"Yeah, I guess her parents had a sense o' humor."

"Are you two done yet?" Red interrupted his face a twisted mask of disapproval.

"What?" Mark asked, smiling slightly.

"What? Really? We're stuck on this planet and there may be hundreds, or even thousands of Agalum warriors here with us and you two are playing name games. *That's* what."

"Look, Red, sometimes you need a few moments of levity to lighten the mood in a bad situation."

"I'm not seein' it, Mark, especially not now. Things are looking pretty grim to me."

"Things are always lookin' grim to you," Eddie smirked.

"Maybe that's because I'm the only one not looking at the world through rose colored glasses."

"Okay enough," Mark blurted out. "Here's why I'm not that concerned, Red. Things are not that bad. The ship is being repaired. Even though we may have some time stuck here as of yet, we will get off this planet. Secondly we just befriended the natives, who are even now eating more of the food we provided to them. Thirdly, somehow we lucked out and fell upon a major Agalum base only a day or so from Earth, their most forward base."

"That we know of," Red amended.

"Yes, that we know of. Though I'm pretty secure in saying it's probably the closest one, period."

"Okay I'll go with that."

"Alright Red, so tell me in your estimation, since you are security, what happened to us out there? How come we were attacked first by a fast attack ship we managed to defeat in a pitched battle and then by reinforcements that just happened to be in the area? The G'Kor class ship is another matter entirely."

"As far as I'm concerned the whole cluster muck up is just coincidence. That fast attack ship was probably on patrol in that sector, scanned us and went on the attack because we were relatively close to their base. Or it was returning there and its crew knew it had to stop us."

"Okay, what about the other ships?"

"The fast attack called for help, those others responded, which would explain why small two man vessels would be out this far in the first place."

"Because it wasn't really that far with this hidden base smack dab in the middle of everything," Eddie added.

Red nodded. "That's right, short stuff. You got it exactly. Those guys were the back up."

"Fine. What about the G'Kor though?" Mark pressed.

"What about it? It may not be here for us at all. It could be on a supply run or something. Or it could simply be passing through."

"Do you believe that?" Mark inquired.

"Not for an instant, but I had to put it out there because it is a possibility," Red finished.

Mark nodded. "Understood."

"So what do we do about this base?" Eddie asked.

"I don't know," Mark replied. "To be honest I'd rather be able to get the hell out of here and back home, and then point the Fifth Fleet out this way to clean that thing off the face of this planet."

"What's stopping that from happening?" Eddie queried.

"It depends. I can't send a signal from here, even a fast encoded one. They'll find us instantly. One thing we've been able to learn is that a lot of their tech has gotten very good of late."

"Yeah, they've probably been stealin' our stuff," grumbled Dan.

"Of that I have no doubt, Danny. There've been lost ships on both sides of this mess. I'm sure, no matter what precautions we've taken with self-destruct mechanisms and other anti-tampering devices that they've gotten their claws into our stuff."

"Okay, so they stole some tech you and the other big wigs developed. What does that do for us in the big picture?" Eddie asked.

"Real easy, Eddie. There are several 'fingerprints' I've put into my own tech. Things that could help us if the situation gets dire enough."

Dan growled, "But it ain't anything you wanna rely on unless ya have to, huh?"

"I don't want to play that hand unless we're really in dire straits, Danny. That's an endgame gambit that we could go far with. We hold that in reserve as long as possible."

Dr. Troiano's voice interrupted over the comm.. "Mark, you better get down here. Something's up with Ariel. Bring Red with you."

"On our way, Doctor."

Mark exchanged nervous glances with everyone and headed for the maglovator door.

"Maybe we should all come with you," Danny stated.

"I won't argue," Mark shouted over his shoulder as he ran into the waiting maglovator, followed by the rest of the command crew.

They all exited upon the medical deck and ran down the hall toward the glass doors of the medical lab, which slid open at their approach.

Everyone ground to a halt when they entered the medical lab. Ariel floated vertically above her bed, standing in mid-air with her long blonde hair streaming wildly about behind her as if blown in the wind. Her eyes glowed like stars.

"What the hell?" Mark blurted out.

"Mark, she just started doing this," Troiano advised. "She won't let me get close enough to even check her. I try and I'm pushed back telekinetically."

"She's a telepath, not a telekinetic," Mark barely whispered.

"I know, that's why I called you."

Then Ariel opened her mouth and a voice decidedly not her own reverberated from it. "You will leave my world, and you will take these others with you. You will drive them from my world, from my surface and skin, or none of you will leave this place ever again."

With that the entire ship lost power and went dark, cold and dead.

Chapter 7

Mark took a step toward the floating Ariel. "Who, what are you?"

"I am Chakix, Goddess of this world. I am this world's spirit, its soul. I am Chakix."

Dan quickly took a step forward behind Mark. "Yeah, you said that already. Put Ari down. She don't need ya runnin' around her brain."

The creature that was possessing Ariel turned her body toward Dan, "You are the one who hurt my child."

Lightning seemed to burst from Ariel's glowing eyes, and Dan was flung across the room to land hard against a wall.

"Dan!" Troiano shouted as she ran to his side.

Red whispered, "This just took on a whole new level of weird."

"No kidding," Mark replied. He turned toward Ariel. "Chakix or whoever you are, what have you done to Ariel? What have you done to my ship? I want answers now, lady, or whatever you are."

The creature possessing Ariel O'Connor laughed. "I am Chakix. I am this world. Your kind has come to my pleasant shores and brought devastation. This will be tolerated no longer."

"You confuse us with our enemies, who inhabit a hidden base somewhere on this world."

"It does not matter if they are with you or against you. You are all the enemy of Chakix."

"We are not your enemy, Chakix. We *had* to land here. Our vessel was damaged from doing battle with our foes. We merely wish to repair our ship and be on our way back to our home world."

"I do not believe you, pale skin creature."

Mark took another step forward. Behind him Danny was slowly getting to his feet, while Troiano and another member of the medical staff fussed over him. He waved them off, annoyed.

"Chakix," Mark began, "we mean you no harm. You are inside Ariel. Check her memories if it will do her no harm. She is special to me. Please, do not hurt her."

"You have no say in this at all, pale skin creature. I will do as I please."

"Don't become our enemy Chakix; think on this before you go any further. Check Ari's memories."

Ariel's intruder said nothing more. Its demeanor became almost blank. Then after a few silent moments it looked down upon Mark and the others before replying, "What you say is true. You and this one, this 'Ariel' hold special feelings for each other. She regards you very…highly. But she is battling me even as we speak. She does not want me to know all about you."

"Ari, let her know what she needs to," Mark implored, grasping her by the forearm now.

Ariel/Chakix looked at him imperiously at first, and then her demeanor changed and softened.

"Ariel…loves you. She would do anything to protect you and she feels you would do the same for her. Her memories, they are chaotic. These invaders, they are called the…Agalum? Is that correct hu-mon MarkJohnson?"

He nodded grimly in reply.

Behind Mark, Dan forced the sliding glass doors open easily and disappeared down the darkened hallway of the great ship.

"Where is he going? The one who hurt my child."

"Forget him and talk to me. What do you want?"

"I have already told you, I want you and your adversaries off of my world."

"Look…Chakix, we mean you no harm and would gladly leave here now if we could. Those…adversaries damaged our ship in battle and they have a world destroyer class ship in orbit around you right now. That class of ship is no joke. They've been trying to get something like that to my world for over a year now, and we've beaten them back at every turn. But they outnumber us in bodies and in ships. We're fighting for our very lives and existence. Our world can't build ships fast enough to keep up with them."

Chakix/Ariel tilted her head and asked simply, "Then how are you still in existence?"

"We are holding our own through our design and manufacture of weaponry and ships. As a race we are builders. We shape what we need and use it against our enemies. Never before in the history of my world have we faced a foe from beyond the stars. All our internal conflict has led to this. There is no doubt; we are a warrior race in many ways."

"I have no…difficulty with that. My children here are warriors as well. You are simply more…advanced than they are."

"Yes, we are. Again, we'd much rather repair our ship, the *Cagliostro*, and simply leave this place."

"You cannot leave until you remove these enemies," she barked harshly.

"Chakix, we did not bring them here. They outnumber us greatly we fear. That great ship in orbit can and most definitely will destroy you if they learned of your sentience."

"I-I..." Chakix/Ariel stammered.

"Think, Chakix. We would rather aid you in defeating these enemies but we cannot do it alone."

"My children. All my children would...die?"

"If the Agalum learned of what you truly are, then yes. They would blow you out of space killing every living creature upon you."

She paused a moment and seemed to look inwardly, her face down toward the floor, then her face lifted. "Why would they do this thing?"

"Because the Agalum are a petty and small minded race which attacks those different from them. They fear those who represent something other than their way of thinking, or who in their small minds might pose a threat to them. They surreptitiously infiltrated my world for over a century weakening and sabotaging our space program."

"Are you saying they deterred you from leaving your world mother?"

"If you mean a being like yourself, there is no such voice upon our world."

She was silent a moment, then began to speak again after a moment of reflection. "That is blasphemy. There are other worlds, other voices like mine throughout the beyond."

"Not that we have encountered, Chakix."

"You lie. I do not believe you." The words were vehement this time. Ariel's face contorted angrily.

"Uh oh," Eddie murmured.

The creature called Chakix floated toward Mark who put his hands up and tried to stop her forward movement.

"There must be others like me, there must be more. I am not...alone. I cannot be." Her voice turned almost sorrowful.

"We've never encountered another like you, Chakix. That does not mean others like you do not exist. It means simply we have not encountered them as of yet."

Troiano and Eddie both looked at Mark and nodded their approval almost imperceptibly. Red merely scowled, tightening his hand on his blaster pistol's grip.

Without warning the lights flared back to life and all the electronic equipment in the ship with them.

"What?" Chakix/Ariel was stunned.

"Dan," Red turned to Eddie and mouthed.

Mark held Chakix/Ariel by both arms now, making sure her attention was focused on him and him only. "Release Ariel, Chakix. We mean you no harm. We want these adversaries removed as much as you do. From your surface as well as from this quadrant of space. Help us do so."

"No," the not Ariel voice continued. "You will all leave my skin, my surface, my world. You will take those...Agalum with you, or you will all die here."

Troiano moved surreptitiously away from Mark with Red and Eddie knowingly blocking her from view. Red tapped his left sleeve, which pulsed a red light twice at the cuff faintly.

"We don't want to be your adversary, Chakix," Mark continued, "But we cannot leave here as of yet, and you cannot stay within Ariel any longer."

A half dozen security men burst through the med lab's doors on each side, surrounding the possessed Ariel.

"No! You will all leave!" Chakix/Ariel shouted.

Her eyes flared brighter and the entire security detail was lifted into the air and hurled against the walls.

But at the same time Troiano made her move, slipping up behind Ariel and injecting her with a powerful sedative.

Ariel's eyes rolled up into her head. Her eyelids fluttered like a butterfly's wings. Then her body dropped toward the ground. Mark deftly caught her before she could impact the hard, gleaming floor.

"What'd you give her?" he eyed Dr. Troiano.

"The equivalent of a horse sedative," She answered grimly.

"Are you serious?"

"Yes I am, Captain Johnson. She *will* be all right. If you had seen the life scans my equipment had on her you would have done the same thing," She paused a moment and then continued with a strange look upon her face as she looked at Ariel. "Hell, after looking at the readings I'm getting on her right now I'm not certain I used enough."

"I'm not condemning you for what you did, Doctor. I know it had to be done. I'm just concerned for Ari, that's all."

"We all are, Mark," Troiano replied.

Simultaneously Dan Sledge thundered through the doors. Medics were helping the security people back onto their feet all around the crew.

"Everybody all right?" Dan asked.

"Yes, Danny. What happened? What allowed you to get our power up and running again?"

"The ship was bein' enveloped by this frequency from the planet itself. It was some kinda power dampening field. Hand held scanners still worked, an' if you noticed so did our suits' protective qualities. I powered up a frequency jammer outta some stuff in the engineerin' lab an' isolated that frequency, puttin' up a counter frequency. I used my suit's power supply to get it started, an' once it was in place I tagged it onta the ship's power. She's not gonna be able ta do that again to us. I got the ship's systems scanning for frequency changes. We can match her just as fast as she changes 'em, now that I know what we're lookin' for."

Mark patted him on the shoulder. "Good man. I always said you were the smartest guy I ever met, except for myself. Today you were smarter."

"Naaah, Boss. I just had my head clearer. You were worried about Ari."

Mark turned and watched as the medics picked Ariel up off the floor and placed her onto a gurney. She was unconscious and her eyes were closed.

He turned toward Dan and Troiano. "Is there any way to use that same procedure to remove this 'Chakix' from Ariel's mind? Perhaps block whatever signal she's transmitting to Ari?"

"Do you think Ariel is receiving a signal from this Chakix?" Troiano asked with wide eyes.

65

"It's either that or she's possessed by it. We won't know until we run some tests I suppose. Danny, can you rig something up to see if Ari is being used to receive some sort of telepathic commands or something?"

"I could, Mark, but would that explain the telekinesis?"

Mark sighed. "I suppose not. But I want you to run that test anyway. Perhaps Ari is possessed by this thing, this world mind, or whatever the hell it is. Or perhaps she's just being given commands from afar that are being overwritten onto her mind. It doesn't really matter either way. I want this thing's influence out of Ariel's head as fast as possible."

Troiano looked stoically at Mark. "What if I can't remove it?"

"Either that thing gets out of Ari's head on its own or we're going to force it out of there. I'll do whatever it takes, even if it means killing that thing."

Chapter 8

Mark sat alone in the command meeting room, a glass of bourbon in his hand. Slowly he spun the ice around the glass, watching the crushed cubes swirl in the dark colored liquid. Then he took a drink. He clinked the tumbler heavily upon the surface of the meeting room table.

"Are you all right?" a male voice called from the doorway.

Mark turned toward it, smirking slightly as he did. "Yes, Red, I'm fine. I just needed a few minutes in a quiet place to get my thoughts together."

"Good. Get them together, because everyone on this ship needs you."

Mark rose creakily from his seat, arching his back as he did. "Do you ever remember stuff like this being easier than it is now?"

"Stuff like what? Hurtling through space in the fastest ship known to mankind, and maybe the whole damned universe? No, last I remember it was always pretty tough."

Mark grimaced as he rubbed his back. "Yeah, I guess you're right."

"Got any ideas about Ari?"

"I'm having Danny fabricate a multi-band signal scanner. I'm hoping that will do what we need in allowing us to discover if there is an outside or controlling force being projected into Ari's mind. If it doesn't, then I have to assume something is already living inside of her."

"Like something possessing her."

"Yes, exactly. He said it'll be ready in the next few hours."

"What about the engine repairs?"

"Dan said they've run into a snag. They need a specific type of ore to smelt down and create a certain component for the magno disc propulsion system. He's used the ship's sensors and found some in a volcano about two hundred miles from here."

"So under a minute in one of the shuttles or the *Stargrazer*."

"Yeah or whatever time we want to take getting there."

"Okay, so why aren't they jumping on it?"

"Because somewhere out there lurks our enemy."

"Could you be any more dramatic?"

"Don't laugh, Red. This is serious. I'm having a shuttle outfitted with the upgraded camouflage stealth system right now. The problem is we're not sure where our enemy is. Neither are our newfound friends. We could be flying right past or over them. Not something we want to do."

"This turned into a mess really fast," the burly security chief sighed.

"Yes, it did. For once luck was not on our side."

"When is it ever? Think about the last two years. We've made our own luck every step of the way."

"Yeah, like I don't know that."

Red sat down at the table and reached for the bottle of bourbon. Mark pushed it toward him, then reached behind himself and removed another glass tumbler from a cabinet. He filled it with ice from an ice machine, which was also inside the cabinet. He handed it to Red, who nodded in thanks.

Red poured himself a glass of bourbon, then took a pull off of the glass. He placed the glass back upon the table, then looked back at Mark. "I've been thinking, maybe we should send the *Stargrazer* home to get reinforcements."

Mark nodded slowly. "We could, if they could get out of the system without getting caught. But there's no guarantee of that happening."

"What about that new camo system you were just talking about?"

"I don't know, Red. As a last ditch effort, maybe. But I don't have any interest in sending anyone to their possible death."

"You really think it will come to that?" Red asked.

"Yeah, I do. We don't know what's out there. There could be a hundred ships massing behind the sun in this system. The *Cagliostro* is fast enough and tough enough to cut through anything and escape if need be. But the *Stargrazer* might get cut to ribbons out there. Sure its shields are first rate and cutting edge, but it doesn't have the hull density of the *Cagliostro*. If we can't get this girl off the ground anytime soon I'll consider it, but not before."

"Why not use the '*Grazer* to go to that volcano and mine the ore you need?"

"For the same reasons that we just discussed. It's our last ditch effort and our final card to be played. We hold it in reserve until we can't do anything else, then we let it go and send it home."

Red took another pull on his glass before speaking. "Yeah, but it may be too late by then."

"I know. It's a chance we'll have to take. I do not want to give away our location if I don't have to."

Red nodded stoically. "Understood. What do you want me to do?"

"You're leading the mission to the volcano. Take Eddie with you, and Lori Westin as well."

"Anyone else?"

"There will be five others going with you from the geology lab. They'll be handling the ore mining. I want you to pick two more security officers as well to take along. Take as much weaponry as you think you'll need, just in case."

"These geo guys know what we're looking for?"

"Yes they do. They're the ones who pinpointed what we needed inside that volcano."

"Is that thing live?"

"It's bubbling, but it appears like it's been that way for a very long time."

"Great. I just gotta make sure I'm not setting it off."

Mark smirked. "That would be a start, Red. Get in, get out, get back here. Get it done."

Chapter 9

The shuttle bay of the *Cagliostro* opened slowly, and an instant later a small shuttlecraft flew out of it, turned in mid-air and zipped away. Almost immediately the skin of the ship seemed to shimmer and the small shuttle's lines became blurred. An instant later the shuttle disappeared.

It was a small craft holding all eight of its crewmembers in tight confines. The shuttles were modular in nature. This allowed maintenance crews the ability to remove or add rows of seating. This compromised carrying capacity, but at times it could not be helped, such as now. The shuttles were just twenty feet long, with a seven foot ceiling. They held emergency rations only. These were not deep space faring vehicles, merely for use on short hops between the *Cagliostro* and a planet's surface if the *Cag* could not land for one reason or another. They were also sub-light only vessels. Anti-grav disc powered, Mark's precursor to the magno-disc. No exhaust trails were present with either design. Once started, they created their own energy and could run almost infinitely, the magno-discs more so than the anti-grav discs.

But none of this mattered to Red Robinski. The shuttle slid silently through the atmosphere, save for a slight hum at its passing.

"ETA to volcano?" Red growled.

"At present speed three minutes longer, Sir," Lori Westin replied professionally.

"Good, Miss Westin. Are you picking up anything on your comm unit?" the large security chief grumbled.

"Nothing Sir, from the *Cagliostro* or from anywhere else."

Red nodded silently.

Lori Westin was flying the small shuttle. Eddie sat next to Red at the next console in the shuttles nose. He spoke in a low tone in Red's right ear. "You okay, Chief? You seem, I dunno, nervous or outta sorts."

Red snorted then replied, "Naahh, I'm good, Eddie. Just thinking things through. We're in a pickle, if you know what I mean. Things are not great right now. We need to get whatever it is the scientist types need to repair the *Cag* and get outta here fast. I'm not liking this whole thing. Something just seems, I don't know, Eddie, off somehow."

"Off how?" Eddie questioned in a low voice.

"It's nothing, pal. I just have a bad feeling, that's all."

"I don't like 'bad feelings'. Mama DiGenovese didn't raise no superstitious fool, but she always told me what to be wary of, and one of them was normally tightly wound men acting squirrely all of a sudden. Just like you are."

Red chuckled in a low, deep tone. "Don't sweat it, Eddie. Just keep your eyes open. I have a feeling we may run into the unexpected, that's all."

Now it was Eddie's turn to laugh. "Dude, we're out in space battling nasty aliens. Our whole lives are the unexpected now."

"Good point actually." Red agreed.

The boxy little shuttle approached the volcano and slowed to a hovering halt.

"I'll take it from here, Lori."

The young red headed woman nodded her head as Red took control of the shuttle.

"I want to fly around the cone once or twice and check it out before we land, so be aware of anything that might seem suspicious."

Everyone nodded and affirmed Red's orders.

The boxy little shuttle slowly flew around the cone of the volcano, still maintaining its camouflage, which reflected the ships surroundings back onto its hull so it was seemingly invisible.

"How are we gonna get down there?" Eddie asked.

"We're not. The scientists are going to lower a robotic tool that will scoop out exactly what they are looking for from that thing's cone and bring it back to the storage compartment below. Once onboard it will be cooled to room temperature, thus allowing it to be handled more easily. Onboard the *Cag* it'll be mixed with other ingredients that will be added to that soup. Then it will all be added to whatever other pieces they need to get the *Cag* back into space at hyper-warp speed."

"Oooff. I don't even like the sound of that."

"Relax, Eduardo, the *Cag* has a fully fitted and stocked chemical lab. Between that and the other departments on the ship we can recreate any component on the ship."

"Yeah I know, Red. Though that doesn't mean I have to be happy to be in the situation we're in."

Red nodded. "Agreed, buddy. Let's just get into position and hope this fixes the *Cag* up. I don't want to be hanging around this place any more than I have to."

"I'm in total agreement, big man. The sooner we get off this planet the better."

"You both are forgetting something," Lori Westin admonished.

"Oh yeah? What's that Lori?" Red asked.

"There's an Agalum base hidden somewhere on this lush green world and they probably know every square inch of this place."

Red nodded. "Yeah, I'm well aware of that Lori."

"I'm keepin' an eye on things out there Red," Eddie interjected. "First sign of trouble I see I'll be blastin' 'em with both barrels."

"Yeah, just be aware this damn shuttle's only got the two forward guns. It would be a fantasy to call what's on this ship 'canons'."

"Understood, Red."

Red turned to Lori. "Lori, tell the science geeks to get to work. We're right over the spot we detected the monotriglicine we need to replenish the coolant. They can start lowering the collector now."

Lori talked quietly into her comm microphone to the men in the back of the shuttle who were already controlling the robot arm. It lowered with a great amount of precision, dipping carefully into the molten ore, then removing itself with a full scoop of brightly glowing molten rock and metal. After four more scoops of the stuff the scientific crew announced they had enough.

Red nodded and began to lift the still fully cloaked shuttle away from the volcano, when he stopped it and turned its nose back around to face the volcano's side.

"What is it?" Eddie asked.

Red said nothing, but pointed to an image on the viewer.

"What the heck?" Eddie muttered.

Cut into the side of the mountain was a slot cut into the mountain itself. It was illuminated with landing lights along both the roof of the manmade, or in this case, alien made cave as well as on the floor. It seemed to be a fairly large cave. One that was big enough for at least medium sized ships to land in.

Before either man could say another word a small two man flyer zipped through the air right below them and entered the impromptu landing bay. An instant later the hole in the mountain's side disappeared again.

"How come we didn't see that until just now, and where'd it go?" Eddie asked.

Red shrugged. "Probably for the same reason they didn't see us. They've got it cloaked somehow."

"I figured as much," Eddie admitted. Then he turned back to Red, "Now what do we do?"

"We get back to Mark and the others and tell them what we discovered. The enemy is living right under our noses, inside a hollowed out volcano. And from the look of things they have already established a forward base on this world. One that's within striking distance of Earth."

Chapter 10

"Their base is inside the volcano," Mark repeated.

Eddie and Red looked at each other, then back at Mark and nodded.

"At least we know where it is now," Mark commented as he slid back into his chair at the conference table.

"That's not going to make things any easier," Red added.

"No, it's not. At least the ore and chemicals you managed to acquire seems to be exactly what we need, according to Dan. The final repair parts and coolant are being manufactured as we speak."

"How long until we're off this mudball?" Eddie asked.

"It should only be another day or two at worst."

"Yeah, but then we have to get by that G'Kor class monster out there, the Agalum's planet killer. That's not going to be easy you know," Red advised.

"I didn't think it would be, Red. But what choice do we have? We can't stay here forever. The natives already know we're here and while they are friendly now, all it takes is one of them getting captured and then interrogated for whatever reason and bam, there goes our secret."

"That's for sure. I guess it's better to get out of here and take our chances out there." Eddie waved his hand toward the ceiling and the depths of space beyond.

"I don't know about 'better', but it's more of the devil we know as opposed to the one we don't."

"Why? You think there may be more to this place than just a base?" Red asked with a furrowed brow.

"It is possible, Red. Though sometimes the most obvious reason is all the reason you need."

"Yeah, understood," the big security chief acknowledged.

"So what do you want us to do in the meantime?" Eddie inquired.

"System checks and training exercises. Let's make sure everyone is in top shape for our mad escape from this world."

"I guess that's one way of putting it," Eddie muttered.

"That's what it's going to end up being, Eddie. A mad rush out of here. I'm sure well have plenty to contend with on the way back up to the stars."

"You know that's probably an understatement." Eddie smiled.

"I'm well aware of that, Mr. DiGenovese."

Red held up his hand to silence both of the other men. "Now that that stuff is out of the way, I have the important question. How's Ari?"

Mark sighed and deflated. He looked at the tabletop, then back toward his two friends. "She's the same. Not good. Dan's signal blocker did not work or maybe it's not a beamed in signal and maybe she's really been possessed. I don't know. We have to keep her sedated, otherwise that thing inside her begins to rave like a lunatic under a full moon. But how long do I really want to do that for? This gets worse and worse." Mark shook his head, exasperated.

Eddie leaned forward. "What? Do you really think this is any worse than anything else we've faced the past few years? C'mon, Boss, think about it. We've always prevailed before. What makes this time any different?"

"Nothing, except we don't have Ari and may not again if this goes on. Hell, what if I can't sever the ties that Chakix thing has on her? What happens when we head out to space? Is that going to kill her?"

The three men exchanged worried glances and for the first time Eddie and Red actually knew what was bothering Mark, the entire truth of it.

"What does Troiano think?" Red queried.

"She's not sure. She's worried that if we leave the planet's atmosphere Ari will die."

"Wait, I think we're all jumping the gun." Red raised his hands up before himself. "We don't know either way what will happen. The entity or whatever the hell it is may end up being stuck here when we leave the planet."

That was what Mark hoped for deep inside. But he also knew that forcibly separating Ariel and this Chakix thing could be disastrous, especially for Ari.

"No matter what we do, if it does not want to let Ari go, it won't, period. We have to work around that conclusion. We have to drive that thing out of Ari, without hurting her."

"I don't think forcing it out of Ari is going to be any picnic," Eddie interjected.

"So what, Eddie? Are you going to ask it nicely to get up and leave Ari's body?"

"Well, not really. But something did occur to me."

"Are you going to share, Di Genovese?" Red asked.

"What if we make it uncomfortable for this thing to stay inside of Ariel?"

"Hhhmmm, not bad, Eddie," Mark replied while stroking his chin in deep thought. "The question is how?"

Chapter 11

Chakix/Ariel awoke in restraints. Steel bands were wrapped around each arm and leg and bolted to a platform that was in turn secured to the floor of the med-lab.

The creature that commanded Ariel's body looked around, perplexed.

"What is this? You seek to trap me here? I cannot be restrained thusly. I am Chakix." The alien presence spoke to Mark who was standing staring at Ariel's body with his arms crossed.

"What you are now is my prisoner. I already proved to you we can keep you sedated indefinitely. But that doesn't do me any good. I want Ariel back, without your presence. So you're going to accommodate me and leave her body."

"I will do nothing you ask, MarkJohnson."

"Access Ariel's memories to see how stubborn I can be."

"Stubborn?"

"Yes, Chakix, stubborn. Pig headed. Single minded. Dogged. Persistent. All of those words have the same definition or meaning. Do you know what those words mean? Can Ariel's memories tell you that? Don't bother looking. I'll explain it for you. I am 'unreasonably determined'. Meaning I do not give up, ever. I do not bend a knee to a supposed 'superior' foe. Ask your enemies the Agalum about that. They thought we were easy pickings. By 'we' I mean the Earth, my home world, but you already knew that by going through Ariel's memories. I find a way to defeat an enemy and I finish the job."

Chakix/Ariel cocked her head sideways. "Then why have you not dealt your enemy the Agalum a mortal blow they cannot recover from?"

Mark walked slowly about the room before answering. "The reason is simple; I'm not trying to eradicate that race, or rather races. There are at least three we know of that are heavily involved in the Agalum empire."

"Yet as a race against superior forces you fight alone and you hold them off?"

"You have Ari's memories, you know we do."

"How?"

"Access Ari's memories again, so you know what I'm telling you is true. Our technology is better than theirs. This is why they fear us. What we have done as a race in a few hundred years has taken them much longer. Our weapons are stronger, and now our ships are faster. *That* is why they fear us."

Chakix/Ariel moved her head side to side in short, quick motions. "They will eventually wear you down and overwhelm you. They have the beings to do so."

"You mean they have the numbers on us, correct?"

Chakix/Ariel nodded in the affirmative.

"I figure there's got to be a few races out here somewhere that have had enough of the Agalum and want revenge on them or just want to see them beaten so far back that they never come out of their solar system again."

"As they tried to do to you."

"Don't you think that it would be apropos?"

Slowly Chakix/Ariel nodded her head in the affirmative.

"Good. Now leave Ariel's body."

"I will not, not until you comply with my demands."

"Your demands hold no meaning now. You are held captive. I can pump sedative into you with a nod of my head. Not only that, but I came up with a little something that will make your stay within Ariel agonizing. Leave her body and we can speak to each other respectfully as civilized beings should."

"What is this 'civilized'?"

Mark rolled his eyes. "This is going to be a long evening, isn't it?"

"I refuse to leave," Chakix snapped.

"Very well. Let's see how you do with this new toy."

Mark touched his sleeve and a virtual pad sprang to life before him, anchored at his right sleeve. He touched a few spots on its surface and then looked up above Chakix/Ariel's head.

The creature inhabiting Ariel's brain followed his stare and her eyes grew wide as a helmet began to lower in place around her head from above.

"What is this?" the strange voice shouted. "I will shatter this device and destroy both you and this vehicle!"

"I don't think so, Chakix. Right now you're still sedated enough to not be able to concentrate sufficiently to use your telekinesis. Once I activate that helmet your brainwaves will be scrambled. You'll be the helpless passenger inside Ari's brain and not the other way around. She won't even be affected. You see, we were able to separate your brain patterns and since we already had Ariel's on file, it was a simple matter to come up with the correct frequency to neutralize your own. The tables are about to be turned. You're about to learn what it feels like to be on the receiving end of what you did to Ariel."

Mark touched a button on his virtual control panel and the helmet instantly hummed to life. Chakix/Ariel began to scream silently then went limp.

Before Mark could even get to her side, Ariel sprang back upward. "Mark! I-it's gone, I mean I still feel it within my mind, but it's now trapped, and it can't escape."

Mark rushed to her side and hugged her tightly. "What is it Ari? What does it want?"

"Mark, i-it's frightened. I can feel it. It's not an act. Chakix is a frightened parent looking to protect its children."

"What? What children?"

"Everything on this planet is Chakix's child. At least that's how Chakix sees things."

"That's not good. Mothering instincts are some of the most powerful known to man. If this sentience is seeking to protect everything on the planet, it only can lead to disaster."

"It already has. Chakix had no defense against the Agalum. They had no telepaths with them at all. Not even one of those horrible Quels they used on me, at least none that Chakix recognized."

"Okay, go on."

"The only reason she attacked was because she realized I was a telepath, or psi. My mind was attainable to her. She was as surprised as I was when she entered my mind. She's been guiding her children or the beings on this world against the Agalum since they arrived here a few months ago, but it hasn't done much good."

"I can see that. What about 'Red Kong' out there?"

"She can guide his actions as well. But it's sort of aiming a bull at a red flag and letting it go. She can basically coerce these beings to do what she wants, but they are not mindless. It's different than you would think."

Mark nodded. "Okay, are you all right now?"

Ari nodded in return. "Yes, good looking, I am." She leaned forward and kissed him, then withdrew slowly, touching the helmet on her head. "Gets in the way, doesn't it?"

"Afraid so, honey. Tell your passenger that we mean her no harm and we want off her world as much as she wants us off of it. The *Cagliostro* is almost repaired enough to make a run for it off of this planet."

"Mark, she *still* wants us to drive the invaders off as well. She's adamant about it."

"Tell her we're not here to run a suicide mission on her behalf. We have a crew of one hundred people against who knows how many that the Agalum have stationed here."

Miss Wallflower's voice rang over the comm system. "Captain Johnson, please return to the command deck immediately."

"Uh oh. Does your passenger know anything about this?"

"N-no. She's not really saying but she seems more frightened, as if fearful something bad is about to happen to her 'children'."

"Stay here, Ari."

"I'm restrained. I can't go anywhere, remember?"

"Okay I'm sending Troiano back in. I'll be back as soon as possible." He leaned forward and kissed her again, then bolted out of the room. Mark turned toward Ann Troiano as he ran past and said, "Doctor, see to Ari. I have to get back to the command deck."

Less than a minute later he exited the maglovator and re-entered the command deck once again.

"What is it, Miss Wallflower?"

The buxom redhead pointed at the view screen in answer. He followed her finger to see several of the red skinned natives jumping up and down gesturing wildly, while talking to the security team by the ramp.

"What the hell?" Mark exited the command deck and was out of the ship a moment later trotting down the ramp toward Red who was standing there trying to calm down the red skinned natives of Chakix's world.

"What's going on here, Red?"

The leader turned to Mark before Red could reply and began to speak quickly, his words instantly translated by the ship's systems into Mark's tech suit. "Our tribe is under attack. They come for us again, from the sky. Help us," the alien warrior begged. "Help us please, or they will kill us all!"

Chapter 12

The *Stargrazer* flew free of the shuttle deck of the *Cagliostro*. At the controls Red Robinski piloted the sixty foot long sleek ship with the swept back side wings close to the tree tops. Instantly upon leaving the *Cagliostro* he activated the *Stargrazer*'s camouflage device and, like the shuttle before it, the ship faded from sight.

"Ya gotta love the way the new camo unit works compared to the old one," Eddie DiGenovese commented. He sat in the co-pilots chair next to Red.

Red nodded grimly as was his wont. "Yeah, Mark worked out all the bugs. After the last iteration of that thing failed us around Mars two years ago he made sure he got it right this time."

"ETA thirty seconds, big guy," Eddie announced.

Red stole a glance back over his shoulder. Behind him and strapped in was the red skinned alien who had implored them for aid.

"What's your name, fella?" Red asked.

"I am Derombu," he replied stoically.

"Okay, Derombu, are you the chieftain of your people?" Eddie inquired.

Derombu shook his head negatively. "No I am a warrior, but my feet are swift so the chieftain, Procolectu, sent me from our village."

"Okay, Der, when we land, find Procolectu and point him out to us." Eddie concluded.

The native nodded his head nervously in agreement.

Behind them all stood thirty security men, basically soldiers and warriors who were a permanent part of the *Cagliostro*'s crew who answered to Red.

"You men get ready, we're landing in five."

The ship touched down silently, displacing little plumes of dust. It was still invisible to every known type of sensor. But those on the ground were not invisible to the crew aboard the *Stargrazer*

"Oh man, we got trouble," Eddie muttered.

"Get it together, DiGenovese," rumbled Red. "You men activate your suits' camo units now," he shouted toward the back of the *Stargrazer*. The thirty security men did as they were told and disappeared into a shimmering haze.

Nearby could be heard the sounds of fighting and screaming, most of it coming from the severely out matched and outgunned natives.

"The ship is clear for fifty feet in every direction. You men clear out first and head right toward the battle. I'll be joining you on the ground. Der, you're with me. Eddie, take this bird back up and power up the cannons. As soon as we separate the natives from the enemies, do a strafing run."

"You got it, Red."

The rear door of the *Stargrazer* slid open silently and the cloaked men exited like silent wraiths. Red nodded to Eddie and activated his own camo unit and disappeared as well, dragging the fearful native behind him, hiding him within his own camouflage field.

The battlefield near the village was chaos. Purple skinned aliens fired plasma beam weapons at the natives, blasting them off their feet to land in unconscious heaps upon the ground. Once unconscious they were bound and collected. They were then dragged to an awaiting ship where they would be brought back to the hidden base under the volcano and used as slave labor. All of this Red processed almost instantaneously.

But then the crew from the *Cagliostro* joined the battle. Blasts of energy enveloped the surprised Agalum troops, dropping them to the ground with one shot. Now the battle was joined.

"Sweep them up, guys," Red ordered. His men complied standing in a staggered formation and firing in an A group B group pattern one after another so that there was always someone firing upon the alien intruders.

Startled, the Agalum fired back upon their invisible foes. But even if they scored any hits the super durable blue and silver suits, light armor that shunted energy as well as projectile attacks, each member of the *Cagliostro* crew wore deflected most of the energy damage from the blasters. While the wearer was discomfited, he wasn't mortally wounded or rendered unconscious.

The Agalum troop leader, a 'Salad head' according to the *Cagliostro* crew for the way their hair, or whatever it was that grew out of their heads, resembled a head of lettuce, hurried up the ramp of the ship that had the natives packed into it. He ordered the ramp closed with quick barking commands.

"Red, they're rabbiting," Eddie called over his comm.

"Don't let 'em get away, Eddie. It's all on you. We have our hands full."

"Thanks, Chief. I appreciate the added pressure."

"My pleasure, short stuff," Red grunted in reply.

The cargo ship lifted off the ground and shot ahead, but almost instantly the cloaked *Stargrazer* was on its tail. Both ships rocketed just above tree level. Eddie aimed the forward cannons and fired, nailing the escaping ship's primary engine. Instantly the Agalum ship lost altitude and slammed into the trees, flattening dozens of them as it slid to a smoking, sizzling halt.

"Woo-Hoo!" Eddie shouted over his comm to Red, "Got 'im!"

The natives who were in the heavily fortified ship ran from its shattered hull, some carrying those who were too hurt and could not run. They all disappeared into the dense forest surrounding them.

But Eddie's glee was short lived, for flying over the horizon was a much bigger, much deadlier looking ship that did nothing to hide its approach. It was sleek, a long rounded body with a stanchion on each side that rose up above the hull, then dipped down toward the ground. At the end of each stanchion was mounted an engine and at the forward section was a heavy canon of some type. It was much larger than any weapon Eddie had ever seen on a small Agalum ship.

Eddie hovered the *Stargrazer* in place silently, still cloaked. Cloaked or not the enemy ship was looking to draw him out.

Its weapons began blazing near where Eddie and the ship had been hovering. The sleek *Stargrazer* with its pointed nose and rearward swept wings lifted upward above the attack.

"Holy mother of God! Those are some kind of machine gun blasters," Eddie exclaimed.

Rapid fire bursts of plasma tore the trees below the *Stargrazer* up, turning the ground to jelly with their power.

Eddie slid the *'Grazer* around to the side invisibly and opened fire on the predatory ship, tearing the solar cannons across its hull in explosive blasts, scoring the Agalum ship's hull repeatedly.

"Whoa, that thing's heavily armored, it's some new kind of 'Predator'. At least that's what I'm going to call it."

The enemy ship spun on its axis surprisingly and fired its weapons at the spot the *Stargrazer* was hovering managing several direct hits across the 'Grazer's shields, immediately weakening them.

"What the hell? My shields are down to seventy percent from one attack. This thing is brutal!"

Eddie spun the *Stargrazer* around counter clockwise, then shot the ship toward the stars.

As the *'Grazer* gained altitude, Eddie fired off two star core missiles, which arced away from the *Stargrazer* and impacted against the enemy ship's shields and hull.

The Agalum craft immediately rose up and began racing upward.

"As of now I'm recording all of this, includin' my commentary, for tactical purposes. Camo is still holding; let's see how fast this thing is."

Eddie throttled the *Stargrazer* up as it shed the planet's atmosphere, its enemy pursuing it closely and strafing space with its rapid fire energy weapon. The Agalum ship scored hits on the rear shields of the

Stargrazer. Each time it lit up like a flashbulb, telling the Agalum gunner exactly where its quarry was.

"Oboy, I may be in trouble here," Eddie grumbled.

He spun the *Stargrazer* around, flipping it and rolling it side over side, repeatedly avoiding the powerful blasts from the Agalum vessel. Eddie turned the *Stargrazer* on its own axis and rolled the ship clockwise, firing a steady stream of death at the Agalum ship, pounding its central hull repeatedly.

The predator ship returned fire and its blasts roared into and finally through the *Stargrazer*'s shields, then slamming into its armored hull.

"Shields are down!" Eddie shouted. No one was there to hear him, but the ship's recording system took in his every word.

Again he rolled the *Stargrazer* first clockwise, then corkscrewed her down and under the Agalum predator.

"It ain't gonna be that easy," Eddie shouted as the *Stargrazer* slipped under the enemy ship upside down and blasted its lower hull with twin streams of destruction.

Again the Agalum predator returned fire from those deadly rapid fire blasters, pounding on the '*Grazer*'s hull.

An emergency klaxon began to chime loudly. An automated voice warned, "Hull breach. Decompression imminent."

"Oh that's just wonderful," Eddie barked.

He dropped the *Stargrazer* into full reverse and fired four star core missiles, two at each engine/weapons pod on the Agalum predator. The stanchions that held them rocked explosively with each impact.

Now crippled, the Agalum ship turned slowly, streaming energy from its damaged engines.

"Enemy shield status?"

"Enemy shields at twenty five percent," the automated voice replied.

"Great that's twenty five percent more than I've got."

Again the predator fired where its crew thought the *Stargrazer* would be hiding, but this time missed entirely. Eddie let loose with both solar cannons, aiming directly at the right side stanchion.

The engine and weapons pod exploded spectacularly, disintegrating under the *Stargrazer*'s attack.

Eddie fired again, both cannons focused on the remaining stanchion. The ship exploded in a ball of pyrotechnics, turning space as bright as a star for an instant.

Eddie wasted no time, aiming the *Stargrazer* back toward the planet's surface and where the *Cagliostro* was hidden. The '*Grazer* limped badly through the sky, still invisible but streaming a burning trail of oxygen from the ruptured hull. Further it was re-entering the atmosphere without its shields and the interior was getting decidedly hot.

"*Cagliostro*, this is *Stargrazer*. I'm coming in hot and out of control. I have a hull breach and I'm losin' oxygen fast. The '*Grazer* is badly damaged. Repeat, I'm coming in hot *Cagliostro*, do you copy? *Cagliostro*, do you copy?"

Chapter 13

"Mark," Shouted Lilly Wallflower, "the *Stargrazer* just went down!"

"What? Where?" Mark jumped from his command chair and hurried to Lilly's console.

"Right here, about five miles from us."

"Ari-, I mean Miss- Lilly, Lilly was there any communication from him?"

"No, but his comm may be down."

"Shuttles two and three get to the *Stargrazer* immediately. Medical staff on two and security team, heavily armed, on three. Get Eddie and bring him back here."

"I'm going, too," Red's voice announced over the comm.

"I'm not going to argue. Go," Mark agreed.

"What about the '*Grazer*?" Red inquired as an afterthought.

"If you can't tow it back here, scuttle it completely. I don't want the Agalum getting their hands on any part of it. Shuttle three is on its way to pick up you and your men, Red."

"Good, we're done here. Come and get us."

Mark turned toward Lilly Wallflower. "Get Mr. Marek up here and on the security console."

She nodded. "Will do, Sir."

"In the meantime you scan for enemy vessels heading toward Eddie."

Lilly Wallflower nodded nervously and turned away.

***

The two small shuttles streaked across the alien sky from opposite directions, both in camouflage mode, both undetectable. Less than a minute later they converged and landed in a smoking, ruined tract of forest. There were downed trees and fires burned across the area freely. The *Stargrazer* sat smoldering at the end of a half mile long tract of devastation.

Red was out of Shuttle three at a run, followed by a dozen of his security men. Hot on his heels from Shuttle two was a medical team led by Dr. Troiano herself.

"Good lord, the '*Grazer*'s been through one hell of a battle," Red growled, "Eddie! We're comin' for ya bud, hang on!"

He worked the hatch controls to the right of the doorway and the door slid open slowly. Inside everything was askew. Seats were broken off of their mounts to the ship's hull, and control panels smoked.

"Where's Eddie?" Red barked.

In reply a moan issued from under a console along the ship's front wall.

"I've got it," Troiano shouted, getting ahead of Red with two of her medics.

"Ooohh," the voice under the console moaned once again.

Medics pulled away the debris and removed Eddie carefully from under the console once Troiano checked him to her satisfaction. The medics placed him on an anti-grav gurney, and headed toward the shuttle they had landed in.

"Get him to the shuttle quickly. I want him under a med scanner as soon as possible."

"All right, Doctor," one of the medical staff concurred, holding the anti-grav gurney with another medic. The two men walked the barely conscious Eddie to the shuttle with Troiano right behind them. "Red, we're heading back to the *Cag* immediately."

"Go, Doc, don't worry about us. Get Eddie stabilized."

Red turned to his people. "Get out the anti-grav lifts and get them attached to the hull. I don't want to give up this ship. The *Stargrazer* has been great to us for the past two years."

The men began to work immediately, setting up the two anti-grav discs and attaching them to the ship's hull.

"They're attached, Red," a man named Barker informed him when the work was done.

"Good let's get the *Stargrazer* out of here, and let's all get back to the *Cag*."

Moments later the shuttle lifted off. Within its command area Red activated a small pad he held. "Let's see if this all works now."

He activated the pad and a holographic control interface popped up from its surface. Red began working the controls and the *Stargrazer* rose unsteadily into the air, the anti-grav discs attached to its hull slaving it to the shuttle.

"All right, let's get out of here before the Agalum show up."

The shuttle took off and headed back toward the hidden *Cagliostro*, the *Stargrazer* following behind it, shakily mimicking the shuttle's movements by remote control.

"Red, this is Lilly," Miss Wallflowers voice streamed from the ships comm system, "We have incoming ships headed right toward you."

"Wonderful. We're picking up the pace, Lilly. What's their ETA?"

"At their present speed, about forty seconds."

"We'll be there in twenty."

Red accelerated the shuttle and the *Stargrazer* being flown by remote control followed accordingly.

"Are we camo'd yet?" Jenkins, one of the security people asked.

"Yes, and I'm extending the field over the *Stargrazer* too. We're arriving at the *Cag* now."

Smoothly the shuttle flew into the shuttle bay, followed by the *Stargrazer*, which rocked side to side and landed heavily, even sliding a few feet across the shuttle deck floor.

Shuttle number two was already in place and emptied. Red and his crew walked out toting their weapons. Mark entered the shuttle deck as they were all approaching the exit.

"How's Eddie?" Red inquired, concern written all over his face.

"Troiano is looking him over now. We'll all know more in a short while." Mark's eyes played over the

Stargrazer. "She looks like hell. What the heck did Eddie run into?"

"We won't know until we download her files."

Mark nodded. "I'm having the techs go over her now. Whatever did this to her may still be out there."

"Is Eddie awake?"

"No. He got banged up in the crash, but Troiano thinks the safety protocols saved his life."

"When he does finally wake up we'll know what we're up against," Red grunted.

"Let's get those files out of the '*Grazer*'s security systems," Mark ordered.

Red nodded slowly, almost absentmindedly. It wasn't lost on Mark.

"What's the matter, Red?"

The big warrior turned to him. "Eddie's down, Ari's down, hell both the *Stargrazer* and the *Cagliostro* are down, the '*Grazer* maybe for good. We're in trouble now."

"We'll get out of this. We will. This is a tough spot we're in, Red. I'm not belittling it. But we've been in worse. We'll get out of this one, too."

"I hope you're right, Mark. I don't wanna be stuck here for the rest of my life, however short an amount of time that may be."

Troiano's voice broke over Mark's comm unit. "Captain, please come to sick bay. We have a situation."

"Eddie?" Red asked.

"Let's go." Mark ordered.

Both men ran from the shuttle deck to the maglovator. They were whisked almost instantly down a level and across the ship to come to a soft halt on the medical deck. The doors shushed open and the two men emerged in the med lab's hallway. They pushed their way through into the med lab itself, the doors not sliding open quickly enough.

"What is it, Ann?" Mark asked Dr. Troiano.

"It's Ari. She's needs you. Better get in there."

Mark turned and ran toward the room Ari was in. Mark found her up against the wall holding her head. The helmet was still in place, but she was obviously fighting the thing within her.

"What happened to her restraints?" Red asked.

"She was fine with the helmet in place; she wasn't a problem or a danger to herself, so I let her out of the restraints for a while." Troiano answered.

"Ari, honey, it's me, Mark. Talk to me, baby."

"M-Mark… this thing, this Chakix… it won't leave and it's fighting against the helmet, and against me." She stumbled across the room and landed on the hospital bed in a fetal position, still holding her head. Mark got on the bed behind her and held her arms.

"Honey, what does Chakix want?"

"S-she…it wants the helmet off. It's in pain, an-and now it's feeding that p-pain to me. It s-says it won't stop u-until I'm dead, or the Agalum are d-driven from t-the p-planet."

Mark stood silently, dying inside at having to watch Ariel suffer. He touched her long blonde hair gently, then put a cover over her on the bed.

"Doctor," he called to Troiano.

The diminutive physician appeared almost instantly in the room's doorway. "What do you want me to do, Captain?"

"Administer another sedative. Let her rest. Then remove the helmet once she's out cold."

Troiano looked at him in surprise. "Are you sure, Mark?"

"Yes, Doc, I am. Ari's going to get permanently hurt this way if she has to keep fighting this Chakix's influence and the helmet keeps harming this alien creature as well. Chakix is sending that pain right back into Ari's mind."

"I know, Mark. I am a doctor."

"I can't have Ari continually hurt like this. There has to be another way to get this thing out of her."

"Okay, I'll be right on it."

Troiano and a nurse approached the quivering Ariel in her bed. The nurse handed Troiano a hypodermic, and the doctor shot Ari full of sedatives again. A moment later Ariel was silent and asleep.

"Okay. I'll remove the helmet now." Troiano looked at Mark for approval and he nodded his head. Troiano, with the help of her nurse, then slid the helmet off carefully.

"Keep her sedated, Doctor. Keep the helmet off of her for now. If this Chakix attempts to control her again, put the helmet back on, but keep her sedated anyway. I have to drive that thing out of Ari's body. I'm not going to let it win."

"It's beating us at every turn, Mark. I was sure the helmet's frequency should have been enough to drive that thing out of her body."

"So was I, Doctor. How could I have been so wrong about this?"

"Stop blaming yourself," Troiano ordered. "This is all unknown territory, Mark. And to be honest, I don't think it has any intention of leaving until its demands are met."

"I want the Agalum off of this world as much as this invader in Ariel's mind does. But her ways of coercing us are not the best ways to gain my attention or my trust."

"Agreed, Captain. But what else are we going to do right now?"

"I'm open for suggestions, Doctor. Do you have any?"

She sighed heavily. "Sadly, Mark, no."

"Neither do I, Ann. But I keep thinking I'm missing something, some way to clean up this entire mess."

"Keep working at it, Mark. You're the smartest guy I've ever met. If there's a way out of this, you'll find it."

"We're only a hundred people on this ship. We can't storm a mountain base full of Agalum."

Troiano nodded in silent agreement.

"Not to change the subject," Mark began after a pause of several seconds, "but how is Eddie?"

"He'll live. He's going to be hurting for a while though. He's bruised up and he hit his head pretty hard. Hard enough for a concussion."

"Nothing broken though?"

"No, he got very lucky. Plus the safety protocols saved his life. Of that I have no doubt."

Mark grinned grimly. "At least something worked right on this trip."

"Something of your design, don't forget that part." She patted him on the shoulder. "Now go get some rest.

You need it more than anyone and to be honest, you're starting to look and smell like hell," Troiano wrinkled her nose.

"All right, I hear you, and you're right. I've been burning the candle at both ends and the middle since we landed here. Hell, that landing was just about the last thing to go right since we've been here." He began to walk toward the exit when he turned back to Troiano. "Is Red still here?"

"No, he looked in on Eddie, and then left when he saw he was still unconscious."

"I figured. Those two may argue and fight like cats and dogs but they're brothers inside."

"Go get some rest, Mark. Something will come to you."

"Okay, Ann. Call me if there's any change to either of them."

She nodded while he walked out into the hallway and made his way toward the maglovator.

Within the maglovator his communicator activated on the sleeve of his uniform, beeping slightly and glowing a faint blue.

"Mark here."

"Mark, it's Red. You better come outside."

"Outside? Why'd you leave the med-deck so fast?"

"That's what I'm trying to tell you. Come outside."

Mark shook his head in annoyance. "All right. I'm on my way." Mark turned and headed toward the maglovator and the world outside the *Cagliostro*.

Exiting the ship and walking down the entry ramp, Mark came to a grinding halt halfway down. He continued after a moment to the ramp's end where Red was standing with a half dozen security men.

"What's going on here?"

"They're scared and want to set up camp here."

Before them were at least a hundred of the native aliens camped outside the force field protective zone. Some were making fires and others were huddling against the coming cold of night.

"This isn't good." Mark sighed heavily. "Get them under the ship and put those fires out. Any who wants to stay within the ship, set up in Cargo Bay two, which is empty. The rest set up with the thermo conductive sleeping bags and let them sleep out here. I'm sure at least their women and young children will want to stay within the warmth of the ship. Get them more food, and make sure it's already cooked. I want those fires out. The last thing we need is to draw attention under this canopy of trees we're hidden in."

"All right, Mark. I'm on it."

"Good. When you're done go get some rest."

"What about you?" Red asked.

"I'm going to do that now. Marek is in the big chair at the moment, or will be as soon as I tell him. I need sleep at this point. I'll check in with you in a few hours."

"Sorry I buggered out of there, but I got a call about this from Parsons." Red nodded toward a dark skinned security officer with close cut black hair.

"It's okay, Red, you're doing your job, which I appreciate."

"How's Ari?"

"The same. We're still dancing with that thing inside her head."

"Okay. I figured as much." Red paused a second, then continued, "Go get some rest. You look like hell."

"I'm starting to feel like it too."

Mark turned and walked up the ramp and into the *Cagliostro*.

He had one more stop to make, and that was within the engineering deck.

"Danny, how are things looking?"

Dan Sledge turned around and nodded with a slight smile, "Better, Boss. The monotriglycine was added ta the coolant mix and the components for the magno-disc counter balancer are almost complete. Another day at most and we'll be back in business. There were some stressed out components here; stuff that went beyond its life cycle, way beyond. But everything is bein' taken care of. We'll be in good shape when we get offa here."

Mark nodded stoically. "Good, good. Has there been any word from the crew looking over the *Stargrazer*?"

"Not yet, I'll let ya know when I hear somethin' though."

"Okay, Danny. Thanks."

"Get some rest, Mark. You look like hell."

Mark chuckled, "You're the third person in the last ten minutes to tell me that."

He turned and disappeared within the Maglovator, its doors whispering shut behind him.

Chapter 14

Eight hours later Mark awoke, showered and dressed quickly. He exited his suite and made his way to the command deck.

"Mr. Marek, I'll relieve you now." Mark stated. His secondary crew leader. Matt Marek stood, smiled and exited the command deck.

"He's quiet. Been that way since I got back in here an hour ago," Red commented.

"Why'd you come back here an hour ago? I thought you were going to get some rest, and I know your morning routine; two hours of exercise before you take your post."

"Relax, Boss. I had six hours sleep."

"And a half dozen cups of coffee?" Mark smiled.

"Yeah, at least." Red returned his grin.

"How are our guests out there? Behaving themselves yet?"

"So far so good," the big security officer shrugged.

"Okay. Don't let them start any cooking fires. I don't want to bring any attention at all to this position. We're buried deep in the foliage here, and it's been serving its purpose. But we are literally under the nose of our enemy. After Eddie took out that ship yesterday in the *Stargrazer* I'm surprised this place isn't swarming with Agalum."

Mark stopped and looked out the view screen, then returned his gaze to Red. "What happened to Red Kong?"

"Disappeared during the night. He got up quietly and skulked off according to Marek."

"Huh. I thought it was brain damaged from the beating Dan gave it."

"Yeah," agreed Red, "There was no reason to post guards around it, when we could have watched it just as closely from here."

"Very true, Red. Besides the way it was lying there I doubt it would have wanted to cause us any more problems once it awakened." Mark mused.

"Or that Chakix thing inside of Ari might've ordered it to remain still and sleep. We don't know what kind of control that creature has on the animals on this world. Hell, it may have control over the natives as well."

Mark nodded silently. "You are right, Red. We really don't know the extent of that thing's power. Danny said we'd be spaceworthy by the end of today. I think it's time to start getting the ball rolling on our exit strategy here."

"I hate to be the one to mention the eight hundred pound gorilla in the room, but what about that base that's in the volcano? Are we just going to leave here and not help these people?"

"Red, we're damaged. You know I have the utmost faith in this ship and more importantly the crew. But we are in the deep end of the pool here without a life jacket. The ship is damaged, and while Danny and the engineering staff can get us up and running to close to full capacity, I'm not sure I want to go into battle without a full refit on Earth, especially against an entire base full of Agalum."

"You do not have a choice, MarkJohnson," Both men turned toward the Maglovator door to see Ariel walking in, but it was Chakix speaking. Behind her was Dr. Troiano waving her hands frantically.

Mark put his hand up, halting Ann Troiano in her place.

"What do you want, Chakix? I cannot drive these invaders off of your world. We are one ship and a damaged one at that. They outnumber us by a vast number. I have complete faith in my crew, but I refuse to send them to their death, just because you want me to. That's not going to happen."

"You will remove them from my world MarkJohnson or I will make sure ArielO'Connor never leaves here."

"That's something else that is not going to happen."

"You force my hand, Earthman."

 Telekinetic lightning flared from Ariel's eyes and slammed into Mark's chest, throwing him across the command deck. Everyone on deck scattered.

Red leaped through the air, and tackled Chakix/Ariel, knocking her to the floor, but her telekinetic power instantly hurled him away, to land unceremoniously next to Mark.

"Ow. That hurt," Red mumbled painfully.

"No kidding. Oh no," Mark exclaimned.

His eyes were fastened onto the rear of the command deck, where Chakix/Ariel had Dr. Troiano by the throat and was holding her a foot above the ground by the neck.

Troiano's feet kicked frantically as a hypodermic needle clattered to the ground from her outstretched hand.

"She's gonna kill Troiano!" Red shouted frantically, fighting his way unsteadily to his feet. Mark grunted and stood painfully as well. But before either man could move the maglovator doors slid open and a blaster bolt rang out, striking Chakix/Ariel in the back squarely.

The maddened possessed woman dropped Dr. Troiano to the ground, then turned slowly toward the figure now pulling itself painfully out of the maglovator. Another shot rang out, catching Chakix/Ariel square in the chest, but the woman did not fall. She stumbled backward and began to walk toward the figure in the doorway again, her eyes sparking.

A third blaster bolt rang out again directly to Ariel's chest. Mark screamed, "No!"

Like a puppet with its strings cut, Chakix/Ariel dropped to the ground, unmoving.

Immediately Troiano was on her feet and checking for a pulse.

"She's not breathing," she called out.

Mark was at her side instantly. He turned to the man in the maglovator doorway, who finally fell into the command deck himself, collapsing on unsteady feet.

"Eddie! What did you do?"

"I-I was tryin' ta save the Doc, Mark," he moaned painfully.

Behind them Troiano called for a medical team and an anti-grav gurney. An instant later both sets of maglovator doors opened and disgorged security teams along with a medical team.

Eddie was helped to his feet and placed on one gurney while Ariel's unmoving form was lifted to another. Red limped to Mark's side.

Everything was a haze now for Mark Johnson. It was as if he was watching a program and not something that was happening before his eyes.

"Mark..." Red began.

"No, Red..." Mark slurred.

Troiano attached pads to Ariel's chest and fired up her defibrillator unit. Ariel jumped once on the gurney, but lay silent immediately afterward.

"Clear," shouted Troiano as she fired the defibrillator a second time. Again Ariel's body bounced up and down, and yet again lie still.

"Don't do this, Ariel, dammit," Troiano muttered, slapping her across the face twice before pumping her chest. Again Troiano charged up the paddles and slapped them onto Ariel. One last time her body jumped up off the gurney. Again she lay there silently.

Troiano began to charge the paddles a fourth time but felt a gentle hand on her shoulder. She turned and saw Mark standing there, his face grim.

"Ann, don't... Let her go.... She's gone already." He barely spoke.

"But..." Troiano began, then stopped as Red put a hand on her shoulder. Eddie had already been taken back to the medical deck during the commotion.

Mark walked over to Ariel's still form and brushed his hands over her eyelids, closing them. Then he collapsed onto her, sobbing softly.

Chapter 15

Mark sat silently in his suite in the dark, staring at nothing save his interwoven hands.

A soft knock came from his door.

"What is it?" he grunted hoarsely.

"It's Danny an' Red. We wanna seeya, Mark. We need ta talk to you. Open up."

Mark sighed and tapped the remote on his table top near where he was seated. The door hissed open and both men cautiously entered.

"Mark..." Dan began, before Mark raised a hand to stop him.

"Look, I know you two mean well, but I need to be alone. After what happened, I can't think straight right now. This whole mission has been one disaster after another, and now this. My poor beautiful Ariel." He sunk his head into his hands and began sobbing again. "Boss..." Dan started again.

"No, Danny, I-I'm all right,"

"Look I need to talk to you about Eddie," Red cut in. "He feels terrible. He said his gun was only on stun. She shouldn't have died from it. I checked everything including vids of the command deck and he's right. He used a low stun."

Mark raised his head, his eyes were red and he had a day old stubble. His hair was unkempt, and he had been in the same uniform at least a day and a half.

He looked at his friends incredulously. "I'm not holding Eddie responsible for this. He saved Troiano's life, maybe yours and mine as well. I know he didn't mean to kill Ari. I know he didn't," he repeated.

Dan fidgeted uncomfortably. "Look, Boss, we need ya to take command again. I mean if you can't Red or I can do it. But this ship, this crew needs you, not Red or me, *you*. You get me? You're its heart an' soul."

"You're our leader," Red added.

"Yeah, you are. An' right now we need ya to lead," Dan finished.

"Guys…"

"Look, man, I know yer hurtin', we all are. Everyone on the ship. Not just the command crew. Everyone loved Ari. The five of us were a team. We were like a family of dysfunctional siblin's."

"What the illiterate Jovian ape is saying is true, Mark. I'm not a guy who can talk about feelings and stuff so easily." Red fidgeted. "But Danny's right. We all loved her. Eddie's tearing himself up over this. Troiano is like a robot since it happened. The crew is barely speaking to each other. The *Cagliostro* is like one huge mausoleum right now. We need our captain back. All of us do. We're not going to be able to get off of this rock without you."

"All right. Let me clean up. Wait for me in the kitchen area. I'll be out in ten minutes. Make yourselves coffee or something. In fact make me something. I haven't eaten in two days. But I have to get out of this room. Danny, what's the status of the repairs to the engines?"

114

"Everything's done, Boss. Everything's complete. We just need to run a few tests and we can get the hell away from this place."

"I can't believe a simple exploratory mission turned into this nightmare," Mark murmured.

"I know," Red agreed. "All we were doing was looking for a mineral rich planet close to Earth, relatively speaking to establish a base on."

"Yeah these Agalum bastards beat us to this one," Dan Sledge added.

Both men turned and looked at him with furrowed brows.

"What?" Sledge asked, surprised.

"Nothing, Danny. You're right. They beat us here" Mark replied.

"This place would have been perfect too. I bet we could've even come to some kind of an agreement with the natives or that Chakix thing."

Mark looked at Red and agreed with another nod.

"Where is Ari?" Mark suddenly asked.

"Med deck, in a suspended animation pod. You know how that works. We bring bodies back to Earth if we can for burial there. Hell, you wrote that rule."

"Yeah, I know," Mark replied glumly, and then continued, "I'll be out in a few minutes."

Fifteen minutes later the three men walked onto the command deck from the maglovator, a newly shaven and showered Mark Johnson at the forefront, wearing a clean blue and silver tech suit.

"What is Mr. DiGenovese's status?" He turned and asked Lori Westin, who was on comm duty.

Shocked at seeing Mark there and trying to hide it she answered, "Dr. Troiano thinks he's fit for duty. But he c-can't bring himself to come up here since the, um accident," she finished in almost an inaudible whisper.

"I don't care. Tell him if he wants to keep his job I need him on the command deck of this ship."

Mark turned to a young black man who was sitting at the weapons console. "No offense Hoskins, but I need DiGenovese back up here."

The young man smiled. "None taken, Sir."

"Good. I have to get this ship and crew back to running order as fast as possible. By throwing DiGenovese back into the fire may be the only way to do it. We need familiarity on this command deck today."

"Sir," Lori Westin called him quietly. Mark turned to look at her. "Sir, I-I know I can't replace Miss O'Connor, but I'll do the best I can to serve this ship until we get back to Earth. Lilly feels the same way. W-we both wanted you to know."

Mark relaxed a bit, he softened as he looked at her. "I know that, Lori. I never doubted you or Miss Wallflower for a moment. I'm sure both of you will perform your jobs with professionalism and grace."

"T-thank you, Sir."

"No, Lori, thank you."

The maglovator doors hissed open behind Mark and Eddie DiGenovese uncomfortably walked in. Hoskins saw him and stood immediately, clearing the weapons console for Eddie, who immediately sat and adjusted the seat and controls for himself.

Mark Johnson cleared his throat, and then began to speak slowly. "Systems check, Mr. Sledge?"

"Engines are started, an' runnin at nominal, Mark."

"Security?"

"We moved the indigenous species away from the ship earlier today. We've also supplied them with more food and cold weather gear until they rebuild their village the Agalum destroyed," Red answered.

Mark nodded, "Weapons systems, Mr. DiGenovese?"

"E-everything seems okay."

"Well is it or isn't it, Mr. DiGenovese?"

Eddie nodded affirmatively, "It, it is Sir."

"Drop the 'Sir' crap, Eddie. In all the years I've known you, I can't remember you ever calling me 'Sir'."

"A-alright, sorry Mark."

"Are we ready for liftoff?"

"We are Mark," Dan answered.

Mark leaned forward onto his fist, his elbow on the console before him. "What about our eyes in the sky? What do they have to report?"

"The two probes saw that Agalum G'Kor move off several days ago and disappear into space."

"Yes, I remember the report," Mark acknowledged.

"It musta been a supply run," Dan offered.

"Probably, but there's only one sure way to find out, right? Let's get off of this planet. I don't ever want to be back here again."

"Mark?" Eddie interrupted, "What about these people here? We can't just leave 'em to the Agalum, can we? They did nothing to us. They're livin' in fear. If we leave 'em behind, the Agalum will scoop 'em all up for slave labor in no time."

"I'll send a fleet of war ships back to free this planet Eddie. I, no, we just can't do it, not right now."

"Mark, think about it before we leave," Dan advised.

"Take us up and out of here, Mr. Sledge," Mark ordered coldly.

Dan shook his head and touched his virtual control panel. "You're the boss."

The ship began to lift up, but suddenly as if a gigantic hand had slapped down upon its outer hull, the *Cagliostro* bore back down to the ground.

"What's happening?" Mark growled angrily.

"I-I can't get enough thrust to get us off the surface." Dan turned toward Mark and answered. "It's like local gravity has increased a thousand fold."

"How is that even possible?" Mark rumbled.

"Look!" Lori Westin pointed toward the view screen.

There, in front of the ship, stood all the remaining natives as well as the giant red ape creature, and all their mouths were moving in unison. They were all speaking, including the giant red ape, and they were all saying the same thing.

"What are they saying?" Eddie asked.

"Lori, outside audio, on."

"Yes Sir," the brown haired girl acknowledged.

The audio came through the speakers and it instantly chilled them all to their very souls. The natives were repeating, "You will not leave. You are bound to this world by the will of the goddess Chakix. You will not leave until your mission is complete. Such is the will of Chakix." They repeated what they were saying over and over again, until Mark finally got up and shut off the audio feed at Lori's console.

Chapter 16

The conference room was almost chaotic. Everyone was trying to speak at once, including Mr. Marek, there at Mark's order. Marek ran the secondary crew and his opinion was a trusted one. The third shift crew had been called to the command deck and was staffing it now while this meeting was going on. Dr. Troiano sat quietly with her arms crossed over her ample chest. She was not happy.

"Everyone calm down," Mark shouted. "This Chakix is holding us here, but that's a temporary thing. We'll be able to get out of here, I'm sure of it."

"How do you know, Mark?" Lori Westin inquired. "Have you ever run up against anything like a sentient planet before?"

"No Miss Westin, I have not and neither has anyone here. But that doesn't mean this is an unattainable position. We've been in tougher spots, we'll get out of this one. The ship is fully functional again and that's the most important thing right now. That's what's going to give us a fighting chance."

"So what do we do?" Dan asked. "Do we go out there an' try to talk to this crazy planet ghost or whatever it is?"

"I don't think talking to it will do any good at this point. The damned thing killed Ariel and I was hoping it had died with her somehow. At least that would have been some modicum of revenge. Yet there it is again, this time talking through its natives."

"How do you want to play this, Boss?" Red queried.

"What are you asking me, Red? Should we go guns blazing and try to break free of the planet's gravity field?"

Red shrugged, cocking his head to the left as he did. "Yeah that about sounds right."

Mark leaned back in his chair and steepled his fingers in front of his face before speaking. He sighed and continued, "Oh how I wish, Red. Right now that's exactly what I want to do. I want to take this Chakix monster and lash out at it, and don't kid yourself I still might, but where would that leave the native people here? Would they be able to survive without Chakix?"

"We survive without some deranged guardian spirit," Eddie offered.

"You're right, Eddie, we do. But will they? *Can* they? Their whole history has this Chakix acting as their guardian angel."

"Not the way I woulda put it, but yer point is taken," Dan grunted.

"So it all comes back to what do we do now?" Red summarized.

"I think we have to drive the Agalum off of this world. I don't think we have a choice at this point." Mark summarized.

"How are we going to do that? There are a hundred of us, and there could be as many as thousands of them inside that base. We could really be going face first into a wasps nest," Red barked.

"You're right, Red. It's a no win situation any way you look at it. Unless we get some help."

"What are you thinkin', Mark?" Dan asked.

"I'm thinking we get Chakix to help us."

"Do you think that's possible?" Troiano joined the conversation, after sitting silently for the past several minutes.

'I don't think we have a choice, Doctor," Mark answered. "And I don't think she does either."

"I keep thinkin' this is gonna blow up in our faces," Dan exclaimed.

Mark nodded. "You're probably right, Danny."

Red sat back, rubbed his eyes and then sighed. "Let's go talk to this Chakix and see if we can strike up some kind of amicable deal."

"I have my doubts," Dan replied.

"I think we all do," Troiano agreed.

Mark stood, with everyone else following suit. But he still gripped the edge of the table top heavily as he did so.

Dr. Troiano stopped him before he exited the room and pulled him to one side.

"Mark, tell me you are not going to do anything stupid in dealing with this creature."

"Ann, I couldn't do anything stupid even if I wanted to. Answer this for me. What is there for me to do? This Chakix thing is some kind of world spirit. It's alive and inside the planet and its inhabitants."

"Are you saying it's a god of some kind, Mark?"

"Ann, for all I know it could be a viral infection carried through the air on spores that are breathed in."

"If that's the case anyone who's been outside the ship, including both of us would be infected. But since we're both fine I think that shoots down that theory."

"I think you're right," Mark agreed.

"So what do we do then?"

"We go deal with this thing, this living planet and try to make some sense out of this. In the meantime I'm going to have every scientist on this ship working to figure out what this thing is and how to overpower it."

"Are you sure you're all right to go back out there and actually talk to Chakix? Ariel died yesterday, Mark. Not last week, not last month. This is more than a little soon."

He turned and looked at Troiano. His lips formed a grimace before he replied, "No, Ann, I'm not okay. I can't forgive this thing and if I find a way I *will* kill it for what it did to Ariel. I will not let this living, sentient planet get away with killing Ariel. But right now I do believe we need this creature and her inhabitants if we're going to drive off the Agalum."

"Wait, Mark. You are really going to trust Chakix to aid us against the Agalum? Have you lost your mind?"

"Honestly Ann, I'd have to say yes. Since Ariel died, I most definitely have lost my mind, which Chakix is about to discover."

"Mark, wait..." Troiano called after him. But he ignored her. He entered the maglovator and descended to the boarding ramp. He began to walk down it as the maglovator doors sighed shut behind him, only to re-open only a scant few seconds later. Dan, Red, and Eddie followed him down the ramp.

"You three stay on the ship. I've got this," Mark called over his shoulder.

"Like hell you do, Mister," Dan Sledge answered.

Mark looked over his shoulder, his brow furrowed in surprise, "Dan, You're fired. Red, take him into custody."

Red looked at Mark's face impassively. "Do it yourself."

"What? You three are here to what? Mutiny against me?"

"Not the word I'd a' used, amigo, but hey whatever shoe fits," Eddie replied.

Mark was stunned, but he pointed up the ramp toward the entry way door. "This is not funny you three. Turn around go back up that ramp and wait for me inside. We'll work this out."

"We ain't goin' anywhere without you, Mister," Dan growled.

"Are you three out of your damned minds? I've given you all direct orders."

"Yeah, we know. We just ain't obeyin' them." Dan stepped forward, closing the distance between them in four steps.

"Listen, Mark, You're too hot headed for this right now. You gotta relax and give yourself a chance to cool out. Ari dyin' hurt us all, every one of us on this ship, but especially us." Sledge waved his hand as if to encompass the four of them. "She was family to us. The five of us were more than crew members, we were a team. Now if you're goin' out here to deal with this thing, we're goin' witcha. It's that simple, deal with it."

Mark stood there, not knowing what to say, or how
to respond. Finally after at least half a minute he deflated
and sighed, "I don't know whether to start hitting you
three idiots or hugging you all right now,"

"No hugging," Red grunted. "I don't 'hug'. Not now,
not ever, got it?"

Mark smiled and nodded. "Yeah I got it, big guy. To
be honest, I'm not that big on hugging another man
myself."

"Good," Red agreed. "Remember that and we won't
have any problems in the future." He half smiled as he
brushed past Mark and took point down the ramp where
the alien natives and the hundred foot tall red ape with
the 'V' shaped head stood silently.

The four men spread out across the bottom of the
ramp, and then Mark began to speak. "Chakix, show
yourself now. I order you to come face me."

As one all the aliens and the ape spoke. "You order
me, human? I who am goddess and world to those who
dwell here? You are impertinent, MarkJohnson."

"No, you monster. I am angry. How dare you think
you can hold my crew here and make us fight your war.
How dare you think you can force us to drive your
enemy off of this world's surface, something you
obviously don't have enough power to do yourself."

"You are wrong, MarkJohnson," the strange unison
voice replied. "I could drive them off, but many of my
children would die."

"Oh you mean like the way Ariel died? Ariel was
special to me, I loved her. She was going to be my wife
someday. We were going to spend the rest of our lives
together when this war was over. I hate the Agalum. I

124

despise them for what they did to my world. I have no interest in anything they have to say. I'm not interested in doing anything where they are concerned save forcing them back to their own solar system and closing the door on them, much the way they had intended to do to us."

Mark paused a moment and walked a few feet, looking away from the gathered natives and into the sky. Then he returned his gaze to the waiting aliens and through them, Chakix.

"But you?" He continued, "You I hate more than I do them. Infinitely more. You took the love of my life from me. You took my future from me. That's something I'll never forgive or forget. Ariel made me a better man just by being in the same room as me. I looked at her and all was right with the world no matter what situation we were in. She calmed me just by being there. I can still see her face smiling at me. That's something I'll never be able to do again, because of you. I'm going to drive the Agalum off of this world, but after I'm done with that, I'm going to destroy you, no matter what it takes. For killing Ariel I'm going to kill you."

If a being who considered herself a goddess could know fear, than certainly Chakix was feeling that emotion now. But instead of recoiling, Chakix's minions merely stood their ground and spoke as one once more, every being present replying, "MarkJohnson, you misunderstand. ArielO'Connor is not dead. She is here with me."

Chapter 17

"What do you mean she's here with you?" Mark exploded, thundering off the ramp and running until he was face to face with the native chieftain.

"When your Eddie shot at her/I, the pain was awful. I retreated back to my body, back to my world and children, and I took Ariel with me. She is not dead. She is here, all around you."

"You crazy psychotic thing, you release her immediately," Mark roared.

Behind him, Eddie, Dan, and Red looked at each other and then at Mark, surprise etched across all their faces at Chakix's proclamation.

"Free her or I'll free her myself from your grip. I promise you it will not be pleasant for you. If you know anything about me, I'm a man of my word, and nothing, *nothing* will ever stop me from attaining whatever goal I set for myself. You've merged with Ariel. You know what she does. You know I mean every word I say. Release her because I swear if you don't I'll tear her mind from your grasp and rip you apart in the process."

The gathered aliens were silent a moment, as if considering Mark's demand. Then as one being they all looked upon him. "I never meant any of you any harm. It is not my way. But these Agalum had hurt my children and had blocked themselves from my wrath, in much the way I cannot affect your ship other than holding it here."

Danny looked at Red and Eddie and mouthed silently, "The force field."

They both nodded in silent agreement.

"Release her," Mark demanded again.

"Will you help my children? Will you drive these Agalum from my surface? From my skin?"

"No promises. Release your hostage or I'll force her from your grasp, whatever way I have to. Once you do we can discuss what you want. All you've done so far is show us all how much you cannot be trusted. You haven't been dealing with us from a position of power as you may have thought, but from one of threats, as a usurper would. You have not made us respect you, Chakix. You have made us despise you instead."

"B-but my children," the world mind stuttered.

"You put them in this position, one of danger. Not us. We were forced to your surface, driven to land here. If the Agalum had not forced us to land here we would have never bothered with your world, with you. You have given us no reason to aid you. All you have done is filled us with contempt for you. But if you release Ariel without any further delay, we'll begin discussions on aiding you. There are no promises though. I am making that clear to you before we start."

"Very well," were the only words the aliens uttered before they all closed their eyes.

Mark touched the right cuff of his silver and blue uniform, which immediately began to softly glow and called, "Dr. Troiano, I need you to check on Ariel and tell me what you see immediately."

Troiano's voice replied without hesitation. "Captain, I was just about to call you. All of Ariel's life signs have come back all at once. She's alive, Mark. I don't know what you did, but she's alive."

"Doc, get her out of the suspended animation tube ASAP." He clicked his right cuff again, which stopped glowing.

Mark turned toward the closest alien native. "You, you will accompany us onto the *Cagliostro*. Do you understand, Chakix? You'll be allowed this one body aboard my ship and you will speak through him."

Mark softened as the realization of what had just transpired seemed to finally wash over him. He turned and headed back up the entry ramp to the *Cagliostro*, calling over his shoulder as he hurried toward the ship's entryway. "I'll call for you in few minutes. I'm seeing to Ariel first myself. If she's fine, you can come up and join us."

"I understand, MarkJohnson," The eerie voices all spoke at once. "I will await your call here."

Eddie, Dan, and Red followed in Mark's wake, which was as powerful as any sea going titan at the moment. The four men burst out of the maglovator and onto the medical deck, walking quickly and purposefully toward the sliding glass doors.

The doors opened as they all approached. A crowd was gathered near a gurney. The heads in the crowd of people turned one by one and stepped aside when they saw who it was that was approaching. They all parted like the Red Sea at Mark's approach, without hesitation.

Then Mark saw her. Behind him his three closest friends looked at one another and smiled.

Mark threw himself at Ariel and wrapped his arms about her, practically smothering her with his affection. They kissed for several minutes as the crowd turned and left slowly, leaving the two people alone save for their three friends and Troiano herself.

"I thought I lost you," Mark choked. He ran his hands through her golden hair.

"No. Never. I'm still here, and always will be. I'll never let you get rid of me that easily."

"Good, because I was about to turn this world to dust to get you back."

"Always gotta have the last word, don't you?" Ariel snickered before kissing him again.

Eddie, Dan, and Red moved closer when Ariel looked up at them and smiled.

The three men hugged her one at a time. Dan had to turn away and wipe tears from his eyes.

"You're crying? You, the big tough super strong Jupiter colony native?" Red teased.

"Watch your mouth, strawberry, or I'll forget how fragile you really are," Dan answered, grinning.

Mark turned toward his security chief. "Red, show Chakix to the conference room."

Chapter 18

The small shuttle landed two miles from the Agalum base, its camouflage system hiding it perfectly. Mark, Red and three of his best security men exited the shuttle with light blast rifles hanging off of their shoulders and pointed straight ahead, aimed from the hip.

The men looked around silently as the door on the side of the shuttle slid silently shut. Mark tapped a few buttons on the virtual control pad he had hovering over his right sleeve, and the shuttle faded from sight. He tapped another button, causing the virtual control pad to fold up and disappear seemingly into his sleeve.

Mark nodded to Red and the security team and began walking silently through the forest, following a holographic map that had sprung out of his right sleeve in place of the control panel.

The five men walked for a half hour and emerged adjacent to the Agalum base. They all knelt as Mark pointed to various spots around the cliff face. This was the entrance to the Agalum base. It remained hidden to them by some sort of stealth technology. But every so often a small ship would approach and enter the runway built into the side of the mountain volcano. When a craft neared the right location, the entrance would spring into view and then fade from sight the instant the ship passed through the maw-like opening.

Mark silently scanned the hidden entrance with devices built into his suit. The Heads Up Display that appeared above his right sleeve now showed the height and width of the mountain cut away, as well as what depth stretching back within the facility that could be read. Figures could be made out within the cave entrance moving around. *'Maintenance men'*, Mark thought.

Indistinct sounds came from the east, behind them, now and getting closer. Voices talking. The language was unfamiliar. Mark muted his suit's vocal system and went strictly to visual. He made slashing hand motions and everyone else followed his lead. Red nodded silently and waved two of his men to follow him, leaving Mark with one man.

Red and his team disappeared into the thick underbrush walking north, using the compass and 3D HUD on his sleeve to guide them silently.

High over the forest a floating sphere probe was feeding information to both Mark and Red simultaneously. Before the shuttle had landed Mark had released the probe and programmed it accordingly. Its mission was to feed data and telemetry to not only the surveillance team, but also to the *Cagliostro*.

* * *

"Dan, I've got a clear feed coming back from the probe. It looks like that landing bay they built into the side of that volcano goes on quite a distance," Lori Westin announced.

"Good, Lori, glad ta hear it." Then after a moment, he continued, "Umm, not about the size of the base, but that ya got a clear view I mean."

Lori smiled. "I know what you meant, Dan." She dipped her head and winked with a smile.

Dan returned her smile, but nervously. Then he quickly turned away from her and stared intently at his console's holo-display. He was getting the same feed from the probe Lori was and his eyes widened at what he saw.

"Holy…Are they gettin' this too?"

Lori nodded. "Yes Sir, they are."

"Okay, good. I'm not gonna notify them then at what I'm seein' here. I'm just gonna hope we ain't the only ones what seen this."

"Shouldn't we try to tell them on a discreet channel?"

"No matter how discreet the Agies may pick up on it. Maintain signal silence, blondie. We'll trust in Mark an' the boys bein' half as savvy as I think they are."

***

Mark pointed to his right and the guard with him nodded, silently sliding into the dense foliage. Mark moved left, crouched down and held the powerful weapon before him, aiming through its sight at where his sensor told him the Agalum would emerge.

His sleeve warmed slowly, drawing his attention to its display once more. He saw Red in the display gesturing a warning in the direction Mark was facing. Red held up six fingers. Mark tapped his sleeve and Red nodded in reply.

'Here they come.' Thought Mark.

Almost immediately a purple skinned Agalum walked right toward him out of the brush. Without any hesitation he fired six quick blasts, missing only once.

133

Five bodies dropped to the ground, unmoving. "Graaaaggghh," snarled the remaining Agalum. He whipped his weapon out of its holster, but Mark fired first. His second blast caught the enemy warrior in the face, dropping him to the ground.

Red and the other three men thundered up as sirens began to wail all about them in the woods.

"So much for silence," the big security man commented.

"Can't be helped now," Mark began. "We have to make it back to the shuttle as fast as possible."

The five men ran with Mark leading the way, his HUD display showing the exact location of the shuttle.

They bounded over a hill and ran smack into another patrol, which immediately opened fire on them.

"Run!" shouted one of the security men, the instant before an Agalum blaster bolt cut him in two.

"Martin!" grunted Red.

They ran backward, trying to avoid enemy fire as they did.

Each of the remaining four men took turns firing at the group that was slowly gaining ground on them.

"Any second now that group behind us is going to get us, then we're really going to be in trouble!"

"I know Red. I'm working on it," Mark growled.

The two remaining security men fired before them while Red and Mark took aim at newcomers behind them and returned fire. Several times blaster bolts scored hits on their miraculous uniforms, and each time they shunted the blast, saving the men from instant death.

Now they were all kneeling down in the thick foliage, firing all around themselves at unseen foes who fired back repeatedly. The air burned with blaster fire.

"What now, Boss?" Red asked.

"Duck," was Mark's only reply.

The shuttle sprang into view from behind them, rising up over a ridge and firing blazing death down remotely upon the Agalum.

"Hit them hard, now!" Mark roared.

Everyone found targets and with the shuttle's help they obliterated them all.

Thirty seconds later they were aboard the shuttle and streaking across the treetops in the small camouflaged ship.

"That was close," Red admitted.

"Closer than I wanted it to be, Red."

Mark hesitated a moment while looking over the information the probe had fed back to them.

"What the hell..." he muttered.

"What is it?" Jacoby, one of the security men asked.

"Red, look at this. This is a deep black light/infrared scan the probe did. Everything appears in negative. Watch what I see here when I zoom in."

Mark brought the image into a much sharper, much more magnified view.

"What the hell is that?" Red rumbled. "What are they doing to those natives?"

"It looks like they're placing some kind of device into their necks with a hypodermic of some kind and turning the natives into drones controlled from this base. They could build an army this way and are doing just that."

"It looks like they're not just using this base as a supply depot. This is going to be a launching point for an all-out invasion."

Chapter 19

The shuttle door was still sliding open as Mark turned sideways and slid through it.

"What's the rush?" Red shouted after him.

"I want to get a better look at that base," Mark replied over his shoulder.

"How are you going to do that?" Red hurried after him into the maglovator before the doors shut.

"What'd we leave out there, Red?"

"Huh? Nothing that I know of."

"Think, man. The probe. A fully camouflaged probe. Next time that cloaked entryway of theirs opens I'm flying that probe in to get better pictures of the inside of that thing."

The two men exited onto the command deck and both found their stations. The secondary crewmen at each station stood and moved aside. In Mark's case it was Dan who sat at his station. The big Jovian moved over to his own pilot/engineer console where another man quickly stood and moved toward the back of the command deck and the left side maglovator doors.

Mark sank into his command chair and punched a few buttons on the left side arm of his chair. He pulled the desktop over his lap from the right and instantly a virtual display sprang to life before him.

"Here we go," he muttered quietly.

The feed from the probe took up the view screen in the front of the command deck.

The image of a blank rock wall on the side of a volcano filled the screen.

"Nothing happening yet," Red announced.

"What're we looking for?" Eddie inquired.

"Something going in or out of there," Mark quietly replied. His concentration was fully focused on the images playing out before him and nothing else.

Long minutes passed. After several more had gone by, the maglovator door slid open again and Ariel exited from it and into the command deck.

Everyone turned to look at her. Everyone except Mark, who had not realized she was standing there.

Eddie, Red, and Danny's eyes followed her as she walked up behind Mark and wrapped her arms around his neck, letting her fingers play across his chest from behind.

"Hey, good looking. What's going on here?"

Mark turned, obviously surprised at seeing her there. But his look of shock instantly changed to a smile. He stood up, pulled her toward him and kissed her passionately, not caring who was watching.

Miss Wallflower stood up discreetly from the communications console and slipped away, entering a maglovator on the right side of the command deck. Before the doors slid shut she gleefully caught Ariel's eyes, then smiled and waved.

Ariel giggled as she broke Mark's embrace. She walked over to her console and sat down behind it, sliding the desk portion in before her.

Mark continued to smile while he sat back down, either oblivious to all the eyes on the command deck staring at him, or simply not caring.

His eyes strayed from Ariel back to the view screen at the front of the command deck and his demeanor changed in less than a heartbeat.

"Dammit!" he blurted out while recalling the virtual interface before him.

On the view screen an Agalum cargo shuttle was entering the landing bay built into the side of the volcano. The image broadcast from the probe began to move, falling in behind the cargo ship and entering the base.

"Anyone want to bring me up to speed?" Ariel asked with a smirk.

"Short story," Dan began, "is that's an Agalum base built inta the side o' that fake volcano-"

"It was probably a working volcano at one time," added Mark, "meaning the Agalum somehow terraformed it, either venting it out somewhere else or shutting it down all together."

"Right," Dan continued. "That's a cloaked probe we got followin' that cargo shuttle in. It's gonna tell us what's really goin' on in there."

"Actually, Ari, it's just going to confirm what I already suspect and get us a better look inside," Mark concluded.

The unseen probe moved further inside the rock hewn hangar bay. It silently flew over the heads of Agalum purple skinned men as they injected something into the necks of struggling red skinned natives. Once they were injected with the mysterious item within the hypodermic they all went stiff, as if they were now mechanical men. They moved only when commanded to by those called the 'salad heads' by the crew of the *Cagliostro*.

At the front of the cavern stood a yellow skinned Agalum, who spun on his heel quickly and entered a long cavern, the probe following invisibly at a safe distance.

"That's one of those leader caste Agalums," Eddie announced.

Mark nodded his head. "It is. As we've seen over and over, they are the captains of the ships and leaders of larger bases. The salad headed purples run smaller bases and espionage. The bald headed purples are the grunts or foot soldiers. But you all know that anyway."

"It's good to be reminded, Mark. This stuff is important for all of us to know inside and out," Eddie added.

"What are you havin' the probe do now?" Dan queried.

"Following that black eyed bastard back to his den if possible and seeing if we can get any more info out of what's going on here."

All eyes upon the command deck focused on the view screen when a warning light began to blink on Red's station. The big security officer refocused to his own console and his eyes went wide.

"Mark, you better see this." Red touched a virtual control and the view screen split in half, the left side showing the view everyone had already been watching, the right side showing space from the view of the probes they had sent out days earlier and into close orbit. In the blackness of space several large ships had already appeared and were locking into orbit. But an instant later a massive cruiser, bright and gleaming, appeared from hyper-warp and settled into orbit, the other ships encircling it protectively.

"What the hell is going on here?" Eddie asked.

"That's someone important," Red replied.

"I think that ship holds someone far more than just important," Mark announced. "I believe that ship holds the Agalum supreme leader."

Chapter 20

"We're in trouble with all that firepower above us, never mind the base they already established here," Red offered.

Mark Johnson leaned back in his command chair on the command deck of the *Cagliostro* and for several very pregnant moments steepled his fingers in silent thought.

"No, Red, I have to disagree with you on this one," he finally replied. "That base is our number one priority right now. It's going to be our best way to survive all of this and maybe, just maybe end the Agalum threat once and for all."

"What are you plannin'?" Dan grinned.

"I need sixty five armed and ready people prepared to go to battle."

"We only have thirty security people on this ship. The rest are going to be techs and people from all over the ship," Red offered.

Mark nodded. "I know but just about everyone who serves on this ship is ex-military as you well know, no matter what position they may be filling right now. Thirty five people left aboard the Cag will allow us to operate normally if need be. Right now we need ground soldiers who hopefully will not have to fire a shot. Red, I want as many men as you have suited up in heavy battle armor to lead the charge. I need to speak to Chakix. She's going to have to do her part as well now."

***

"You wish me to put my children in harm's way? No I refuse." The native alien who housed Chakix' mind spoke in the same hollow, eerie voice they had all heard emanating from Ariel's mouth when this adventure had begun over a week and a half ago.

Mark, Red and Dan stood opposite the Chakix Alien, varying degrees of annoyance playing across their faces.

"You don't have a choice, Chakix," Mark rebuked her. "This is no joke. I need every able bodied native you have upon this world. If they want this world free from these invaders, they have to be willing to fight for it. *You* have to be willing to fight for it. We can't do everything."

The bare chested, red skinned male who housed Chakix's mind snorted derisively but did not refuse Mark's request a second time.

"You say this will eliminate these invaders from my lands? Why do you now agree to help so quickly?"

Mark shrugged. "I told you before we would help you get rid of the Agalum. But the situation has grown more dire."

"You speak of the recently arrived vessels in my orbit."

"Yes I do, and the one vessel that gleams like a polished diamond amongst the rocks up there? That's a yacht of some type; someone very important to the Agalum is on that vessel. From the looks of things I'd say that's the Agalum supreme leader's vessel. They want this planet, of that I have no doubt. This world, your world is meant to be a staging ground in their attacks on my world, Earth."

Chakix bristled with what could only be described as rage. "I will reach out and destroy that ship and all of those around it."

"That's all well and good, Chakix, but why haven't you done the same thing with the invaders who are here in that base they created?"

"I cannot. They have my children captive," the native Chakix was speaking through simply replied.

"I wish I could get word through to the Earth Protectorate Interstellar Command," Mark mused. "We'd have a fleet of space navy ships here in a day."

"You could do such a thing?" The native eerily asked.

"I could, but not here. They would be upon us in minutes. We have to be far enough away from here to not draw attention to ourselves."

The alien native cocked his head sideways and asked, "Why?"

"Kinda thick, aintcha Chakix?" Dan asked with some annoyance.

"Because they would destroy us on this spot. They would decimate us before we could get space bound."

"So?" The alien continued, "You do not matter; only my children do."

"That's not how it works," Mark angrily replied. He stood and punched the conference table for emphasis. "We're partners in this. You have to work with us if you want our cooperation. It's reciprocal."

"What is 'reciprocal'?" the alien world-mind asked.

"It means you help us, we help you," Eddie added.

For a moment the red skinned, bare chested alien Chakix possessed sat quietly in his seat. Then it raised its head and its eyes met Mark's.

"I do not like this 'reciprocal'. I order you to do as I command, and you obey. That is how it has always been, and how it will always be."

Mark leaned back in his chair and locked his steely gaze with Chakix's host. "No. That's not how it's going to be. Not this time. You're not calling the shots and sacrificing us, Chakix. We're not your cannon fodder. We are partners in this endeavor, nothing less."

"I will crush you and your precious '*Cagliostro*'," the alien leaned forward and sneered.

"No. No you won't. Do you think I sat quietly and awaited you to order my crew, my friends to our deaths? Especially after what you had done to Ariel? Not only can you no longer affect us, but I can also destroy you if I was so inclined."

"You would destroy me and all my children?" The alien stood and shoved the chair he was sitting on out from under himself, banging it against the wall behind him.

"I didn't say I would, Chakix, only that I could. Oh and by the way, I could do it easily too."

"I -I do not believe you," the alien stammered.

Mark stood and everyone followed his lead. "Fine. Prepare for lift-off."

"I will detain your ship," bellowed Chakix.

"No, no you won't. Not anymore," answered Mark. He turned and exited the conference room. An instant later Chakix followed them all out to the command deck.

The command crew relieved the secondary crewmen and took their seats. Ariel was already there, having not been part of the meeting. Mark didn't want Chakix anywhere near her.

"Red?" Mark queried. A moment later two security men appeared and stood on either side of the possessed alien.

"You will not leave, I will not allow it!" Chakix screamed belligerently.

"You don't have a choice this time."

The *Cagliostro* began to rise off of the thick forest floor. The gigantic trees that had hidden it up until now swayed and snapped as the ship rose.

"No, I will stop you!" The Chakix possessed alien closed its eyes and concentrated. Instantly the *Cagliostro* felt like a hand had closed around it.

Mark looked at Dan and nodded.

A wave of energy passed through the hull and out of the ship. Simultaneously the alien host for Chakix fell to the ground as if it were a puppet with its strings cut.

The *Cagliostro* rose upward once more, now completely free of its confines. Its hull seemed to shimmer, almost as if it were hard to see. To the naked eye it looked as if it were almost liquid and not a solid star cruiser.

"What did you do?" Chakix asked weakly.

"Something you won't understand or be able to defend against. You may have great powers and abilities as a living planet, Chakix, but my great ability is finding solutions to problems. It's what I do best. I found the solution to you, and it was right under my nose." Mark nodded to the security personnel who were holding a severely weakened Chakix up by the arms. They walked the alien to the maglovator and entered it together, heading toward the security cells.

"What'd you do, Mark?" Ariel asked.

"We went to hyper-warp without any forward motion. You see, hyper-warp is not a speed related state. We actually slide a small part of our mass into another dimension."

"Is that why it looks like we're in a star filled tunnel when we're in hyper-warp?"

"Yes. Usually we only enter this other dimension with about point zero three percent of the ship's mass. We effectively stand between dimensions and are immaterial in both of them, for the most part. All of this is accomplished with the magno-discs. The other dimension is one of insubstantial nothingness. We are never seen or perceived by anything that might exist there. As of now I believe it's a dimension without any form of life existing within its confines. I've never seen anything, and believe me I've spent many hours searching through it via probes, right, Danny?"

The big Jovian smiled and nodded. "That's right, Ari, an' always made me help him out with the calculations, just to make sure he was right."

"So what just happened?"

"I slid us seventy five percent into the side dimension. Danny and I worked it out over the last few days. We have more of a hold in that one than we do in our own at the moment. That's why Chakix collapsed.

148

Its tether to its own flesh as it were, the planet itself, was severed."

"Is it dangerous?" Ariel asked.

Mark nodded slowly, his head leaning to the right. "It could be, if we stay this way for too long."

Eddie pointed to the view screen. "How come I'm still seeing the planet, and nothing looks different?"

"Our eyes and brains are used to our own dimension and have not acclimated to this dimension of mist and fog, which is all I ever see in this place. There appears to be no up or down. No ground or planetary mass. It's a purple colored void, which if you notice now, things have begun to take on a purplish hue, even though we still see Chakix, the planet, itself."

"So we're not going to need those sixty five crewmen anymore?" Red asked.

"No. Now I'm going to bring an army from Earth instead."

Mark turned toward Dan. "Take us into space, Mr. Sledge."

Dan grinned and nodded. "With pleasure, Boss."

The great ship rose completely upward and engaged forward thrust, bursting free of the planet's gravity field and flying unseen past the Agalum fleet massing there.

"Take us away from here, Danny. Red and Ariel, find us a nice empty sector of space with no Agalum vessels within a few light years. I want to send EPIC all the information we've attained."

"You got it, Mark," Dan agreed.

The powerful Jovian engaged the hyper-warp fully and in a burst of light, like a new star bursting to life, the

Cagliostro glowed blindingly bright and then slowly blinked out of existence.

Chapter 21

"Uh oh," Danny rumbled, "I don't think we're in Kansas anymore, Mark."

"What the hell…" Mark trailed off. He was staring at the view screen in stunned silence as was the rest of the command crew. Even the extra command deck personnel that were constantly coming and going from the command deck stopped in shock and stared at the view screen.

On it was pictured a thick, cloying purple fog as far as the eye could see, which was not very far at all.

"W-what happened?" Eddie DiGenovese stuttered.

"We must have been pulled into this other dimension completely," Mark hypothesized.

Dan turned toward him mirthlessly. "You think?"

Mark's dirty look silenced Dan momentarily while both men returned to staring at the view screen in awe. Puffs of purple clouds rolled by in the void they found themselves in.

Mark finally shook himself out of the shock of the moment. "Dan, status report on all systems?"

"Hyper-warp is down, but it's nothing mechanical, it's just…down."

"What does that even mean?" Eddie choked.

"It means we may be stuck here for a while," Mark sighed.

Ariel looked at Mark and their eyes connected.

'Are you all right?' she asked telepathically.

'Ari, your telepathy is working again?' Mark replied, surprised.

'Just now Mark, since we left Chakix' world.'

Mark mentally sighed. *'I'm glad to know whatever effect that world had on you wasn't permanent. How are you feeling?'*

'I think I'm fine. I feel normal again.'

He nodded and smiled. *'Good. I'm very relieved, Ari. In fact, you have no idea how much.'*

'Oh, I'm sure I do.' She smiled softly.

"Mark," Dr. Troiano's voice filled the area around his command chair, "come down to the med deck when you have a minute please."

"Are we secure here, Red?"

The big redheaded man nodded. "Sensors are a little wonky, but we seem to be okay. It looks like this purple void dimension is filled with a whole lot of nothing."

"All right, let me go see what Troiano wants."

'Dollars to donuts it's that Chakix again," Eddie opined.

"Of course it is. I'm curious to see what it is this time. Danny, join me. Red, you're in charge. We'll be back in a few minutes." He spun on his heel and left the command deck with Dan right behind him.

The maglovator doors slid closed. "What is it, Mark?"

"Nothing, Danny. I just wanted to get your opinion and thoughts on everything so far, and where we should go from here."

Dan shrugged. "Well we're kinda trapped in this crazy purple void, though I'm sure you have a plan to get us outta here. Once we do we should make a bee-line for

Earth, an' then come back with maybe the whole fleet if possible an' wipe these bastards offa that world."

Mark nodded. "My thoughts exactly, though I'm going to start sending the emergency broadcast long before we get home. Perhaps not even return home until we clear the Agalum off of that world."

The maglovator doors opened, and both men exited onto the med deck. They walked into the main med bay. But even before the doors slid open they could hear a screaming from within. Looking at each other they hurried in.

The native who housed Chakix' consciousness was being restrained by several members of the medical staff. The alien native growled and cursed, at one point shrieking madly. All the while Troiano was fighting to get near enough to anesthetize the man. Dan immediately leapt forward and lifted the madly struggling alien up, swinging him around and slapping him upon a waiting gurney with enough force to knock the air out of the wild man, but not do any grievous harm.

Troiano placed the pressure fueled hypodermic apparatus to the man's arm and pushed the button. Instantly a dose of sedative was pumped into him. Within a few seconds the native was docile.

"What happened?" Mark blurted.

Troiano turned to face both men. "When you left the planet's atmosphere Chakix went nuts, kicking and screaming like a lunatic."

"Doc, are you sure that *is* Chakix yet, an' not just the native himself in there?"

Troiano nodded slowly, "I see your point, Dan, but a few of the things the native screamed definitely sounded like Chakix."

"Care to enlighten us, Doctor?" Mark inquired.

"Sure. The alien spoke of wanting to tear your guts out for dragging her away from her world."

"The native himself could have been yelling that, not Chakix." Mark said. "And why did you refer to the creature as if it were a female?"

"It's referred to itself as a female all along, Mark. It possessed Ariel first, indicating a preference for women."

"Actually, Doctor, I assumed it possessed Ari because she was a telepath, making her more susceptible to a powerful world mind's influence than one of us."

Troiano turned her head, bit her lip slightly and then agreed with a nod. "You're probably correct Mark, I had thought of that as well."

"But anyway, why do you think Chakix possessed this native, a male, for any particular reason over any other?"

"Probably because it needed someone to speak through quickly, once Ari was freed, and this man was camped outside."

"Making him an easy choice. Sounds about right, to me at least," Mark confirmed.

"What do I do with him when he awakens?"

"You can keep him/her/it sedated, or maybe see if the creature within can act like a civil being and speak to us normally. I want this creature to eventually trust us. Keeping it tied up and shouting at it just isn't accomplishing that objective."

Troiano nodded her agreement. "Understood, Captain."

"Let's give Chakix another chance to act like a modern human being instead of a savage animal. Maybe we can reach an agreement with it."

"I think you're missing one point here, Captain."

Both men turned back to face Troiano.

"What is it, Ann?"

"That creature, Chakix is basically a god to those people. It does not have to bargain or make deals with anyone. It's in charge. Now we come along and that authority means nothing to us. You've found ways to stymie it right along. You are probably the only serious challenge this creature has ever faced."

"You're forgetting something, Doctor. The Agalum have been on its planet for a while already and have basically ignored Chakix completely. I would say with force fields and anti-gravity devices they've been able to make Chakix irrelevant. The natives have probably been praying for salvation from Chakix for God only knows how long, but it's been helpless against the Agalum. We have to become Chakix' ally, and in turn it our ally. We're heading back up to the command deck. Keep me informed if Chakix wants to talk, but definitely keep its host restrained. For the time being at least."

Troiano nodded grimly as the two men exited the medical bay.

The two men entered the maglovator, and Mark turned to Sledge. "You were quiet in there. What are you thinking?"

"That this is getting' stranger an' stranger, Mark. Also I'm thinkin' I have to get the ship out of this purple dimension an' back home, wherever we really are."

"Yes, let's get to working on that immediately."

The maglovator doors slid open, both men stepped within the command deck area and the entire *Cagliostro* seemed to shudder and shake, as if hit by something.

"What the hell?" Mark exclaimed. He slid into his command seat, while Red took his own seat once more at the security station. Dan slid into his pilot's station.

"Red, what was that?"

"I don't know, Mark. We were attacked by something, but our scanners are still having problems acclimating to this dimension. Something is out there though."

As if in response to Red's comment the entire ship shuddered once again.

"There, look!" yelled a tech pointing at the view screen.

"What the hell…" muttered Dan.

An image floated by on the view screen, obscured by static. It was just a shadow, but it seemed to mimic the *Cagliostro*'s lines and general shape.

"I don't know what that was but it attacked us, so return fire!" Mark ordered.

"You got it, Boss," Eddie replied.

The forward solar cannons roared to life, illuminating the pea soup they were flying through. Both blasts missed, but by what distance no one knew.

"Not easy aiming in this mess, Mark," Eddie blurted out over his shoulder.

"Just do your best, Eddie."

The ship rumbled again as something hit it once more.

Alarm klaxons were blaring loudly all about the ship.

"Shut those off, Red. Leave the red alert lights blinking throughout the ship corridors. Not here though."

"You got it, Mark," Red acknowledged.

The command deck was silent as everyone was trying to discover what had attacked them either on sensor readouts or on the view screen.

"I got something, Mark," Red announced.

"What is it?"

"Believe it or not I'm scanning on infrared."

"That shouldn't work in space, not in a vacuum like this."

"That's just it, Mark, this isn't a vacuum. I don't know what this is, but there's weight and depth here. This thing is swimming through it."

"But we can sense its body heat using infrared?"

"Only up close, Mark. About a few hundred feet away at best."

Mark jumped up from his seat and leaned into Dan's console. "Reconfigure sensors for a wide pattern. Three hundred foot range maximum, Heat imaging on main viewer. Three hundred sixty degree view of the *Cagliostro*."

Dan nodded.

The static filled view screen showed nothing but the white noise images they had been staring at for the last few minutes when something eerily appeared as if from nowhere.

"Whoa, look at that," Eddie whispered, wide eyed.

"I am." Ariel shook her head.

"It looks like the *Cagliostro*," Eddie proclaimed.

"No," Mark interrupted. "It looks like a Manta Ray."

"Mark, it's not alone," Red growled in surprise.

The view screen showed the static filled images and blurry lines, but it also showed more and more of the deep space manta rays that were now encircling the ship.

"There must be half a dozen out there," Red declared.

"And probably more coming," Mark added. "Prepare all weapons systems. Let's make this place too hot for them to handle."

"What are you plannin'?" Dan queried.

"According to the sensor readouts I've been watching since we came here, this purple pea soup appears to be combustible. We're going to set it all ablaze and then hopefully get out of here."

"Wide spread pattern on the solar cannons. I want shields at one hundred percent before we fire."

The *Cagliostro* was engulfed in a ball of luminescent energy that played over its hull the instant the shields hummed to full life.

"Pick a target, Mr. DiGenovese, and fire at will."

Eddie nodded. "Will do, Mark."

The solar cannon glowed a moment and then unleashed its energy directly at the nearest swimming space-ray, catching it across most of its body.

The creature flipped over in space and stopped moving its fins. It just lay there and floated away, seemingly dead.

Immediately the rest of the space-rays turned and directly converged on the *Cag*.

"Fire at will Eddie, this is all you," Mark shouted.

"I'm on it Mark, I'm firing at anything that gets close." Eddie's hands played deftly across the fire controls quickly targeting and firing the shgips powerful solar cannons again and again at the space-rays. After several minutes of this the remaining giant creatures spun away on the purple clouds and floated off, away from the *Cagliostro*, but all about the ship the otherworldly dimension now burned. In fact the entire expanse of space around the *Cagliostro* burned as more and more of the purple clouds caught fire.

"Uh-oh, I'm not likin' this at all," Dan mumbled.

"You're not the only one. Back us away from this mess," Mark ordered.

"Good idea, Boss," Dan replied.

The *Cagliostro* slowly backed away from the burning area of dimensional space.

Once free from it the ship spun about completely and moved away from the burning quadrant of the purple void.

"Are you seeing any more of those creatures, or anything similar?" Mark inquired.

"Not as of yet," Red replied cautiously.

"Are our sensors clearing up at all? I'd like to get a better idea of what we're flying through."

"Yes Mark, the sensors are recalibrating on their own. It's just taking a bit longer than usual because of whatever this is around us."

"That's what I want to find out, what this…muck is we're surrounded by."

"All I can tell you now is that this stuff is not space. It's not a vacuum, Mark. It's got mass to it," Dan said.

"So what is it?" Eddie asked.

"Well judging by those space-rays' movements through this void, it appears to be a gaseous environment of some kind," Mark concluded.

"How do we get out of here?" Ariel asked the question everyone feared the answer to.

Mark tipped his head to the right. "I'm not sure yet. The simple thing would be to just reverse our mass, swapping between dimensions back to our own. But to be honest when we slid out of hyper-warp we should have simply reverted back to our own universe already. I'm really not sure why we haven't."

"Well that's just great, because if you don't know I don't know who will," Ariel nervously replied.

"Hey we've gotten out of tough situations before. We will this time as well. Don't sweat it."

"I know Mark. But we always seem to go from frying pan to fire."

Mark looked at his girlfriend and shook his head slowly in agreement. "You're right, Ari. We do. Especially the last two years. But that will stop once we drive off the Agalum once and for all."

He turned toward Dan. "Danny, any other anomalous readings out there within our buffer zone?"

"You mean like more o' them space-ray things?"

"Yes, and whatever else might be out there."

"No, Mark, nothin' else is out there. At least not anywhere near the ship that I can see."

"Ari, Red, what about you two? Are you picking up anything we should be wary of?"

"It's nothing but dead space as far as I can see," Red confirmed.

Ariel shook her head. "No, Mark. I'm not picking up anything on any frequency. It's like those things are the only creatures alive in this entire universe."

"Which means they must feed on the purple clouds somehow." Mark leaned back and rubbed his jaw in thought.

"So what are you thinking, Mark?" Eddie asked.

"I want to run some projections. Danny, make sure we're in the same area we entered this dimension in. I don't know how much our straying will affect us back in our own dimension."

"Right," Dan agreed. "We could end up light years away."

"Yes, and that would not be a good thing."

"No, Mark, it wouldn't," Ariel commented.

Mark Johnson stood. "Okay here's what we're going to do. I'm going to go down to the engineering lab and run some projections. Dan is going to accompany me. The rest of you are going to get some rest. I'm calling in the secondary command crew for the next six to eight hours. When Danny and I are done we'll call the rest of you back and we'll get the heck out of here. I just want to make sure we're doing this as safely as possible. The next eight hours may end up meaning nothing when all is said and done, but I want to take every precaution before getting us back home, and you notice I said 'before getting us back home', and not 'trying to get us back home'."

Mark and Dan exited the command deck onto the maglovator and headed to the engineering level.

Mark turned toward his friend. "What do you think?"

"Hhmm? About what? Gettin' us outta here?"

"Well what else? Of course getting us out of here. Am I being overly cautious by not just reversing what we did on Chakix's world? Or am I doing the right thing making sure we'll be safe?"

"Look, Mark, I ain't never second guessed you before an' I ain't gonna start now. You come up with what you think will work an' I'll run the numbers, makin' sure it's all safe. That's the way we've always done it an' that's the way it's always worked."

Mark nodded and grinned. "Agreed, big guy. I keep thinking if we just reverse what we did back there the ship will blow up."

"Nobody's gonna know the chances o' that happenin' better than you. If you got a gut feelin' about this whole thing then I'm a hundred percent behind you takin' the cautious approach."

"I know you are, pal. Let's just get this over with. Have you gotten any progress reports on the *Stargrazer*'s repairs?"

"The '*Grazer* was hammered, Mark. I'm not sure we can repair her onboard."

"Okay we still have shuttles that are working anyway."

"Yeah, that's true, but unless we need 'em I'm gonna keep those repair crews on the '*Grazer* anyway, Just in case we need ta reach home an' not aboard the *Cag*, if ya know what I mean."

"Understood, Danny. I always like having the *Stargrazer* ready for a mission involving a smaller ship, just in case we need something a bit less conspicuous."

"To hell with not bein' conspicuous, Mark. If we need ta get the cavalry or even if we have ta go back ta

Earth ta get some parts or equipment the '*Grazer* gives us another option. You know, just in case this baby is in bad shape."

Mark laughed. "Danny, we've never been in as bad a shape as we just were a few days ago. Yet you put the *Cagliostro* back together and even created replacement parts in the machine shop. I doubt this ship can be waylaid permanently, especially with you here taking care of things."

Dan shrugged. "Hey whatever, man. I'm just glad to have been of service," he answered with a lopsided grin.

The two men exited the maglovator into the engineering deck.

They headed toward a set of computer interfaces that were back to back with each other. They each placed a helmet with a blacked out face screen over their heads and plugged the headsets into the interface.

Mark asked, "Ready to log in?"

Dan nodded. "I'm ready for you ta get inta my head if that's what you mean."

"I do, big guy. Let's go work out these scenarios and see which one is our best bet."

A virtual control panel popped up before Mark, and he immediately began typing parameters into it. A moment later both men's perceptions were radically changed. They found themselves seemingly standing in a barren black room.

"V R system is working at one hundred percent efficiency. Our mind link is strong. Let's see the best way to get out of this void."

"Yeah let's get to it. The sensors are still sendin' us info on this place."

"I know, I'm seeing the telemetry."

***

Seven hours later they removed the headsets and both of them almost collapsed where they sat.

Mark exhaled, "I don't think I've been this exhausted in years."

"Yeah I agree, Boss man. I feel like I'm gonna pass out right here. But at least we got our answer."

"I know. It took us long enough to get the parameters just right, but it was a good thing we just didn't try to cross back over. C'mon let's get back to the command deck."

"I'm starvin'," Dan mentioned.

"Yes, me too actually."

Both men exited the engineering deck into the maglovator, and both of them felt the hairs at the back of their necks rising.

Dan turned to face Mark. "Did you notice…"

"That the engineering deck was empty? Yes I did. C'mon."

A minute later they exploded onto the command deck from the maglovator and stopped short as soon as they entered the command deck.

"What the hell? It's empty!" Dan exclaimed.

"We have to find out what happened here." Mark slid into his seat and activated his holographic control panel.

Dan did likewise an instant later. "Last eight hours?"

"Yes. Start with the command deck, then work our way around the *Cag*."

Dan nodded stoically.

On the main viewer a vid feed of the command deck appeared and began playing very quickly. Hours passed in minutes as the two men watched silently and intently.

"There," Mark shouted at the six hour indicator.

The video instantly stopped, then Mark rolled it back in increments.

"What the hell *is* that?" Dan asked.

Mark shook his head incredulously. "I don't really know. Whatever it is, it's making a chill run up my spine."

On the view screen the two men watched as a roughly man sized amorphous cloud of black smoke appeared and disappeared constantly about the command deck almost instantly. Chalk white arms would dart out and grasp a crew member and then the entire cloud enshrouded mass would blink out only to reappear a heartbeat later at another spot on the command deck to drag someone else unwittingly within its smoky miasma.

Again and again this happened until the command deck was cleared of all personnel.

"Do you think it got everyone?" Dan queried, fear coloring his voice.

"Let's find out," Mark growled.

Mark punched a glowing red button on his console. Instantly the ship's warning klaxons exploded with sound, a female voice began blaring 'red alert' over and over in between the klaxons' bellows.

In twenty seconds the sounds quieted and Mark spoke into a microphone at the communications console. "All crewmembers check in immediately."

After a moment he growled, "Ah, screw this."

Mark punched buttons and the scene on the viewer was replaced by a grid pattern with every crew member's name upon it. Next to their name was an indicator.

Only a dozen indicators remained lit. The rest were dark.

Calls started to come into the command deck, one on top of another. "This is Maxwell on the hangar deck reporting in."

"This is Dr. Troiano in Medical reporting."

"This is Robinski reporting in," Red's voice thundered.

"DiGenovese reportin' in," Eddie's voice followed.

'Mark, what's going on?' Ariel's telepathic voice filled Mark's mind.

'We've been boarded by…something and they took most of the crew. They seemed to ignore everyone who was asleep or buried deep within the ship. Best you come to the C-deck immediately.'

'On my way.' she replied.

Six more crew members from various secluded positions about the *Cagliostro* replied, with the largest concentration coming from the hangar deck where the *Stargrazer* was being repaired.

"Mark," Dan began, "Whatever that was slipped through our shields like they weren't there. Somehow it teleported in an' out of here, an' took our people with it."

"I know, Danny. Do a wide spectrum sweep of nearby space or void or whatever the hell this place is. Also check the sensor log at the time of each appearance, I want to know what energy signature to look for. There should be a bundle of it at each appearance of our mystery guest."

Mark punched up the inter ship comm again. "All personnel report to the command deck immediately."

Ariel whisked into the command deck before Mark had finished speaking.

"What happened?"

"We were boarded. Take your console, Ari. I'll explain what we know when everyone else is here."

"Mark, I've got it," Sledge interrupted.

"What, Danny?"

"Every time this thing appeared there was a huge burst of tachyons across the 'C' band. That's the tell we needed."

Mark nodded and then continued, "Reconfigure the shields to block against tachyons at that frequency, specifically. Also prepare an internal force field to lock onto our guest should he reappear within the ship."

The remaining nine people entered the command deck, led by Red and Eddie.

"What happened?" Red barked.

"We were boarded while we slept. It looks like by one and up to a hundred of these smoky apparitions. They took everyone on the command deck as well as all sections of the ship that were busily in use at the time. Dan and I were locked in our private lab within the engineering deck, and we were ignored or never found."

"Can we find our people?" the tech named Maxwell asked. He was a man of average height and weight with short cut brown hair.

"What are we going to do?" Dr. Troiano asked.

"We're going to get our people back anyway we have to, Doctor. As of right now we are at war with an unknown foe. Woe be unto them for what they have done here."

Chapter 22

"Battle stations. All weapons to full power and loaded positions. Magno-discs to full power. Let's rock this town," Mark ordered.

All across the *Cagliostro* systems immediately converted to battle ready status. The shields now glowed blue within the purple clouds. Lighting all about the *Cag* shifted to a battle ready state, meaning only lighting necessary for battle was lit and glowing. The ship took on a menacing, angry tone, looking more like a predator itself than a vessel of science or exploration.

Red advised, "Mark, those tachyon teleportation bursts seemed to be coming from five hundred miles within the cloud cover, or whatever this purple mess is."

"Dan, take us in."

The big Jovian nodded. "You got it, Boss."

The *Cagliostro* entered deeper within the swirling miasma of the purple void, covering the five hundred miles in less than a minute. It still seemed like an eternity to those on the command deck.

A warning beacon began to blink on Red's console. He immediately announced, "Something just impacted on the shields. Something that was trying to teleport in. I think they noticed us."

"Good. Drop the shields and prepare to raise them on my mark again."

Red nodded and did as he was ordered. The shields dropped about the *Cagliostro*. The color of the ship's hull returned to the bright, clean white it normally appeared to be.

Almost instantly a cloud of inky blackness appeared on the command deck, carrying with it a horrible loud thrumming sound. It began moving instantly toward Mark.

But even faster were the ship's containment systems. A glowing force field encased this apparition, holding it in place.

Simultaneously the shields outside the ship sprang back into place.

Within the command deck the inky cloud of blackness in the force field roiled and turned. After a moment pale white fists began beating against the force field as the inky darkness seemed to dissipate, seemingly drawn back into the body of the alien perpetrator within the force field.

Within a moment all the cloudy darkness was gone, absorbed back within the body of the alien creature standing on the command deck.

The creature sent a shiver down the spines of almost everyone assembled. It was tall and gaunt. Its skin was a bleached white. Its head was shorn of all hair and its eyes were large and luminous. It wore what amounted to jet black rags which covered its body from neck to toes. They seemed to flow and pulse about the creature with a life of their own.

"What the hell is this thing?" Red asked.

It turned toward him, snapping its head quickly his way. Then it cocked its head sideways and mimicked his words in a high pitched, creaking voice, "What the hell is this thing?"

The chilling hands of an unnamed fear spread throughout the remaining command deck crew.

Mark stood and walked up until he was facing it, only the force field and mere inches separated them. He stared it directly in its glowing black eyes.

"Ignore its circus act. It's just trying to rattle us."

The creature stood for a moment as if measuring Mark's worth, then smiled and bowed slightly, holding the edges of its tattered rags and spreading them wide.

"Where are my people?" Mark spat.

The chalk white creature sneered at him repulsively, but said nothing.

"Okay, we'll play it your way. I'm sure there are plenty more of you out there."

Mark turned and walked back to Dan's station. "Did the scanners get a read on its physiology?"

Dan nodded grimly. "Yeah, they did. Like nothing we've ever seen before, but we got a read, a good solid one."

Mark grinned. "Good." He turned back toward the entrapped creature. "Fill the force field with a gas that will kill this thing, and slowly. I want to see it suffer."

Ariel and Eddie exchanged nervous glances and then turned back toward the horrible creature within the force field cylinder.

From above it a sickly green gas began to seep into the force field. Almost instantly its horrifying grin faded as it tried to teleport out again and again. The black wisps sprouted from its body once more and enwrapped its form, repeatedly and violently exploding off the force field to no avail.

Slowly the tendrils of darkness withdrew into its ghostly pale body and it sank to the floor, clutching its own throat, its eyes distending from its face in pain.

Mark waited a few seconds more until the creature was barely breathing within the tight confines of the force field, and then commanded, "Clear it, and return the atmosphere."

Instantly the force field cleared out and air filled the cylinder of energy holding the repugnant creature. It lay upon the floor grasping at its own throat wide eyed, staring in new found recognition of the man who now knelt down before it. Mark Johnson's face was unreadable as he stared at the thing trapped in front of him.

For long moments he locked eyes with it, while the creature massaged its own throat, and then Mark asked, "Where are my people?"

Chapter 23

The *Cagliostro* streaked through the void space, following the trail of a vessel that had been hidden by the purple clouds within the void.

"Status on our quarry, Red?" Mark inquired.

"Estimating two thousand miles out and closing fast."

"It wasn't that hard to find these bums now that we know what ta look for," Dan offered.

In the forward left corner of the command deck stood the alien, still trapped and sneering angrily within the force field.

"Good idea keepin' that thing where we could see it," Dan remarked.

"Yes, thank you, Danny. We're a skeleton crew right now, and I don't need to have this thing alone in the detention levels. Best to leave it where we can keep an eye on it for the time being. Who knows? It may even get a chance to go home if its people are smart."

"We're closing on the enemy vessel," Red announced.

"Funny how they rabbited out of there once we had their guy here." Eddie jerked his thumb in the direction of the creature within the force field.

"Yes, I know. We have to be careful though. We're alone in a hostile environment right now."

Eddie snorted, "So what else is new?"

Mark nodded. "Point taken, Eddie. When we get within range fire a blast of the solar cannons across its bow. I want their attention."

"Entering firing range now," Eddie confirmed.

"Fire at will, Mr. DiGenovese."

Eddie nodded and thumbed his firing control. Twin blasts erupted from the solar cannons, both passing within fifty feet of the ship they were pursuing.

Almost instantly it slowed to a stop and began to turn to face the *Cagliostro*. The image on the view screen grew clearer the closer the *Cagliostro* drew.

"Holy…" Eddie began

"Why is it that every ship we face off against has ta be bigger than us?" Dan asked.

The ship spun slowly ahead of them and finally faced the *Cagliostro*. It was perhaps twice as long as the *Cagliostro* with a bow that sloped forward from the bottom upward, like a boat's. It showed hundreds of lit windows along its sides. But the most disconcerting thing about this ship was its make-up and color. It seemed to be a dark burgundy with tendrils growing all about its outer hull. The entire ship seemed to pulse with a light from within, as if it were somehow organic matter and technology mixed together and alive.

The crew sat silently within their stations, repulsed and intrigued somehow at the same time by what they saw.

"We really *ain't* in Kansas anymore," Eddie muttered.

"That things gotta have a hundred decks," Dan blurted out.

"It's firing weapons," Red shouted.

Mark stood up and spoke in a commanding voice, "Heads up and eyes front, people. We're in a fire fight right now, we're not sightseeing."

Blasts of energy leapt from the alien ships weapons and engulfed the *Cagliostro*, spraying across its shields.

"Whoa, shields are down to eighty percent on one shot," Dan announced in surprise.

"Eddie, return fire to their weapons systems and engines. I want that thing crippled if we can. Dan, try to pinpoint our people using their tech suits' transponders."

"You got it Mark," Dan agreed.

"Ariel, try to make contact. If they answer tell them we want our people back and nothing more. If they don't answer or refuse tell them we'll make it a blood bath."

"You got it, Mark."

Twin blasts of energy arced away from the *Cagliostro*'s guns, this time shattering across the larger ship's bow shields.

"They felt that, I think," Eddie commented.

"Fire the star core missiles at their engines, Eddie."

Eddie complied without hesitation. Two missiles arced away from the *Cagliostro* and collided explosively with the enemy ship's rear shields.

"Danny, move us around to their rear, I want a clear shot at those engines."

Sledge nodded. "Working on it."

The *Cagliostro* vectored away quickly, then spun about, flipping end over end so its forward guns were facing the rear of the much slower turning behemoth.

"That thing is starting to turn," Red announced.

"Fire at will," Mark ordered.

"With pleasure," Eddie agreed.

Star core missiles leapt from the *Cagliostro*'s bow, followed by intermittent bursts of the solar cannons. The enemy ship's rear guns fired sporadically, splashing against the *Cag*'s forward shields, when they hit them at all. Most of their shots went wide, while Dan continued to move the smaller, more maneuverable *Cagliostro* about, zig zagging it back and forth behind the larger ship.

"Updated status, Red?"

"Shields are down to fifty percent. But theirs are down to forty."

Mark nodded. "Dan, keep us moving. Red, double up the forward shields if you can."

"You want to leave the rear unprotected?"

"Yes, for now. We'll rely on our armored hull for a few more moments at the back of the ship. I want to make sure our forward section is protected."

"You got it, Mark."

"No reply on any frequency, Mark. Though I am hearing a clipped form of static of some kind on one band," Ariel advised.

"Put it on speaker."

An instant later a clipped sort of clicking sound played through the command deck speakers.

"That's code," Mark appraised. "Block all their communications, Ariel. They're calling for reinforcements."

Ariel immediately complied, then looked at Mark once more. "How can you be sure?"

Mark nodded toward the alien prisoner. "He's smiling, or was at least when he heard that sound."

"Well he ain't smilin' no more is he?" Dan growled.

The creature jammed its amorphous hands into the force field trying to break free once more, and failed yet again. It snarled at Dan as it balled its pale white hands into fists and pounded them repeatedly against the unyielding force field.

"You ain't getting' out o' there anytime soon, Nosferatu," Dan antagonized.

Eddie continued to fire the ship's weaponry. Finally the shield at the rear of the mammoth ship shattered. Arcs of energy flew across the purple void like fingers of lightning thousands of miles long.

"It's down," Red proclaimed.

"Continue firing, Eddie. I want those engines out of commission."

Eddie DiGenovese pressed the firing control again and again, this time strictly the solar cannons. The powerful energy weapons blasted the enemy ship's engines repeatedly until the port engine exploded spectacularly with a large eruption of debris.

"Mark they're trying to contact us now," Ariel declared.

"Yes, of course they are. That didn't take long did it? Put them on screen."

The viewer showed more of the frightening looking creatures, with their bald heads and pointed ears, their glowing eyes and chalk white skin. Three of them filled the view screen, twisting slowly one way then another horrifically. Their tattered rags seemed to flow around them independently as if alive, or at least a part of them.

Before any of them could speak, Mark commanded, "Stop with the theatrics, you don't frighten us. I want our people back, and I want them back now. If you refuse I'll destroy you all."

"You are over confident and you do not bluff well, strange skin." The creature on the screen cocked its head to the side and slowly licked its lips as it replied. Its black forked tongue darted in and out like a serpent's.

"You don't know me very well if you actually think I'm bluffing," Mark replied.

'I've got a fix on the tech suit transponders, Mark.' Ariel spoke telepathically, to not just Mark but the rest of the command deck crew as well.

'Good, Ari. Let's keep that to ourselves for now. We're going to have to send a six man boarding team over there.'

"You creatures, release my crewmen and do it immediately. This isn't a request. If I have to come over there and take them back it will make your lives a *hell* of lot more difficult."

The lead alien sneered. "Come and get them, strange skin." With that, the screen went blank.

"What was that about? He sneered at us and threatened but nothing more. Why even contact us?" Eddie asked.

"Maybe he wanted to see how many of us they'd missed?" Dan suggested.

"Whatever. Keep our shields up."

The *Cagliostro* rocked again violently. "They're attacking again," Red announced.

"Yeah, kinda got that, Cap'n Obvious," Dan smiled while replying.

"Red, what's their shield status?"

"Rear shields are still down, Mark."

"Okay prepare our boarding party."

Eddie looked at the ship on the screen. "How are you we gonna get on that thing?"

Mark crossed his arms over his chest and turned toward the left side corner of the command deck. "That question's answer is standing over there with a force field wrapped around it."

Dan jerked his thumb at the alien encased in the force field, "That thing? How's that gonna help us?"

"The answer to that is coming up the maglovator in Dr. Troiano's hands right now."

Troiano exited the maglovator holding the helmet they had built and used on Ariel earlier to separate and shut down the Chakix entity.

"You think that thing'll work on this ghoul?" Dan asked.

Troiano tilted her head to the side noncommittally. "It should, Dan. From preliminary scans I've gotten off of this creature's neural cortex we should be able to control it through the helmet."

"Yeah but for how long?" Eddie interjected.

"Long enough to get us over there and get our people back," Mark replied testily.

"What about getting back though? Is this thing gonna be able to take sixty people back in one shot?"

"Again," Mark began, "we'll have to see. I know it took groups at least once according to the vid feed. Even if it has to take three or four trips I'm fine with that. The armor suited security people can run interference in the meantime."

"How you gonna get that thing on its head?" Dan asked.

Mark grinned. "Stasis field. I'll drop one in place and hold it still. We'll put the helmet on its bat eared head then release it. That should do it."

"Let's do it then," Dan agreed.

Mark turned toward Dr. Troiano. "Are you ready, Doctor?"

"Yes, Captain, I am," the diminutive ship's doctor replied, her blue eyes sparkling behind her glasses.

The alien creature began to fidget behind the force field, seeking some form of escape.

"Drop a stasis field in place on it now, Red."

The burly security chief nodded and touched a button in his virtual display. Almost instantly the ghoulish creature froze in place within the force field.

"I'll take that, Doctor." As Mark walked past Troiano, he removed the helmet from her hands. He walked up to the frozen creature, then turned to face Red. "Drop the force field but be ready to instantly turn it back on, just in case."

"Don't worry, Mark. I got this covered." Red and another security man stood holding their weapons aimed at the horrific being.

"Dropping it now, Mark," Red announced.

Instantly the field dropped. Mark plopped the helmet gingerly atop the alien's head, locked a buckle under its chin, obviously repulsed by doing so, and backed away quickly.

"Field back up," he ordered.

Red nodded and the force field sprang back into place.

"Now, drop the stasis field. Let's see if this worked or not."

The color of the beam radiating from the ceiling atop the alien abruptly changed from orange to a soft blue, and the creature began beating at the force field frantically. It hissed and spat, but before it could remove the helmet Troiano touched a control on a tablet she was carrying. Instantly lights across the helmet sprang to life and the creature stopped its movements.

"How are you going to control it? The tablet?" Eddie asked.

Troiano nodded. "Yes, everything can be done through here. It's a simple voice command set up. At the touch of a button we can stop its movements completely, like I just did."

Mark reached over and took the pad from her. He touched his right sleeve and a beam from the sleeve on his blue and silver tech suit sprayed across the tablet. He handed the tablet back to the doctor a moment later. "I've transferred all controls to my tech suit. Anything your tablet could have done can now be done through my suit."

"Yeah but shouldn't you have transferred it to one of us instead of you?" Red asked. "We're going across to that thing, not you."

"No, Red, I'm going too."

Red's jaw dropped. "Who's going to be in charge here?"

"Ariel will take charge here. Six of us will go across with our friend here. You and Dan will wear the heavy armor suits along with one of your security personnel. You three will run interference. You know as well as I do that the tech suits can take a beating and keep us relatively unharmed if we come under fire."

Eddie stood up, "So what's the plan? When do we leave?"

Before anyone could answer the ship shook once again.

"They're bombarding us again, Mark," Red announced.

"Okay, you three to the heavy suit bay on the armory level. Eddie and I will wait here. When you get back, we're going to take a trip over to that ship. We'll follow the tech suits' transponders. Now go. Bring back a couple of solar rifles for Eddie and me too, as well as a bandolier of plasma grenades. In fact bring a couple of hand blasters as well."

Dan grumbled, "Why dontcha just come with us an' get yer stuff yourself?"

"I have to stay here to watch our ride over there." Mark pointed his thumb to the force field entrapped alien.

Dan and Red stood and left, taking Malcom Joiner, a security officer, with them.

***

Fifteen minutes later, the maglovator doors slid open revealing the three men in heavily armored battle suits.

Eddie smirked. "Those things always remind me of the old video game giant robots with all the angular lines they got going on. Except these aren't giants of course."

The three men exited the maglovator and looked very impressive. The suits added a foot to their height, as well as half a foot of width. They were massive and powerful. Their colors were silver and blue, just like the tech suits every member of the crew wore. Each man carried a matching helmet. Across their backs were slung multiple weapons belts.

"Here ya go." Dan held out his hands and handed Mark and Eddie the weaponry Mark had requested. Red and Joiner followed suit as well.

"Thanks," Mark replied.

"Maxwell," Mark started, "you take over the weapons array."

"Yes Sir." Maxwell saluted smartly and sat in the seat Eddie normally occupied.

Mark looked at the young sandy haired technician uncomfortably, "Maxwell, what's your first name?"

The young man seemed to squirm a bit in his seat, his face knotted uncomfortably. "Colm, Sir."

Mark nodded, leaned in and began to whisper. "If you ever salute me again I'll smack you in the back of your head, understand?"

Surprised, the young man looked at him and nodded, wide eyed.

Mark slapped him on the back. "Good man. We're counting on you to keep this ship free of alien infiltration. Aim true and fire. Most of it's automated anyway. You won't have any trouble."

Maxwell nodded. "Thank you, Sir."

Mark nodded and moved closer to their other dimensional captive, "I'm going to release the force field. Train your weapons on it, just in case. Everyone ready?"

They all nodded in the affirmative, their eyes never trailing from the captive.

Dan muttered, "This is one damned ugly Nosferatu lookin' thing."

"Never mind, Sledge. Close your helmets up everyone. I'm going to activate our teleporter."

Mark began tapping a virtual control panel on his sleeve. An instant later the creature shuddered, momentarily fighting the control the helmet was exerting over it, then finally relaxing.

Mark walked up until he was standing in front of the creature. "I have some questions for you before we go to your ship. What is your race called?"

"We are the Tahir Ga'warum," the creature hissed.

"And your name?"

"Barukt, I am called."

"That's a start. How many of us can you teleport at once?"

The creature answered unemotionally, "Forty of you in one group."

"So, we need three trips then," Red whispered to Mark.

"Agreed, Red. Let's see what we can do."

"Okay, Barukt, you are going to take us to these coordinates within that ship."

Mark steered the alien like a remote controlled drone. The horrific creature activated its teleportation ability and its robes swirled about itself. With a snap the world seemed to go black, but in less than a heartbeat it resumed being lit again, this time aboard the alien ship.

"What the hell..." Red droned off staring around at the corridor they stood in. It was a dark red in color and seemed organic somehow, as if portions of the ship were alive. The burgundy lighting seemed to pulse slowly as well.

"Okay this is kinda scary," Eddie commented.

Dan grumbled. "Judgin' by these guys didja expect any less?"

Eddie shrugged. "Not really I guess."

"All right, enough guys. Our people should be right about here." Mark pointed to a blank wall. "I'm still reading their transponders there."

"Want me ta punch our way in?" Dan grinned.

"No need. Our friend Barukt is going to lead us to the rooms entrance. Isn't that right Barukt?"

The alien walked forward to a corner that was hidden in the dim lighting and turned left. The crew stepped over tendrils that lay across the floor from tree-like limbs that lined the walls.

"This place is freaky," Eddie grumbled unenthusiastically.

"Yeah, let's get out of here ASAP," Red agreed.

They followed Barukt another fifty paces down the corridor he had taken them, stepping over more vines and tendrils until the creature came to a stop. It waved its hand over a nodule on the wall and an almost seamless panel slid open. The creature walked inside with the six man crew following. Once inside the room they all gasped almost simultaneously.

Both sides of the room were filled with clear tubes. More of the tendrils wrapped about and nightmarishly covered the tubes.

But it was what was within the horrific tubes that caught everyone's breath in their throats.

"The crew…" Dan verbalized, barely croaking the words out.

"They're here, but what'd these sons of bitches do to them?" Red growled.

Everyone turned at a sound that came from the doorway. Just entering the room and advancing were a group of the creatures, bent over and slinking their way toward the six man away party. They began to crawl atop one another, like reptiles. Their deathly white skin reflected the dim red lighting giving them an even more gruesome appearance. Tendrils of blackness whipped about them, while their tongues lashed in and out. All the while they hissed maddeningly as they inched closer and closer.

Chapter 24

"Hold them off; I'm going to free our crewmen." Mark shouted. He worked quickly at the tubes holding the crew, using his tech suits scanners to quickly ascertain how to open the clear pods.

The horrific creatures leapt toward the away team almost as one unit. A seeming river of the horrid beings frantically crawled atop and over one another just to get to the boarding party before the Tahir Ga'Warum next to him. They were literally fighting for position as to who would attack the human invaders first.

But Red was already swinging his powerful handheld cannon into place from his back. It was Red's favorite weapon to use on boarding or away missions, even if it was big, bulky, and heavy.

The creatures surged toward the group and Red fired. His first blast of explosive energies sprayed across them with the strength to shake the room and send several of the tubes filled with the missing crewmen smashing to the floor.

But the aliens kept advancing, relatively unscathed.

"Uh oh…" Red muttered. "Switching to projectiles," he announced and fired again.

The projectile hit and exploded. The aliens were blown off of their feet and scattered.

Mark nodded his approval. "That's better. All of you go to conventional projectile weaponry."

"That'd work if we all brought some," Dan growled as he took three bounding steps and hurled himself into a tight knit group of the aliens who were still advancing.

Dan collided with them with a bang. He began hammering at them with blows that could shake mountains. But surprisingly they fought back and did not go down under his superhumanly powerful onslaught.

"Uh oh, that ain't good," Eddie muttered.

Eddie brought up his powerful rifle and began firing. He started with energy bolts which again had no real effect, then switched to explosive shells which, while not the same caliber as Red was using, were still powerful enough to do substantial damage and knock their enemy flying backward.

Dan had grasped one of the creatures by the feet and was using it as a bludgeon against its compatriots, hammering away incessantly.

"Guys this ain't goin' so well," he shouted over his shoulder.

Mark replied, "Keep them back, Dan. We'll have everyone freed in a few minutes. As soon as I get the first group of forty free, I'll order Barukt to teleport them back and then return for the next."

Dan grunted, "Just do it already."

"You heard the man," Mark continued. "Let's get everyone free and start heading back to the *Cag*." Mark and the two men with him continued to work feverishly to open the tubes and free their fellow crewmen while the others fought a desperate battle against their terrible foes,

The heavy armored suits Dan, Red and Joiner wore were taking a pounding. The aliens smashed at the three

188

men over and over trying to crack the armored suits open.

"These things must be almost as strong as Dan is," Eddie assessed.

"Keep shooting, Eddie. Danny is starting to falter."

"No I ain't!" Sledge roared.

Dan slammed two of the pale skinned fiends' heads together. His armored gloves were covered in their black blood. His fists worked like pistons, slamming through the oncoming tide of alien attackers.

Nearby Red continued to fire his handheld cannon, sending the enemy creatures scattering in all directions with each pull of the trigger. But less were actually removed from the battle than they had hoped for.

"Mark, these things are tougher than I expected," Red admitted.

"It doesn't matter, Red," Mark replied. "They have to go down. If they don't we're all done for."

"Going down. Good idea." Red smiled. He aimed the cannon at the ground in front of an onrushing group of the Tahir Ga'Warum and fired. The floor exploded beneath the aliens' feet, leaving a wave of them to fall below to the next deck.

A few of the just freed crew were helping Mark release the others. Though all were groggy at first they quickly regained their senses.

"Go, bring them back, then return here immediately for the next group," Mark commanded Barukt. The alien nodded once and disappeared amidst flowing tendrils of darkness along with forty of the groggy and just reawakened crewmen. An instant later the helmeted Tahir Ga'Warum returned, as he was commanded.

"Next group, go," Mark directed.

Again the alien disappeared and returned a moment later.

Eddie was kneeling now, the big gun resting on his knee. He fired again and again, knocking down the creatures, but each time they regained their footing.

"This ain't good, Boss," Eddie cried.

"No kidding, Eddie," Mark admonished. "We're almost done. Barukt's coming back for the final group now."

"Can't come fast enough," Red answered. The big man reloaded his cannon in a heartbeat and fired again, taking out several of the ghoulish aliens that were leaping across the room toward him. "I'm starting to run low on ammo. We have to get out of here."

"I know Red, a few moments longer."

Barukt reappeared in a mass of swirling, whirling alien tendrils, grasped the last group of crewmen within said tendrils, and disappeared once more.

Dan was up against a wall with a crowd of the creatures pressing in on him. With a grunt of fatigue he lifted his foot up and slammed it down, scattering everyone near him with vibrations like an earthquake within the ship. The floor buckled under his powerful stomp.

But still more of the ship's denizens scrambled over their senseless brethren and continued to attack Dan. Meanwhile Joiner fired his rifle repeatedly, scattering the enemy, but only temporarily.

"These things are tough, Captain. Only the Chief's cannon and Mr. Sledge's fists seem to be making any real difference," Joiner shouted at Mark.

"I know, Joiner. Keep firing and fall back to my position, all of you!"

The men closest did as they were bade, encircling Mark. Only Dan was still separated from his companions. Mark removed a grenade from the bandolier he had across his chest and heaved it into the crowd of aliens nearest the doorway. The explosive 'whoompf' knocked everyone, including the landing party to the ground. Only Dan Sledge was immune. Even Joiner and Red who also wore the heavy armored suits were knocked down by the powerful blast.

Dan burst through the remaining aliens and stood between them and his teammates. "You wanna get to them, you gotta go through me, freaks," he growled hotly.

The alien Barukt reappeared then in their midst. "Get us back to the *Cagliostro* now," Mark ordered.

In an eye blink the remainder of the boarding party was standing back aboard the *Cagliostro*'s command deck.

Dan immediately pushed his way to the pilot's station, almost heaving the man sitting there from the seat.

"Get us out of here!" Mark yelled.

"Wit' pleasure, Boss."

Dan punched the controls and the *Cagliostro* arced away, accelerating rapidly and leaving the heavily damaged Tahir Ga'Warum vessel behind.

Mark turned toward the alien in their midst. "You, return to your people and warn them never to cross our paths again, or they won't be so lucky next time."

The creature began to teleport away, its tendrils swirling madly for an instant and then it disappeared in a burst of its black, whirling teleportational power.

"Do you think it made it back to that ship? We put a few hundred thousand miles between us already," Dan asked.

"I couldn't care less, as long as the damned thing is gone and from what I see on ship's sensors it's out of here," Mark rumbled.

"What about the helmet? We lost that now," Ariel asked.

Mark shrugged. "That doesn't matter, Ari. We could build another in ten minutes now that we have the design stored."

Red turned toward Mark apprehensively. "Mark, that ship is giving chase and it's gaining on us."

"Dan, prepare to phase us back to our universe. Let's see if eight hours of calculations and test scenarios pan out."

"I'm on it, Boss. I can't wait to get outta this nutty purple universe anyway."

Mark mused, "Yes, I have to agree. Just for once I wouldn't mind going somewhere and being met by sentient teddy bears with hearts embroidered on their chests."

"Who just want to hug us all?" Ariel smiled.

"Exactly." Mark returned the grin.

Red grunted, "Mark, they're still gaining on us."

"Dan get us out of here."

"I'm on it, Boss."

Dan activated the hyper-warp and the *Cagliostro* seemed to shudder and violently skew to the right, throwing everyone off their feet who was not seated

Then a warm, flush feeling passed over everyone on the ship simultaneously.

"Lookit that." Dan smiled.

Everyone turned to the view screen, relieved to see the familiar stars and deep, rich blackness of interstellar space.

"Status reports, Red and Dan? Ari, scan for communication signals."

"All systems are nominal, Mark," Dan answered.

"Not getting any contacts within range, Mark," Red advised.

Mark turned toward his communication officer. "Ari?"

"I have EPIC command on the interstellar frequency, Mark. They want to know where we've been."

"Advise them that a full report will be sent shortly. Also tell them I will be contacting them shortly and that I'll be requesting back up fleet regiments at the coordinates I'll be furnishing them with."

Ari nodded and forwarded the message.

"Now what?" Eddie turned and asked.

"Now I go down and talk to our guest in the medical bay."

Eddie chuckled. "I almost forgot about Chakix."

Mark shook his head in disgust. "I wish I could have. I swear if this thing gives me any more of a headache I'm going to throw the native host out of an airlock."

"I don't think anyone would blame you for that," Eddie chortled.

"I think you're right, Eddie." He stood from his command chair and grimaced, stretching his back painfully in the process.

"Are you okay, Mark?" Ariel asked, concern written all over her beautiful face.

"I'm just tired, Ari. I think I'm up about thirty six hours now, without any kind of break."

"You have to rest, Mark. Not only for yourself, but for the rest of us as well."

"I know kiddo, I know. After I talk to EPIC and see to Chakix I'm going to get some rest. In fact, where's Marek? Let's get him and his secondary command crew up here as long as nothing critical is facing us at the moment. Everyone take a few hours off."

Ariel nodded and called the secondary crew to come to the command deck.

***

A few minutes later she and Mark were exiting the maglovator and entering the medical bay. Troiano's medical deck was loaded with people. There were many of those who were held within the strange cylinders of the alien ship.

"How are they?" Mark asked.

"They seem to be okay. I'm not seeing anything going on with them that's out of the ordinary." Dr. Troiano replied with a shrug.

Ariel looked at a few crewmembers she recognized and smiled warmly to several before turning back to Troiano and Mark. "So what were they doing to them in those cylinders?"

"As far as I can tell they were storing them."

"What does that mean?" Mark asked, suddenly angry.

Dr. Troiano locked her eyes with Mark's. "They were storing them like pickles in a jar, Captain. Like you would with any type of food."

Mark's lip twitched in disgust. "That is not what I wanted to hear."

"What about Chakix?" Ari asked.

"The native housing its sentience is still unconscious from the sedative I've been giving him. I can bring him out of it at any time though."

"Can you do it gradually? I don't want this thing back to its full insanity at the drop of a hat."

Troiano nodded in the affirmative. "Yes, I can. I can make the native host barely cognizant, if need be. I can also give him something to keep his body almost paralyzed but his mind fully functioning."

"Ann, I don't want this thing to be dangerous. I want to be able to speak to it calmly."

"What are you planning, Captain?" Troiano asked suspiciously.

"Something that will benefit all of us, Chakix and Earth alike."

Ariel squinted her eyes slightly while looking at Mark. "You're planning on making a deal with it aren't you?"

Mark grinned slyly. "You know me better than you think, Ari."

"No," she shrugged her shoulders and then added, "I just know what to expect from you at this point." She returned his grin.

Mark feigned surprise holding his right hand across his chest and over his heart. "What do you mean, oh fair Ariel?"

"I mean I expect the unexpected"

Mark leaned over and kissed her gently. A moment passed and they separated.

Ariel smiled, "Mmmm, I like kisses…" she cooed softly.

Mark moved his head sideways, smirked and replied, "Well they're better than a punch in the mouth."

She slapped him playfully. "You are such a jerk sometimes."

He laughed. "Hey as long as it's not all the time."

Troiano cleared her throat. "Excuse me, but if you two children are finished, what would you like me to do with our guest?"

"I need Chakix awake and lucid but not in control of that body. Can you do that?"

Troiano nodded. "Give me five minutes and you'll be able to talk to it."

Chapter 25

Mark and Ariel sat at a table in a small closed room. The red skinned alien that bore Chakix's intelligence sat facing them. Behind the alien stood two security men, guns at the ready, just in case.

"What is it you want now, MarkJohnson? You have separated me from my body, my world, and children. What more can you do to me to humiliate and hurt me?"

"Hey, Chakix, let's be honest. You attacked us first. You possessed Ariel, you tried to cause death and destruction on my ship and to my crew. None of that was necessary. We were willing to negotiate, you wanted to demand."

"I am Chakix, demanding is what I know. None have ever refused me before," the alien blurted out.

"That's not my problem, Chakix. If you want to play in the big boy pool you have to learn the rules of the game. Now I'm still willing to negotiate getting rid of the Agalum *with* you."

"With?" The alien went wide eyed and exclaimed.

"Yes, with. Like I already previously explained to you, we're not your slaves, or your weapons to point at your enemies. If you want allies to aid you in getting rid of the Agalum, we can do that. But it would be you entering into a long term contract or deal with our world, Earth."

The red skinned native looked perplexed. "What is this…deal?"

"It basically means we will aid you as your allies, and you will aid us as ours. We will require some concessions in exchange for ridding you of the Agalum."

"What kind of...concessions do you seek?"

"We will help you in driving the Agalum from your world, but we get to use the base they already created. We will turn that base into a forward command for the Earth forces. Your people will be freed from slavery by us. We will supply our own people to work the base. We will require natural resources from you, in exchange for freeing your people."

"What are these...resources?"

"Minerals, oil, any other items we can find of use to us that will aid in the war against the Agalum conglomerate. Once we defeat them permanently we will leave your world if that is what you want. If you want us to remain that can be arranged as well, but that we can discuss when the time comes and only if you so desire our presence here."

The bare chested red skinned alien spat, "I do not need your help to defeat these...Agalum. I can do it myself."

Mark smiled as he walked around the captive alien. "No, you cannot. If you could drive them from your world you would have done so already instead of demanding we do it for you. So think on that a while if you must. I'm offering you a very fair deal. It's time to wake up and grow up, Chakix. You can't keep acting like some all-powerful spoiled brat who'll stamp her feet if she doesn't get her way. If you want to win the freedom of your children or people or whatever, you'll have to join us, and come into a long lasting agreement with us that will benefit both of us. That's what I'm offering you."

The Chakix host hesitated. "I…do not know. I do not trust you. Others like you; they have done much harm to my children and myself."

"Those others, the Agalum, are *not* like us. Not at all. We'll leave if you tell us to, once this is over. Though I'm counting on you to be a creature of your word and to allow us to stay and use this already constructed base to keep our mutual enemies at bay. What say you?"

The Chakix host stared up at the blank ceiling a moment, then exhaled before finally answering, "You will allow me to make my mind up when this war is over?"

"Yes, Chakix, once the war is over you can either welcome us completely as your permanent tenant, or tell us to leave. *But* if you choose to tell us to leave after we defeat the Agalum and before the war is over, effectively double crossing us… well, let me put it this way. You'll wish the Agalum were still your tenants and not us. What I'm saying is don't betray us, Chakix. We want to be your allies, not your enemy."

The red skinned alien stared at its feet, then the ceiling again momentarily before returning its host's glare upon Mark Johnson. "You will aid us in driving these Agalum away?"

"Yes, Chakix, as I have said already. They are your enemy, not us. We seek to build a relationship with you."

Chakix looked at them hesitantly. Mark extended his hand, waiting for the alien to take it and shake.

Hesitantly the red skinned alien reached its hand out and grasped Mark's, clumsily shaking it.

Mark grinned and released the alien's hand after a moment. "That's great, now let's get to work."

Chapter 26

The *Cagliostro* dropped out of hyper-warp and slowed to a stop. Its position was deep in the void between solar systems.

"Maintain shields at maximum. Red, any contacts?"

The big security man shook his head negatively. "Nada, Mark. I'm running hyper-warp as well as regular space scans. There's nothing and no one even close to our position."

"All right. I'm going to send a coded message to EPIC about our situation and what we need out here. I'll be in the command conference room. Ariel, join me please."

Ariel thumbed a control on her console and spoke, "Lilly Wallflower to the command deck please." She then rose and followed Mark to the maglovator.

They exited the maglovator outside the command conference room a minute later.

"After you," Mark offered. The door slid open before them and both entered.

Sitting down across from each other, Mark began talking. "Are we doing the right thing?"

"What? What are you talking about?" Ariel asked in total surprise.

Driving the Agalum off of Chakix's world. I mean the Agalum are our foe, no doubt about it, and Chakix agreed to our terms, but you know as well as I do that Chakix can't be trusted. What if this is all a ploy to get a large number of our vessels out here far enough from

Earth that the Agalum can attack and do us some extended harm while we're trying to free Chakix?"

Ariel continued to look at Mark with astonishment in her eyes. "How many ships are you going to request out here?"

"We're going to need at least one carrier and several battle dreadnaughts to take down that fleet they have around Chakix. Plus how do we know they are not going to pull more ships in as reinforcements once the battle begins?"

"You think they would, right?"

"Of course I do Ariel. I have no doubt once the alarms start going off they are going to pull every ship they can into place about Chakix and start trying to protect their investment."

"You're right. They're not going to go easy, I guess."

"No, of course not. In fact this may well be the bloodiest battle of the war, even surpassing what happened two years ago above the Earth when we drove them off."

"What if we could do this, I dunno, maybe stealthily?"

Mark smiled. "Do you have a suggestion, Ari?"

"Well you want to use a ground force to take out that base, right?"

"I don't even know if that's possible. That's a functioning base with hundreds of personnel at least, perhaps thousands. I don't know what it will take to breach their defenses and take over that place. I know we don't have enough manpower to hold it even if we do succeed in taking it."

"What if we really do?"

"What are you suggesting, Ari?"

"That you're overlooking the natives."

"I know. I had considered them earlier, but they're savages with sticks and flint point knives. They're not exactly a major fighting force, all things considered."

"What about the giant red ape?"

"Well, we only saw one of those, and any blast from one of our cannons would have killed it. So unless there's a few hundred or thousand of those things floating around, they're really not going to be a major force that can't be taken out fairly easily."

"Mark, wait. Think about it. The natives under Chakix guidance were pretty formidable, and Chakix already proved that the red ape is under her dominion too. She had it talking in her own voice along with the natives, remember?"

"How could I forget? That was more than a little disconcerting. It was downright eerie."

"Okay, that aside, what do you think about getting Chakix and the natives to draw the attention of the Agalum commanders and their troops while we sneak in and take the base?"

"It's a really bad crap shoot, Ariel. I'm really not sure any of this is such a good idea. That's why I'm having second thoughts about it."

"What else are you going to do, Mark? Dump the Chakix alien back on his world and leave the Agalum in charge? That's like pointing them at the doorway to Earth and handing them the keys to get in."

He sighed heavily and then banged his fist on the table top." Put the call through to EPIC now requesting a fleet. I'll work up an attack plan. Between Chakix's forces and our own we *might* be able to pull this off, but I'm not counting on it."

"You're such a glass half empty kind of guy." She smirked.

"No, seriously, what I am is a realist. I don't take that many chances, Ari, and usually when I do the odds favor us coming out on top. Right now that's not the case. We could be in for a heavy loss, and that alone could seal the Earth's fate. That's something to think about before we go any further."

"So you're willing to just walk away?"

"Now that's something I never said, did I?"

She shook her head side to side, her expression remained neutral "No, you didn't. What are you planning? I already see those gears turning inside your head."

"You're the telepath, Ari. You tell me."

She laughed weakly. "No, no, no. I'll let you surprise me."

Mark grinned like the Cheshire cat. "Don't I always?"

"That's what I'm afraid of."

The ship rocked suddenly. Ariel immediately touched her right sleeve. "Lilly, it's Ariel. What's going on?"

"We're under attack by three fighters approximately the size of the *Stargrazer*. Eddie says it's the same design as the ones that attacked him the other day when he was aboard the *Stargrazer* alone."

"I'm on my way topside," Mark interjected, rising from the table immediately, quickly followed by Ariel. The ship rocked once again from an explosive attack.

"Battle stations, everyone!" Mark called into the tech suit's comm unit on his sleeve. He entered the maglovator with Ariel a step behind him.

He emerged from the maglovator onto the command deck, followed by Ariel.

Matt Marek slid from the command chair. "All yours, Captain."

Mark nodded. "Thank you, Mr. Marek. What's our status?"

Matt answered, "Three of those unknown ships are flying around us and attacking continually."

The *Cagliostro* rocked as another barrage from the attacking ships slammed into the *Cagliostro's* shields.

"That ain't good," Eddie muttered.

"Relax, half pint," Red growled. "Shields are holding steady, so far at least."

Mark nodded slowly. "Danny, it's time to raise some hell."

"An' I'm just the guy to do it," the smiling Jovian replied.

Dan heaved the *Cagliostro* to the right and began to accelerate away. He held his present course for ten seconds and then corkscrewed the *Cagliostro* majestically, rolling it over in space so it was heading back in the direction it had come from.

"Now, DiGenovese," Mark ordered.

Eddie nodded. "With pleasure, Boss man."

The *Cagliostro's* guns opened up, spraying their enemies with the forward solar cannons. In mid-attack Eddie thumbed up two star core missiles. Every weapon was aimed at one of the ships attacking them.

"What the hell?" Eddie exclaimed. "That was three direct hits, and that things still coming. It should've been dust by now."

"Yeah, but it ain't so keep shooting' it," Dan barked.

"What do you think I'm doing you big ape?"

Eddie continued to fire at the one ship, until its shields glowed a bright red. At the same time the other two ships fired upon the *Cagliostro* repeatedly.

"Dan, continue on a heading directly toward them, slide between the two ships, splitting them. Eddie, take that damned ship you nicknamed a 'Predator' out so we can start on the other two."

Di Genovese replied, "I'm workin' on it Boss."

Again and again the *Cagliostro*'s mighty solar cannons lit up space like newborn stars erupting from her bow. Each blast careened madly into the shields of the strangely winged ship. The *Cagliostro* slid between the other two attacking ships, Dan turning it almost vertical on its wingtip to do so.

The instant it slid past, Eddie switched to the three rear mounted solar cannons and locked onto the two ships they had just passed, spraying them with energy beams.

"Those two are turning around again," Red grunted.

"Okay, go back to one at a time, Eddie. Lock onto the one with the most damage and let's cut the odds down with its destruction."

"Locked on now, Boss."

"That one's rabbiting, Mark," Red announced.

Eddie fired a spread of star core missiles again at the now fleeing attack craft. The three missiles impacted brightly against its shields, but then the shields flared bright white. If not for the instantly dimming display the command crew would have been momentarily blinded by the sight.

"Gotcha!" Eddie exclaimed. He fired the solar cannons again and again against the now defenseless attack craft, turning it to free floating atoms in a heartbeat. The resulting explosion lit up the viewer brightly for an instant until the ships systems compensated and dimmed the viewer a heartbeat later.

Mark shouted, "Where are the last two?"

"Turning attack vectors back to us, Mark," Red replied. "They circled around and are coming from the front at us, from opposite vectors, both aiming directly toward us though."

The crew stared at the viewer and both remaining ships could be seen coming from opposite angles toward the *Cagliostro*, one seemingly from the left, one from the right, in a V-shaped attack pattern with the *Cagliostro* itself the point of the V, or the convergence point.

"Danny, it's time for a game of chicken."

Dan looked over his shoulder at his friend and Captain. He squinted his right eye in obvious disbelief. "Yer kiddin', right?"

"Not at all, Mister. Take us on a collision course with the starboard enemy ship now. Red, shields double front. Eddie charge up all weaponry. As soon as we get a visual on them begin firing at your leisure. Red, what is our shield status?"

"Sixty percent, Boss."

"So their attacks *are* taking a toll."

"Yes Mark they are. But it's slow and cumulative."

"Okay Red, let's burn these bastards to the ground."

The *Cagliostro* spun about in space once more. Its gleaming hull gave off sparks when it crossed the debris field left by the remains of the predator craft.

"Eddie, target the 'Predator' on the port side with our forward guns and the predator on the starboard side with our aft guns."

"Ah, okay. I got it. Boss," Eddie nodded his head and grinned.

The *Cagliostro* screamed silently through space, laying down solar cannon fire repeatedly. Both remaining predators concentrated their fire on the sleek manta ray shaped ship, hammering at the *Cagliostro* as it passed swiftly below them. Eddie fired the rearward solar cannons, blasting away at the starboard predator.

Once more the three dueling ships switched positions. The *Cagliostro* flipped about like a ballerina dancing in space. The two Agalum ships crossed each other in an 'X' pattern and returned to attacking the *Cag* once more, again streaking directly toward the gleaming star cruiser, their guns blazing.

"Shields are down to forty nine percent, Mark," Red advised.

"Keep the shields doubled where they will do the most good, Robinski."

Red nodded. "You got it, Mark."

Eddie thumbed the fire button once again. This time the solar cannons punched their way through the port side Predator ship's shields, and were followed by a quickly released star core missile. The resultant explosion filled the sky the instant the *Cagliostro* passed the attack craft. By the time the crew looked back through the *Cagliostro*'s rear cameras, the Predator was burning, glowing dust.

"One left," Red announced with a hint of danger in his voice.

"Not for long," Mark replied, "Eddie destroy that thing."

"I'm on it, Mark."

Once more the *Cagliostro* reversed itself, flying to the left quickly. Dan looped the sleek ship around and accelerated powerfully after the now retreating vessel.

"Concentrate all firepower on its engines."

Eddie nodded. "Will do, Mark."

The solar cannons screamed repeatedly, firing their deadly blasts across airless space, punishing the smaller ship's shields again and again.

Another brace of missiles issued from the *Cagliostro*'s hull and punched through the failing shields. The predator craft exploded in a bright eruption of gasses, fuel and debris.

The *Cagliostro* peeled off and away from the destroyed vessel and its remains.

"Status?" Mark queried.

"Shields are at twenty eight percent right now. Minor damage to decks one through four. No casualties. Some minor injuries from the bumping we took. The crew is fine otherwise."

Mark nodded. "Very good, now let's send that message to EPIC."

Chapter 27

Mark Johnson stared at the man displayed on the viewer in his command conference room and his blood pressure began to rise.

"Admiral Bright, what do you mean you can't send us everything we need? This is going to be a beachhead against the Earth. How can you not understand the importance of what I'm talking about? This world is a day from Earth at hyper-warp. They could mount a never ending attack from here. If we do not take the battle to them and evict them from this planet we'll be signing our own death warrants."

"*Captain* Johnson, and I use the word loosely, do not seek to educate *me* in the ways of warfare. I have been through more battles than you could possibly imagine. Right now our forces are locked in battle in several key sectors of space."

Mark's arms crossed his chest and he furrowed his brow, tilting his head down and forward as he began to reply to the bald headed and heavily bearded Admiral on the view screen. "I'm sorry, Admiral Bright, but you are wrong. Not only are you wrong but your actions will result in Earth's destruction if this forward base is not taken out of Agalum hands. I have already-"

"Mind your place, Captain Johnson." The Admiral stood from his plush desk chair and shouted, pointing a finger at Mark. "I have been placed in command of this war by the President. Your ship operates independently of military channels due to President's orders, but don't think you can just come in here and order me around. I still am the ranking officer here, not you. The fleet follows my orders, and right now I'm ordering them to remain right where they are and continue fighting against Agalum forces at those junctures. Not to run across the galaxy haphazardly at your whim."

Mark bristled angrily. "Admiral, this is not about egos or half assed plans. This is about our survival. I have the approval of the planet's denizens themselves on this action."

"Yes, yes, a supposed 'sentient' planet. Am I actually supposed to believe this poppycock? This is not some comic book adventure, Johnson. This is war. It's something I'm good at and I know."

Mark met the Admiral's gaze with an unwavering glare. "Perhaps at one time you were. Right now you can't get past your own hubris."

"How *dare* you!" the Admiral shouted.

"Oh I dare. I dare because humanity is on the line. This is no joke. If we don't stop this infestation of Agalum so close to home it will result in a conflagration that will engulf the Earth and burn it and its people to ashes. Why can't you see that? Are you another Agalum shape shifter? That can be the only explanation I can see at this point."

"I've had about enough of you, Mister."

"Get us a fleet out here, Admiral, or we're all dead. This is the worst threat since the Agalum surrounded Earth two years ago. Which, may I remind you, I was the reason for victory that day. Myself and my crew. We ensured the Earth's survival. You may be the leader of

EPIC's Earth-side command, but out here in space, in the trenches we need someone who has gotten their hands dirty and knows how to recognize a threat. You obviously have lost that ability. I'll deal with things out here, Admiral. Continue to play with your paperclips and other bureaucracies. I'm going to be saving the Earth, again."

Mark cut off the communication and sat in the command crew conference room seething.

'That didn't go too well, did it?' Ariel's voice sang through his mind.

'No, not at all,' he grudgingly replied to her through her telepathic link. *'That man is a bureaucrat first and foremost. I have no idea why the President appointed him to anything, let alone placing him in command of EPIC.'*

'You forget, you refused the honor, remember? The President had to appoint someone, and Bright seemed like the best candidate at the time.'

Mark snorted lightly. *'You still think I made a mistake turning down command of EPIC?'*

'I think you would have been good at it, honey.'

'I think I did more good out here, and still do than I would have done sitting behind a desk somewhere waiting for the next disaster to overtake us all.'

Ariel chuckled mentally. *'It would have been nice to be out of the line of fire for a while instead of being the Agalum's public enemy number one.'*

'That's a position for a guy like Bright who gets his kicks from going to state functions and cocktail parties where he can push his rather heavy weight around and be impressed by his own stories.'

'That's true,' Ariel giggled. *'We both know how much you love anything you have to wear a suit or God forbid a tux to.'*

Mark grinned. *'I'll be right up, and thanks for making me laugh a little. It broke my foul mood up rather nicely.'*

Ariel's voice rang joyfully through his mind. *'Glad to have been of help, sailor.'* And then she was gone, the telepathic connection severed.

Mark stood and continued grinning. He left the command conference room and entered the maglovator. He had a lot to plan and make ready, and he and his crew were going to have to do it alone.

Chapter 28

"So what's the plan?" Dan asked.

Mark grinned, "A simple one this time, Danny. We camo the ship again and land within walking distance of that base. Chakix has agreed to allow as many of her people as we need as well as the red ape to aid us."

Seated around the command crew ready room table were the entire primary command crew.

"That's not bad except for one thing," Red intervened. "It's still only a handful of us and a bunch of stick wielding savages against a highly trained and fortified army."

Mark nodded. "Right, but we do have a hundred foot tall ape to help us."

Eddie shrugged. "Yeah, amigo. The only problem is one blast from the *Cag*'s solar cannon can punch a hole through its chest you could fly the '*Grazer*' through."

"Well we're not going to be aiming at it, DiGenovese. We'll be defending it."

"Well ain't that a kick in the ass?" Eddie grinned.

"As long as it's not our asses being kicked, Eddie," Mark answered.

Mark turned toward Dan. "Danny, do you have anything to add on the status of the *Stargrazer*?

"It's still under reconstruction, Mark. It was basically destroyed. I'm not even sure we can rebuild it onboard the *Cag*. It may have to be dry docked for a few months back home to get it all right."

"That's not the answer I was looking for, Dan. You and your crew should be able to do anything aboard this ship that can be done at any Johnson Aerospace facility. We need that ship back in working condition as insurance."

Mark's comm unit beeped. He immediately touched the cuff of his right sleeve. "Yes, Miss Wallflower?"

Dan grimaced at the use of her formal name, but said nothing.

"Captain, I'm getting a signal here you might want to see for yourself."

"On my way, Wallflower."

Mark looked at his command crew. "Are you joining me?"

Everyone arose from the table almost simultaneously and headed toward the maglovator.

"What do you think this is about?" Ari asked Mark as they walked.

"You're the telepath, you tell me." He smiled.

She squinted her eyes and reached out with her mind. An instant later she opened them wide and said, "C'mon, someone's trying to contact us."

"Well I knew that already, Ari."

They all stepped into the maglovator, then Ari turned back and looked at Mark. "You don't know the half of it. boy scout."

The crew stepped onto the command deck and Mark froze staring at the view screen.

"What the hell?" he whispered.

Arrayed before them in a semi-circle were a half dozen EPIC vessels of various sizes and fire power. The view screen flashed and the image of the captain of one of the other ships filled the viewer. He was an Asian man, most probably Japanese.

"Captain Johnson? I am Captain Nagata. We heard you were having an issue trying to get back up out here against the Agalum and we'd like to offer you our services. The *Coronado* and its crew are at your service as well as the other five vessels in my fleet."

Mark smiled. "Thank you, Captain. Please join me along with the captains of each of the other ships in my conference room in one hour. Oh and Captain Nagata, thank you again."

***

One hour later the command crew conference room was filled with the captains of each ship that were floating out near the *Cagliostro*.

Mark entered the room with Dan and Red at his side and smiled warmly. "Gentlemen, first I have to say that I can't thank you all enough for coming to aid us. I explained what we discovered to Admiral Bright, and I have to assume you all heard either from him or through other channels what is actually out here."

Nagata spoke first. "Rumor has it that you discovered a fully functioning Agalum base a day away from Earth. Is that true, Captain Johnson?"

"First, call me Mark. Secondly, Captain Nagata, yes it is true. They could re-arm their ships as well as maintain them from this world. It is a fully functioning base to stage attacks from."

Another captain, a grey haired and balding black man, raised his hand and began to speak. "Captain

Carlson, captain of the *Revenant*, How large a force is on this world?"

"Captain, we are not certain. There could be hundreds to multiple thousands. I just do not know for certain."

"Did you engage them in battle?" a third captain asked, a gray haired white man who looked inordinately trim and fit for his age.

"We met them in battle at two instances while we were affecting repairs on the *Cagliostro*. I can tell you all that they have a new type of attack craft, one that actually seems to have shields almost as sturdy as a full sized star cruiser's. My personal craft, the *Stargrazer* was almost fully destroyed in pitched battle with one of those small attack crafts. We nicknamed them 'Predator', or rather my weapons officer did.

He was the one who finally shot it down, at almost the cost of his own life I might add."

"I understand," the Captain nodded thoughtfully.

"What is your name, Sir, and your ship?" Mark inquired.

"Ah I apologize, I should have introduced myself I am Captain Brennan of the *Tempest*."

"Welcome, Captain. What I can tell you all is that not only is this a fully functional attack and resupply base within a day of Earth, but the planet has a few surprises of its own."

"What kind of surprises?" Nagata asked.

"The planet is alive."

"All planets are alive," answered the fourth captain. "Captain Argento of the *Crossbow* at your service."

"It's not alive like that, Argento. It's sentient."

"What?" Carlson barked. "What kind of line are you trying to feed us?"

"It's no line." Mark tapped his right sleeve's cuff. "Bring him in please."

A security officer entered the conference room, and with him was Chakix, or rather the bare chested, red skinned alien native that housed Chakix's mind.

Captain Nagata narrowed his eyes and asked, "Who is this?"

Haughtily the red skinned alien looked at him and replied in its strange hollow voice. "I am Chakix. I have allied myself with this man. He is resourceful and I believe trustworthy. He has agreed to cleanse my world of the usurpers who now trod upon my children and use them as slaves. I trust this Captain Johnson. So should you all."

"What is this? A carnival side show?" Carlson asked angrily.

"No, Captain. This is the truth. Chakix is the life force, the mind of that world which we have begun to call Chakix as well."

The alien native nodded, crossed his arms over his bare chest and smiled, "I am Chakix."

"Foolishness," spat Carlson contemptuously.

Chakix's host slammed his fists down on the table. "The only foolishness is you making light of this. I am Chakix. MarkJohnson has told me you will help my children and I will hold you to it."

Carlson stood, sneering as he shook his head. "I'll be returning to the *Revenant* now. When you have something serious to discuss I'll consider it. Until then I'm going back to my ship."

"Hold up, Captain." Mark stood and held his hand out in the universal stop signal. "Look, I'm not going to try to talk you into anything you don't want to risk your crews' lives on. But we do need your help. Whether you believe my friend here or not there *is* a world with a heavily fortified Agalum base on it that is near enough to Earth to be a threat, and we need every ship we can to take that base. But the base is not the only problem. There are ships in orbit of that world now. The *Cagliostro* can get in and out without a problem because of our camouflage field. But we're the only ship here that has that camo ability. The rest of you are not going to be able to get to the surface without a protracted battle."

"How many ships are you going to need on the surface? How many troops?" Nagata asked.

"It all depends on how many natives Chakix is willing to send to aid our cause."

"Again with this Chakix," Nagata commented. He looked down at the table top and shook his head,

"You better understand, gentlemen. Chakix is for real, as are his claims. Every member of my crew here has seen Chakix's power at work. Chakix even possessed Ariel O'Connor, my comm officer for a short time."

"She's a telepath, isn't she?" Carlson asked.

Mark nodded affirmatively. "She is, yes."

"And also your girlfriend," Brennan added.

"You do your homework, Captain."

Brennan smiled. "I have to. I'm a Captain in EPIC, and we are at war, and not with each other."

Mark grinned as he sat back down. "You're right, Captain. We're not." Mark turned toward the last two captains who had sat silently throughout the proceedings. "What do you two have to add?"

The first shrugged noncommittally. He was a dark haired, dark skinned man who stood about six feet tall. "I'm Captain Jepson of the *Eagle's Claw* and this is Captain Ryan of the *Triumphant*. We both hold you in the highest regard, Captain Johnson. Where you lead, we'll follow."

Ryan added, "Without question." Ryan was sandy haired and fair skinned, six feet two inches tall, "We know what kind of man you are, Captain Johnson. We know that without you Earth would be a smoking rock of a world right now and its inhabitants all but extinct. We're here at your service, as these other men and their ships should be as well."

"Relax, Ryan." Nagata smiled. "We're all here for the same reason. We'll all follow Johnson and his 'wonder ship'. Though I still want proof on this Chakix thing."

The native leaned forward until it was almost nose to nose with Nagata. "You will have your proof, Earthman, when we return to my world."

Mark stood. "Gentlemen, I suggest you return to your respective ships. We'll reconvene by secured signal later to firm up our plans. We have a busy day ahead of us."

"What is your plan, Johnson?" Argento asked.

"The six of you will engage their fleet while the *Cag* returns to the surface to start the assault on the base itself. Once the assault begins I'll need a thousand troops brought to the surface to aid in the attack. Our allies will look like Chakix's host here. The enemy is Agalum in all their various forms which I know you men are up on, especially after two straight years of intergalactic war."

Carlson nodded. "You're right, but what about the actual assault on this base of yours?"

"We'll have to make a full frontal assault. This base is underneath a live volcano with only one way in or out."

"Underneath a volcano? How is that even possible?" Jepson asked.

Mark shrugged. "I'm not sure myself, but it is. Somehow they diverted the lava flow and built a base in the core of the mountain itself. But don't kid yourselves, this base is huge."

"Have you been inside it?" Ryan asked.

Mark shook his head. "No, not physically. I sent in a camouflaged probe. It sent back plenty of information."

"Well that's a start," Nagata concluded.

"We're not going to have time for much more, gentlemen. We were attacked leaving that world by more of those predator fast attack ships. They have heavily fortified shields and almost pack the punch of a full blown cruiser."

"So these smaller ships represent a big improvement in technology for the Agalum," Brennan noted.

Mark replied grimly. "Yes, a very significant advancement over what they had before. Eddie barely won that battle on Chakix, and still barely got away with his life. The *Stargrazer* is still being repaired and we may not be able to complete those repairs on board the *Cagliostro.*"

"You seem very concerned with these new, smaller Agalum vessels, Johnson. Any reason why we should not just consider them more of the same? I mean we have been holding our own pretty well against everything they've thrown at us," Carlson noted.

"Captain Carlson, to be honest we'd be foolish not to consider this a major advancement in Agalum technology. Thousands of these small ships swarming across the Earth would be devastating. They are fast, tough, and have increased firepower. Right now the *Cagliostro* and the *Stargrazer*, to a lesser extent, represent the pinnacle of Earth's space force technologically. All of the advancements to each of your military vessels have come from these two ships, including your shields and hyper-warp technology. Remember, gentlemen, two years ago this was the only faster than light ship from Earth. Now the entire fleet has that ability. These 'Predator' fast attack ships represent a change in Agalum thinking, which before was 'bigger is better'. Now they seem to be going with quantity over size."

"But is it quantity over quality? You defeated several of these ships yourselves you say," Argento asked.

"The quality seemed pretty good," Dan added with a shrug.

"Yeah, they took hits. These were not 'cannon fodder' ships, that's for sure," Red advised.

Nagata leaned back in his seat and steepled his fingers, "So we're up against a potentially game changing weapons advancement. Johnson, have you thought about a countermeasure to these ships?"

Mark met his stare grimly. "It's been on my mind, yes. But to be honest I have not had much of a chance to sit down and come up with something that will deal with a swarm of these things."

"Which is why you should not be out here traipsing around the galaxy getting into trouble. You should be back home designing and building weaponry for EPIC," Nagata countered.

"I do more good out here than I would trapped behind some desk. In case you forgot, Captain Nagata, once again my crew and I are the ones who discovered this very immediate threat, not the military, who by the way I have nothing but respect for."

Nagata relaxed, seeming to collapse within himself, "I...apologize, Captain Johnson. I know of your commitment to ending the Agalum threat. I also know what you have done for the planet in the past two years and how only your timely thinking and intervention saved us all from defeat at that time."

Mark nodded. "Thank you, Captain Nagata. I, as well as you, know the pressure we are all under with this war. I suggest you gentlemen return to your ships and we can begin to formulate our attack plan. I would like to be underway tomorrow morning if possible and commence our attack at that time."

"Agreed," Nagata replied.

"I will speak to you all at 20:00 hours tonight. Hopefully we can come to an agreement on what each of us will be doing during the attack at that time," Mark finished.

"That is amenable, Captain Johnson," Ryan replied, stretching his hand toward Mark, who took it in a strong grip matching Ryan's own and shook it firmly.

Chapter 29

Mark, Red, and Dan watched the shuttles leave the hangar deck and disappear into the six ships ringed around the *Cagliostro*.

"Whaddaya think?" Dan asked.

"We have our fleet, though it's only half a dozen ships of various sizes and firepower." Mark shrugged.

"Yeah kinda what I'm thinkin' too," Dan sullenly agreed.

"What about you, Red? From a security man's perspective are we going to have enough men and firepower to take down that Agalum base and those ships out there? Don't forget we saw an Agalum G'Kor class world crusher in orbit around Chakix."

"That's a big space ship, loaded with firepower. But unless they are going to destroy Chakix, which I doubt since they have a base there, it's really too bulky and slow in a pitched battle. But its guns could probably destroy any ship in this fleet in two blasts. Then again, it's pretty unprotected up close. A few ships circling it close to its skin and blasting off major components, like weaponry, fuel storage, if we can get at it that is, communications, and even their engines and then hangar decks and we should be able to render it useless and helpless if not outright destroy it."

Mark continued to stare out of the hangar deck at the blackness of space. "But the key is getting close enough to it to do so."

Red nodded, "Yeah that pretty much sums it up, Mark. No matter what ships are in the attack, if they don't get up on its skin, they'll be vaporized."

Mark sighed and turned back toward his friends. "Wonderful. Red, did you get any readings on how many other Agalum ships are circling that world?"

"Honestly, there are too many. Upward of a hundred right now, or at least when we last saw it."

"We're going to need a diversion, something to draw some off, hell hopefully most of them off. At least temporarily."

"What are you thinking, Mark?" Dan asked with slit eyes.

"I'll let you know in a few hours," Mark replied. He turned with a grin on his face and entered the maglovator, heading to his office on the engineering deck.

Chapter 30

"Change of plans, gentlemen. Await my signal here and I'll contact you when we're ready to begin the assault, unless there are other changes, which is entirely possible."

On the main view screen of the *Cagliostro* was a large image of Captain Nagata on the left side of the screen and five smaller images running down the right, one above the other.

Mark Johnson's declaration was met with differing responses. Captains Ryan and Jepson merely nodded in agreement. Carlson and Nagata seemed to seethe with anger, but were not quite ready to explode just yet. The rest appeared to have a 'wait and see' attitude.

"What's your plan, Johnson?" Carlson asked.

"You'll see when I return."

"What if you don't? Nagata queried suspiciously.

"Then go on without me and destroy that base."

"Why be so secretive, Captain?" Argento prodded.

"Because I'm not about to let you all try to talk me out of this. Secondly, the *Cagliostro* can fully camouflage itself. With what I'm attempting we're going to need that. None of you can help me with this. This has to be done stealthily. That's something only the *Cag* can do right now."

"How long will this mystery mission of yours take?" Nagata pressed.

"I'm assuming two to three days at most, but I can't be certain. Just keep your comm line open for our call.

When you get it, be prepared to implement whatever information I give you immediately."

Nagata's eyes narrowed. "What are you planning, Johnson?"

Mark smiled. "Captain Nagata, I'm planning to save the day. Again."

Ariel cut the communication off at Mark's command.

"Take us out of here, Danny."

"On our way, Mark," Sledge replied steering the *Cagliostro* away, and accelerating into hyper-warp.

The *Cagliostro* disappeared in a burst of light, leaving the half dozen ships behind.

Mark asked, "ETA to Chakix world?"

"Approximately four hours at present speed, Mark," Dan answered.

"Double our speed. I want to be there in two."

Dan nodded and accelerated the ship even more.

"Red, if you see anything out there, I mean anything, I want to know what it is and how far away. Especially if it's a predator."

Mark turned back to Danny. "How's the camouflage unit?"

"Camo is fully engaged, we are invisible."

Mark nodded and smiled, "Good let's go hunt us up a predator."

***

Three hours later the *Cagliostro* sat in stationary orbit around Chakix and waited.

Sledge turned toward Mark and announced, "Camouflage is at one hundred percent, Mark."

Johnson nodded, "Thanks Dan. We may be here a while. But those big G'Kor class ships out there can't see us. That's a plus."

"Yes it is," agreed Ariel, "Do you have a plan to capture one of those things?"

"I do. I plan to float around up here until one appears on long range scanners and then we'll fly to it. overpower it and magno-beam it aboard."

"That's a plan?" Eddie laughed.

"It is for what we need. We really don't need to get fancy with this. When we find one I'll have Ariel jam all communications coming out of that thing and then we'll take it by force. Once aboard the Cag we'll throw the crew in a cell and engineering will dismantle the thing."

Dan swiveled his seat around to face Mark. "What if it's booby trapped?"

"I suppose it could be." Mark held his chin in thought. "We are talking about the Agalum after all, so anything's possible."

"It's somethin' ta consider," Sledge added. "But that's all. I mean it's probably not anything ta worry about."

"No, but you are right, Danny. Anything is possible with these people. I think that you should do a full scan on that ship when we get it, but do it outside the hangar deck. The last thing we need is for a ship that size blowing up inside the *Cagliostro*. It would destroy us."

"How about we don't take it in and instead send a boarding party after we scan it as much as possible from here?"

Mark nodded. "That works for me, Dan."

"Good. I think that's the safest way we're gonna go with this," Dan agreed grimly.

"When we capture one, everyone who boards it wears a heavy armor suit. I want this to happen as safely as possible," Mark ordered.

"Sounds about right, Mark," Red acknowledged.

"Red, your best men on this, okay? Those ships are small, smaller than the *Stargrazer*. They only hold one man."

"Are you sure about that, Boss?" Eddie asked.

Mark swiveled his seat toward his gunner. "Well you fought one up close and personal, Eddie. What do you think? I thought we were all decided that they were one man attack ships, based on the bodies' configuration."

Eddie shrugged. "Yeah, sure, I think that you're right, but what if they're not? What if there's different models of that style ship? Do you remember a few years back during the first battle with these lettuce headed freaks when we jammed sixty people into the *Stargrazer*? I mean, the one I fought sure seemed like a one man ship, but what if it was just one guy who was playin' hero out there? Trying to take the '*Grazer* down?"

Mark nodded before answering. "I see your point. But the bottom line is we'll never know unless we get one to take apart."

"Are we in the right place to do that though?" Red asked.

Mark swung around to face him. "Meaning?"

"Look, here's a star chart that shows where we were when we encountered those Predators a few days back." Red pushed a few virtual buttons and a star chart blazed to life on the main view screen. "This is where we are now, and this is where we were when we fought those predators."

He pointed out a kidney bean shaped pattern on the main viewer, which a dotted line sprang up at his command and stood out clearly for all to see.

"This whole area in between is where the predators could be. We've only seen Agalum activity in this area in the past, so I'm thinking we should concentrate our search there."

"What do you have against where we are now?" Ariel inquired.

"This could be too congested, too much of a bottle neck. It could work against us. There could be Agalum all over us in no time."

"Well, that is a possibility. But we can't just wander aimlessly through trillions of square miles of space looking for a sixty foot long spaceship. At least here above Chakix we know there's a good chance of us finding one," Mark replied.

***

The *Cagliostro* sat in orbit above the planet they now referred to as Chakix for a day and a half, moving across it slowly from one pole to the other, from one position to another. Sweeping slowly and invisibly across the world, seeking one lone 'predator' ship.

"Mark, I've got something," Red announced.

"A 'Predator'?" Mark leaned forward in his seat and asked.

"Yeah. It just dropped out of hyper-warp about fifty thousand miles out."

Mark nodded, his eyes slits. "Okay. Are they giving any indication that they see us?"

"No, nothing. I think we're free and clear right now." Red spun his seat around and faced Mark. "How do you want to play this?"

"I'd like to just snatch and grab it, but I know nothing's ever going to go that easily. I'm thinking we block its communications if possible and then shoot out its engines as it's entering the atmosphere."

"Make it look like an engine malfunction?"

Mark nodded. "Yep that's the idea, Red. Then we'll tractor beam it into the shuttle deck, take out the crew and start taking the thing apart."

"Once we make sure the thing's not gonna blow up on us," Dan added.

Mark agreed. "Right, Danny, once we make sure it's safe."

"Okay, sounds good," Red concurred.

"Mark," Ariel interrupted, "they're trying to communicate with the base."

"Good, let them. I'm in no rush. When they start heading planetside, we go in behind them."

"What about our heat signature when we start to pierce the atmosphere? You know it's going to make us visible," Dan advised.

"Yes I do, Mr. Sledge. At that point we're going to jam their communications and take out their engines. Remember, we're not so concerned with their propulsion. It's their shield design and weapons we want a look at from that thing. We all know how fast and maneuverable the 'predator' is. This is a definite step up for the Agalum. We need to see one up close. I'm not going to say this is a game changer for them just yet, but it could be."

"What about the base? Aren't you concerned they'll see our heat signature too?" Ariel asked.

"Once we take out their engines we're going to get very tight with them, then pull them inside."

"I think I liked the other idea where we boarded them and checked it out first better," Dan remarked.

"Here they go," Red announced.

"Follow after them, Danny."

Dan Sledge nodded. "You got it, Boss."

The *Cagliostro* dipped invisibly toward the planet's surface, mirroring its prey's movements under Dan Sledge's steady hands.

"Status?" Mark queried.

Dan answered, "Ship's systems are all working at one hundred percent efficiency, including the camouflage unit. They don't know we're back here."

"All right, we have to do this fast. Stay three thousand miles back of them until we begin to drop into the atmosphere, and at that point close quickly. I want to be on top of them before the atmospheric burn begins to show on our shields. Red, you and Ari block their transmissions beginning now. Eddie, as soon as they're done you take out that ships engines."

"You got it, Mark," Eddie acknowledged.

Red and Ariel looked at each other and he nodded. She smiled and touched a control on her virtual control panel an instant after Red had adjusted one on his.

Immediately the smaller ship before them was blacked out from communications.

"Take them now," Mark ordered.

The *Cagliostro*'s solar cannons flared to life emitting powerful blasts with pinpoint accuracy. Eddie's aim was true. Solar blasts sprayed against the engine pods on either side of the hull on the Predator.

Explosions splashed brightly from both engines, lighting the sky up brightly.

But the Predator was not through yet. It swung around and looped overhead until it was facing the invisible *Cagliostro*.

"They're trying to aim at our heat signature," Red announced.

Mark ordered, "Take out their engines, Eddie."

"Working on it, Boss."

Eddie fired the *Cagliostro*'s solar cannons repeatedly, pounding the smaller ship before it could really move in the hot, heavy atmosphere. Here, its unique wing design was working against it. While it was still nimble it was nowhere near as swift turning as it was in frictionless space.

"Their shields are crumbling," Red announced.

"Good, finish off those engines, then get the magnetic tractor beam on it," Mark replied.

"What about their weapons?" Eddie turned and asked.

"Do what you can. We don't need them shooting up the inside of the landing deck, but I also want that thing at least somewhat intact."

"Gotcha, Boss," Eddie nodded.

Turning back to his firing reticle on his virtual viewer, Eddie fired the *Cag*'s solar cannons again and again with just enough power to do damage but not incinerate the Predator craft.

"Its port side engine is down," he announced.

"Good," Mark said. "Now the starboard. What about their guns?"

"Starboard is just about done. "They are beginning to panic onboard that thing."

"Let's hope, Eddie. Red prepare the tractor beam."

"It's been prepared, Mark," the big Security officer replied. "I'm just waiting on your word."

"Its weapons, Eddie?"

"They're firin' sporadically. They're panicked."

"Pinpoint fire control, DiGenovese, take out its guns. Then Red will grab it."

The *Cagliostro* rocked inexplicably. Eddie's blasts went wide, missing their targets. Everyone looked around in surprise.

"Red?" Mark asked, tension writ all over his face.

"We're being attacked from orbit. It's one of those G'Kor class ships, the planet destroyers. It's moved into position above us and is lobbing atmosphere mines at us."

As if to punctuate Red's last sentence the ship rocked again.

"Shields?"

"Ninety percent," Red growled.

"Eddie, take those guns out before that thing crashes."

The *Cagliostro* dove after the spiraling Predator while it streamed energy and flame from its damaged engine.

Again and again atmosphere mines were dropped atop the *Cag*, exploding viciously each time.

"This is getting' old fast," Dan grumbled.

"Eddie…"

"I got it, Mark," Eddie reiterated. This time his aim was true. With a puff of exploding debris and gasses the weapon pods on the Predator disintegrated.

"I snagged it," Red announced.

The Predator hung suspended in the air before the *Cagliostro*, and was drawn in slowly. All the while death in the form of the atmosphere mines dropped from above.

"Make sure that thing is not powering up to explode before we bring it onboard," Mark commanded.

"Everything is saying 'no' right now, Mark. I think we're in the clear," Red confirmed. Then a moment later he added, "It's onboard, let's get outta here."

"Dan, punch it!"

"I couldn't agree wit ya more, Boss," Dan replied.

He slammed the *Cagliostro*'s throttles forward and the ship leapt away, arcing invisibly upward toward space.

Red stood and headed toward a maglovator. "I'm going to the landing deck. I have a full security detail down there already, but I want to see…"

Mark cut him off. "Go, don't explain yourself."

Red nodded with his usual grim demeanor and was gone.

Ariel touched a comm control. "Mr. Marek to the command deck."

She turned and faced Mark with a slight smile, "I'm psychic, remember?"

"I know, darlin', I know."

The maglovator door opened and Marek exited.

"Take the security console, Matt."

"Yes Sir," Matt Marek replied.

The *Cagliostro* broke the planet's atmosphere into the eternal darkness of space.

"Uh-oh," Matt almost shouted.

"I see them," Dan replied, tension coloring his voice.

"Evasive maneuvers," Mark ordered.

Before the *Cagliostro* were two G'Kor class planet destroyers and each was bearing down on the *Cag*'s position.

Dan stared at the view screen and shook his head. "Out of the fryin' pan…"

Chapter 31

Energy blasts slammed into the *Cagliostro*'s shields, shaking the gleaming star cruiser mercilessly from both attacking G'Kor class ships.

"Mark, we're in trouble," Matt Marek shouted.

"Really? How could you tell?" Eddie replied sarcastically.

"Both of you shut up and just keep the ship together," Mark admonished. "Eddie, look for any weak spots on those behemoths and fire at them. I don't care what that is as long as it's a weak spot we can use to our advantage. Matt, rotate shield strength to where we need it most. Danny, get us the hell out of here."

"I can't, they did somethin' to local space. I can't form a hyper-warp funnel. They blocked us somehow."

"What?" Mark leapt from his seat and moved to Dan's engineering and piloting station.

"Look," Dan continued. "We can't form the hyper-warp funnel that the magno-disks create nanoseconds before hyper-warp. They're doing something to local space to stop us."

Mark stood up and stared at the main view screen. The two gigantic G'Kor class world destroyers were closing fast from opposite directions.

"This was all a trap," Mark grunted. "All of it. They knew we were here somewhere. They must have planted that Predator alone entering the atmosphere to draw our attention and to expose us."

"How'd they see us through the camouflage?" Ariel asked.

"They didn't have to. The heat signature we left behind entering and exiting the atmosphere was enough for them to lock onto."

"Dammit!" cursed Dan. "They musta been planning this for weeks."

"It doesn't matter if they started planning it yesterday. We're in trouble if we don't get out of here."

Again and again the *Cagliostro* rocked with enemy fire.

"Shields are at sixty percent and holding, Mark," Dan commented.

Mark looked around momentarily, his mind racing. "Ariel block and jam their communications between the two ships. I don't care if you have to sing to them. Block them from talking to one another."

She nodded and turned toward her comm console.

Mark touched his own console's holographic keys. "Red, what'd you find down there?"

Red's voice replied over the command deck's audio system. "Two purple skinned Agalum, nothing more. Besides the one destroyed engine pod the ship is complete."

"Good, stand by."

Again the *Cagliostro* rocked badly.

"Man, they are doin' a job on us," Eddie muttered.

"Target both of their bridges with a full spread of star core missiles. Fire!"

Eddie complied. The missiles flew free and exploded upon both ships' shields above the command decks of each.

242

"No damage," Matt Marek advised.

Again the *Cagliostro* rocked.

"Mark, I'm receiving damage reports from decks one through four and decks eight through ten."

"Move all nonessential personnel to decks four through seven. I only want the Med bay, the engineering deck, the weapons deck, and the shuttle deck occupied."

"I've got them jammed, Mark. They can't speak to each other," Ariel confirmed.

"Good," Mark acknowledged. The *Cagliostro* shuddered violently again and again.

"Dan, Are we venting anything?"

"No, Mark, we're not."

"We're in space long enough they shouldn't be able to track us on a heat signature any longer. The camouflage should still be hiding our movements. Then how…"

Mark's face lit up like a light bulb as he stabbed at his control console. "Red, scan that Predator ship completely. There's a bug onboard it that they're using to track our movements. Scan the two salad heads you dragged off of it too. The bug may be inside of them."

Mark stopped talking and the moment hung pregnant in the air.

Finally, Red replied, "Mark, this ship is full of bugs, and these guys too. I'm picking up stuff embedded beneath their skin from salad head to toe. We'll never be able to remove them all from the ship or these two clowns."

"Throw them in restraints, tie them down to whatever passes for seats in that thing. Destroy its communications array and add a mark seven welcome package from weapons locker thirteen."

Dan began to rise up. "I better go help him."

"No, stay put, Danny. I need you here right now. Weapons section can take care of that"

"Okay, Mark. You're the boss,."

"Mark," Eddie interrupted, "I have a shield on the port side G'Kor weakening."

"Concentrate all fire on that shield."

The battered *Cagliostro*'s weapons lit up furiously. Its solar cannons fired almost continuously, followed by full braces of star core missiles. Again and again they slammed into the much larger G'Kor ship's shields, hammering unmercifully at them.

But all the while the other G'Kor class behemoth pounded the *Cagliostro* with its own powerful weapons.

"Our shields are down to twenty five percent," Marek announced.

"I don't care. Keep them up and you, Eddie, keep shooting at that other G'Kor. Dan, fly us the hell out of here, whatever you have to do."

"Can't get away from 'em, Mark. No matter how much I dodge and weave the ship, we're getting hit. They keep followin' the trail left by those bugs they got hidden on that Predator."

Red chimed in, "The package is ready and secured, Mark."

"Good. Kick that thing out of the landing deck. Use the tractor beam and push it toward that monster out there."

An instant later the Predator ship reappeared as if by magic, right into the path of the starboard side G'Kor pummeling the *Cagliostro*'s shields.

The *Cagliostro* was suddenly free of attacks as now the G'Kor's massive weapons were firing wide.

Eddie shouted, "Direct hit! We're through the port side G'Kor's shields!"

"Don't let up, breach their hull now!"

Again the weapons on the *Cagliostro* exploded furiously, pummeling the much larger ship's weak spot over and over.

Within in seconds the blackness of space lit up in an explosion of blinding light as escaping gasses burned brightly from the breached hull of the first G'Kor.

"Put some distance between us now," Mark ordered.

"Your wish…" Dan replied.

The *Cagliostro* shot away from the two G'Kor planet destroyers, putting a hundred thousand miles between them in seconds.

A second burst of light filled the view screen, this time much larger than the first.

"Magnify and center on that explosion."

Marek complied, and the G'Kor that had been closest to the Predator when it was ejected from the landing deck now hung in space shattered and destroyed.

"They pulled the Predator inside with their own tractor beam," Matt Marek announced.

"Yes and then the bomb we left them inside of it went off," Mark finished.

"I almost feel dirty about that," Eddie commented. "Almost."

"I don't. They would have taken us captive and slaughtered everyone they didn't deem necessary, worthy or important. They got what they deserved," Mark concluded.

Chapter 32

Two days later, the *Cagliostro* had reconvened with the other six ships in their small fleet in a dead section of space. An area out of trafficked paths and away from any inhabited star systems.

"Very impressive work, Captain Johnson," Captain Nagata smiled.

"Thank you, Captain. We did what we could, as we were all thinking on our feet."

"That seems to be one of your strong suits, Captain," Captain Jepson offered.

"Thank you, all of you. But we have more pressing matters to attend to. I have now a full set of scans we acquired from the predator ship we had captured. While we have no idea how its electronics and computer systems are configured, we do know about its engines, shields, and weapons."

"Do you think this ship is really that important for our mission?"

Mark nodded. "I do. That ship is a huge leap in technology for them. A lot is stolen from my own designs of this ship, but we knew they had a plant in my company two years ago when we battled the first *Cagliostro* clone on our way back to Earth. But this is something more. It's a huge leap for them technology-wise. There are a lot of these systems which are unlike anything we've ever seen before."

"And in two years we've seen quite a lot of Agalum systems," Captain Carlson added.

"Indeed," Mark replied. "Which brings me to another conclusion. There's a new player in the game."

A stunned silence hung between the seven men.

"You believe someone else is supplying the Agalum with weaponry and technology?" Captain Brennan asked.

"I think it's a foregone conclusion at this point. From the scans we did on that new class of ship we've nicknamed 'Predator' that ship this is all new technology for the Agalum. Those shields which were so tough are different than anything we've seen from them before. Different shield frequencies, different construction. Plus they can now do something to trap us in conventional space, not allowing us to access hyper-warp. There is no doubt, my fine captains, that we have a new hand in the soup pot and it is stirring it with increased vigor."

Most of the other six men stared at Mark with a perplexed look upon their faces. Nagata was impassive and Argento smiled, as did Ryan.

Mark grimaced and shook his head. "There's a new player, guys, it's that simple. Someone is supplying the Agalum with new shields and possibly new weapons systems. Hell most of the tech on that Predator was new. We're going to have to get this information back to EPIC."

"So why not just send it?" Carlson asked.

"Because I don't trust Admiral Bright."

"What?" Nagata leaned forward in surprise.

"Did I stutter, Captain? I do not trust him. The man is more bureaucrat than warrior. Hell, I'm not even sure he hasn't been replaced by one of those shape changing things."

"I thought you discovered a way to see through their shape shifting?"

"I did. That doesn't mean they couldn't come up with something new."

Nagata eased slowly back into his chair, his face pensive. "I suppose you could be right, Captain. What do you suggest?"

"Right now I want to come up with a permanent plan to free the planet Chakix from our enemies' grip. Once we do that, we return to Earth and have a chat with Admiral Bright."

The other captains looked to each other and then Nagata, and all nodded in agreement

Nagata turned to Mark and said, "Agreed, Captain Johnson, agreed."

"I'll contact you all in two hours. We'll come up with something workable at that point."

The other men all agreed and shut down their communications except for Nagata.

"A word, Captain Johnson." It was a command not a request.

Johnson turned back toward the view screen in his command ready room, his face twisted quizzically. "What is it, Captain Nagata?"

"A question really, but a simple one and one that needs to be answered before we can proceed."

"Well, what is it?" Mark asked.

"Why are we following you? I know of your past deeds and the things you and your crew have done, but you have no high level military training, as far as I know you've never trained in tactics, and in reality the title 'Captain' doesn't mean all that much where you are concerned. Don't you believe someone like myself should be in command of this fleet?"

Mark looked at Nagata, meeting his stare and locking it to his in a grip of iron. "No. I do not, Captain. While I look forward to your input on this battle plan the way I've done things has worked for my crew and I. I was looking for help and while I will always welcome positive input, I won't be looking to give up the lead position on this mission any time soon."

"Not even when a trained soldier could take over?"

"What's really going on here, Nagata? Why the sudden interest in leading this mission? Yours and five other ships appear out of nowhere offering me exactly what we were looking for, and now suddenly you decide you want to run the show. Perhaps you all were sent here by Bright to keep an eye on the renegade nut job who got lucky a few times out here?"

"The reason I'm out here, Johnson, is to help, not you, but our planet. I'm here to make sure we win."

"Perhaps you are, Nagata, but I find it interesting how after I request Admiral Bright send me a fleet to aid us out here and he refuses me, you suddenly show up with five other ships in tow ready to jump right in. That is until you find out basically what's at stake, then you want to move in and take over. It's a little too pat for my tastes. A bit too contrived."

"So what, you think I'm some kind of spy for Admiral Bright? That we all are? Let's not beat around the bush, Johnson. Do you think we're here to somehow undercut you? Or to keep you in line? I have to remind you, we're all on the same team here, all on the same mission."

"Yes, I would like to think so, Nagata. If this was a military operation that we had flown in on to aid you all, not that the little *Cagliostro* could be so much of an aid to the power behemoths of EPIC's fleet, I would gladly do what was asked of us and follow yours or whoever's lead. But that is just not the case. This is a delicate situation. One we've been deeply engaged with for the past week plus. I'm asking you to trust me, Nagata. We need a scalpel here, not a hammer."

Nagata sighed and seemingly deflated. He leaned back in his desk chair and stared at Mark silently for a moment.

Nagata pointed at Mark. "You better be right about this. I'm putting my faith and my trust in you. Don't make me regret this."

"I won't Captain. Trust me. I won't let you or the Earth down. But I have to ask you one other favor, a minor one at best. I'd prefer to get your word that you or any of the other Captains or crews will not contact Admiral Bright until after the mission is over."

Nagata bristled at this, but then relented. "Very well, Johnson. You have my word. We'll play it your way, because, whether you believe it or not, I *do* respect you and what you have done."

"Thank you, Captain."

Chapter 33

Mark and his command crew sat in the command deck ready room staring at each other across the table.

"Do you trust them?" Ariel asked.

"I think I have to. What other choice do I have?"

Dan shrugged. "Well we could just blast outta here so fast they'd never catch us and go back to Chakix. We could settle things up ourselves once we're there. Don't forget, we're still the fastest ship in the fleet, and so far from what we've seen the fastest ship around period. Don't sell that short."

"No, Danny, I won't. But I don't want to believe our own organization would turn against us for no reason."

"Maybe Bright's been compromised," Eddie commented. "It is possible."

"I know, Eddie, it is. Even with the screening systems we've been able to come up with to defeat their clones and shape shifters they could just have come up with something new."

"Or we're all just getting a little too paranoid," Red allowed.

Mark nodded solemnly. "You're right. Or that."

Ariel turned toward Mark. "Mark, when they were here I didn't break into their minds and scan them. But I didn't get any latent feelings of deception off of them either. Every one of them seemed genuine enough while they sat at this table."

"I understand, Ari. I don't know what to think at the moment. I just know we've been out here for a long time. When this is over I want a vacation," Mark sighed.

"Yeah Boss, you ain't the only one," Dan noted.

Red looked around at everyone seated at the conference table. "So what do we do now?"

"We're going to put our plans in concrete, Red. Let's decide right now how we're going to do this."

Eddie waved his hand toward Mark. "Hey, you're the boss, Boss. You come up with it and let us know what you wanna do. Like always. You command we'll follow. If something doesn't look kosher, we'll let you know."

Mark grinned. "Thanks for the vote of confidence, Eddie."

"What? I was bein' serious."

"I know, DiGenovese, I know. That's the best part of it."

Dan grunted, "Now you guys are gettin' loose? When things are goin' to be their worst?"

Mark smiled. "C'mon, Danny, you know how I work. When things are at their worst I'm at my best."

"It don't always work out fer the best, man," Dan replied.

"I'm aware of things, Dan. You know that," Mark countered.

"Ah, you know I'm just playin' devil's advocate." Dan grinned.

"I do Danny, and actually I thank you for doing that once in a while, just not too oft-"

A frenzied voice cut through the ship's comm system. "Emergency on the landing deck, repeat emergency on the landing deck."

Mark's face immediately turned grim as he toggled the comm unit built into his tech suits sleeve. "This is Captain Johnson. What's the emergency and who am I talking to?"

A voice immediately replied, but in the background shots could be heard firing from blasters all about him. "Th-this is Phillips. I-I'm a tech working on the *Stargrazer* repairs. Th-these things started growing out of the f-floor. Th-they're unstoppable."

"What kind of things, Phillips? What are they?"

No other reply came.

Red exited the conference room and ran straight toward the maglovator. Eddie and Dan looked at Mark, who then turned and followed Red.

Eddie, Dan, and Ariel followed him into the maglovator.

"Red got into the other car ahead of us," Eddie mused.

"He's only got a few seconds on us," Mark answered.

Once again he tapped his right sleeve's cuff, this time on the run, "All available security personnel to the landing deck. Repeat, all available security personnel to the landing deck."

The command crew exited the maglovator on the landing deck, bursting through the sliding doors as soon as they parted.

"What the hell?" Dan barked.

Everyone froze for an instant. Three robots were rampaging through the landing deck. Three robots that no one had ever seen before. Big, blocky things and they were the same light blue as the *Cagliostro*'s landing deck floor.

Red was already ahead of them and sprinting toward the robots, a blaster in hand.

Mark turned to Ariel. "Ari, scan them, make sure they're robots and not men in armor."

"Already did it, Mark. I'm getting nothing. There's nothing organic there. It's all robot."

A man bleeding from a forehead wound stumbled toward them and fell into Mark's arms.

"Cap-tain, I-I'm Phillips. Th-those things, th-they grew right out of the floor."

"What Philips? How?"

Mark shook the man but he was now limp in Marks arms, unconscious, or worse.

Mark propped him up behind some equipment in the landing deck and angrily turned toward the rampaging mechanicals.

Security men had exited the maglovator behind the command crew and were now engaging the three robots. Energy blasters were firing almost nonstop and Red was right in the thick of things, directing his men and firing shot after shot from his own blaster.

"Small arms fire is just bouncing off of them," Eddie observed.

Mark nodded. "We need heavier artillery."

With a terrible wrenching sound one of the robots flipped over a shuttle like it was paper.

"Great, more damage," Mark grunted.

"Where the hell did these things come from?" Eddie shouted.

"They had to be left here from that Predator craft," Mark replied.

"How's that even possible, Mark?" Dan queried.

"Miniaturization. Think about it. Remember what Phillips said on the comm? They came out of the floor. These things were miniaturized and absorbed material from the hull of the ship, or rather the landing deck itself. Look at the floor near where that Predator class ship was being held. See how it's discolored and it looks almost gouged out? There's mass missing from there. They built themselves from some pre-programmed code. We're lucky it's only three. It could have been hundreds."

Red's voice interrupted on the tech suits comm units. "Mark, I'm heading to the armory to get something with more punch. I've got a total of thirty men either engaged here or coming to join the party."

"Acknowledged, Red. Bring something powerful."

"Just what I was thinking, Boss man."

Red disappeared back into the maglovator.

Dan turned toward Mark. "I gotta buy these guys some time."

Without another word he leaped toward the robots. One immediately identified him as a threat and batted him out of the air. Dan smashed into the previously flipped shuttle, and both man and shuttle careened across the landing deck in a heap of twisted metal.

"Danny!" Mark shouted.

"Oh man, that *had* to hurt," Eddie moaned.

In reply the decimated shuttle split apart. Dan crawled from within its wreckage, tearing the rest of it in two. He ran directly at the three robots, while carrying what was left of the shuttle in each hand. The security men continued to fire gleaming blaster beams at them, which careened all over the landing deck.

Dan leaped through the air, roaring, "Eat some heavy metal, you brainless freaks!"

He heaved the shuttle halves at two of the robots, knocking them from their feet and crushing them against the bulkhead wall.

"Get this deck cleared of all non-security people!" Mark shouted.

The other two robots were closing in on the rapidly firing security team. The machines were heavily shielded and the hand blasters were just not powerful enough to tear through them quickly.

"This is not so good," Eddie complained.

"Aim for the joints in the knees and hips. Let's see if it's a weak spot," Mark ordered.

"Good idea, El Capitan," Eddie smirked.

"Red, where are you with that heavy artillery?" Mark spoke into his sleeve's comm unit.

"Coming," was the terse reply.

Across the landing deck, Dan traded blows with the powerful robot he had engaged.

"Holy…Will you look at him go," Eddie exclaimed.

Dan slammed his right fist into the robot, and then followed with his left. Each punch was punctuated by a terrible wrenching sound of steel being damaged.

"C'mon, you pile of garbage, let's see what you've really got!" Sledge yelled.

The robot, in an almost human seeming gesture, paused as if angry, hesitating a second. Then it threw itself at Dan Sledge, both block-like fists raised above its head.

Dan did not hesitate an instant. He squatted down, then leaped straight at the robot, both of his fists knotted together. He swung those mighty club-like fists at the instant he engaged the robot. The impact was like a bomb going off in the landing deck. Everyone turned to see what the sound was, even if they did not mean or want to.

The robot's head exploded from its shoulders as if it had been launched out of a rocket and slammed against the ceiling of the landing deck with a thunderous cacophony.

Dan landed on the deck with his back to the robot in a crouch. He turned to stare at the mechanical monster with a sneer of utter contempt upon his brutish face.

The headless robot took one step, then a second and fell over, unmoving. Fluids began to seep from its body.

Instants later the doors to the maglovator sighed open and Red along with more security men entered. Red was holding his favorite energy cannon, which was strapped to his back in a harness.

He lifted it, aimed, and fired in one smooth motion. The blast rocketed from the cannon's maw and slammed into the nearest robot, sending it careening into another shuttle.

"Wonderful, yet more damage," Mark groused.

'Ariel?' Mark questioned mentally.

'I'm here.' she replied.

'Get upstairs. I don't want you involved in this. This is turning ugly.'

'*No. I'm part of this command crew. If you're all here, then so am I.*'

Mark shook his head angrily. '*Okay, just stay out of the way and near a maglovator in case you have to escape from here. If you're going to stay then link us all up telepathically.*'

'*That I can do.*'

'*And Ari, be careful. I almost lost you once on this mission. That was one time too many.*'

Ariel smiled and blew him a kiss, then ducked low and made her way to the nearest maglovator. From there she reached out with her mind and linked the command crew up.

'*Everyone here? Check in please,*' she asked.

'*Yeah. I'm here,*' Eddie answered.

'*Ditto,*' grunted Dan.

'*I'm a little busy now,*' replied Red.

'*We all are,*' Mark finally commented.

Red turned toward Eddie, who was ducking down behind a shuttle, and threw him a rifle.

'*Here, squirt, try that.*' Red's mental voice flooded the mental link.

'*Thanks, big man,*' Eddie replied while catching the rifle deftly from the air.

Spinning it like a toy Eddie brought it up quickly and fired in a blur. The first blast spun the robot nearest him around, but it did not go down.

Red meantime was hammering at the second robot with his blast cannon aligned with about half of the security force in the hangar deck. Red's cannon was making progress, certainly more than the hand blasters were and even more than the rifles. But even so it was a slow uphill battle.

'I can't believe Red's cannon is not tearing that thing apart,' Dan critiqued.

'Neither can I. All I can think of is that it's made of our armored hull material,' Mark replied. *'Are you okay, Danny?'*

'Yeah, boss. I just need a minute to catch my breath.'

'You got it, pal.' Mark ran off crouched low across the landing deck toward Eddie and some of the security personnel.

The group Eddie was with fired continuously at the robot. So much blaster energy was being thrown at the thing that it glowed bright red in spots.

'How the hell did these things get oils and lubricants inside of them?' Eddie asked.

'It's from the shuttles and what's stored here. Don't forget this is a maintenance bay; everything they need to run on is here. The damned things must have absorbed it slowly somehow.'

'Mark,' Ariel interrupted, *'what the hell are these things? What kind of science is this?'*

'I don't know, baby. I've never seen anything like this. This scares me,' he admitted.

'Everybody clear away from my target,' Red barked, *'I'm ramping the cannon up to a hundred and ten percent.'*

Mark answered immediately, *'Red be careful, you're bypassing the safeties. That thing could explode in your hands and take out half the landing deck.'*

'Kinda hoping this works out, Boss,' was his terse reply.

The cannon hummed dangerously loud in Red's hands, its sound starting at a low rumble and spiraling upward to a screeching, ear-splitting crescendo.

"Try this on, tin can," Red shouted.

He fired, and the cannon's kick back knocked him from his feet and slammed him into the bulkhead behind him. But the blast of energy it emitted was shockingly powerful, akin to a comet being released within the *Cagliostro*'s landing deck. The ball of fury exploded upon the robot's chest, searing a hole clear through it before dissipating. The robot stumbled a step, then two and finally fell over, a melted heap of scrap metal, totally destroyed.

Red dropped the cannon. It was blisteringly hot to the touch and ruined by the powerful blast itself.

'*Red! Are you okay?*' Ariel shouted telepathically.

He waved her off, as he fought his way to his feet, trying to catch his breath and wincing from the pain he was in.

The last robot now moved steadily toward the group of security men Eddie was with. Their weapons were slowing it down, but not doing enough damage to stop it.

"Crap!" Eddie shouted dropping his rifle. It had begun to overheat and glow in his hands.

'*Clear the deck,*' Mark commanded through their link.

Everyone looked around for him but he was nowhere in sight.

'*Move it all of you,*' he ordered once more.

"C'mon, back to the maglovator." Eddie moved the men with him. He met Dan who was holding Red up and the unconscious Phillips in his other arm.

"Where the hell is Mark?" Eddie shouted over the roaring sound of the advancing robot combined with the continued gunfire.

Before anyone could answer, the *Stargrazer* came to life and lifted up into the air. It spun itself into position between the men and the advancing robot, which stopped in its tracks to assess this new threat.

"Fire in the hole!" shouted Mark over the '*Grazer*'s comm system.

The *Stargrazer*'s twin solar cannons fired, obliterating the remaining robot instantly. All that was left was a steaming pile of unrecognizable metal.

The *Stargrazer* hovered slowly back into its landing berth and settled down. Its engines powered down and the ship shut down. Mark exited the '*Grazer*'s doors at a run toward his crew.

"Everyone okay?"

"Some bangs and bruises but for the most part we're all fine," Ariel answered.

"Good. I was able to use a low powered setting on the *Stargrazer's* cannon's, otherwise that might have turned into more of a mess on this deck then just the robots attack. The last thing I wanted was to blow a hole in the side of the *Cag*. I'm glad repairs on the *Stargrazer* got as far as they did. At least I was able to get it off the ground. I want a cleanup crew down here immediately. Make sure our remaining shuttles and the *Stargrazer* are locked down securely. Then from the landing deck I want those piles of junk sucked out into space. Open the deck doors and force field. Let them all be sucked out. Once that's finished I want this deck swept for any more surprises the Agalum might have left behind."

Red nodded. "You got it Boss, I'll get right on it."

"No," Mark interrupted him. "You're going to the medical deck to see Dr. Troiano. You're hurt from that harebrained stunt you just pulled. Someone else can take care of this. Security team, whoever's not injured stay down here while the cleanup crew gets this place in order. Let's move it people, we've got a planet to free."

Chapter 34

"That's what I have for you, Captain Nagata. This is totally new technology. I have no doubt there's a new player aiding the Agalum now. Feel free to relay my findings to the rest of the fleet captains. Since you seem to be the leader of our impromptu fleet I wanted to talk to you first."

Nagata sighed resignedly on his side of the view screen. "That is awful news, Captain Johnson. I am relieved to hear none of your crew was seriously injured. What about repairs to your ship?"

"Engineering is taking care of that now. It's mostly minor damage to the landing deck. I have them reinforcing the deck floor where it was weakened."

"And you say there's been no sign of any more of these miniaturized robotic weapons systems?"

"No Captain, none to be seen. The ship is clean."

"Very well, Captain Johnson. Are you satisfied with your attack plan?"

"Yes, I am. I think it's the most advantageous plan we can put into motion. What are your thoughts, Captain Nagata?"

"No, I have to agree. Use our strengths in the best manner for each situation. I believe your plan is sound. When our part of the battle is completed we'll join you with your beachhead assault upon their base. Godspeed, Captain Johnson."

Mark saluted, "To you as well, Captain Nagata. Be careful out there."

Nagata nodded and broke the connection.

Mark slumped back into his chair in his conference room. He closed his eyes momentarily and breathed slowly.

'How'd it all come to this?' he thought to himself.

'Don't worry about it, Mark. We'll be fine.' Ariel's mental voice replied.

'Sorry, Ari. I didn't realize you were listening in.'

'I really wasn't but your last comment sounded almost painful.'

Mark laughed. *'That wouldn't be far from the truth, but you understand what I mean.'*

She sighed telepathically. *'I do, Mark. But you are the best man for the job, you know that.'*

'Sometimes I wonder though, Ari. Sometimes I think these big starship Captains should be running this show instead of me.'

'Mark, you know that the President has the utmost confidence in you.'

'Sometimes I think Scaleia has more confidence in me than I have in myself.'

'You not being an overconfident ass is a plus, you know.' She chuckled softly.

'Really? Try telling that to Admiral Bright.'

'I think he doesn't like you because you're not military.'

'Him and everyone else who wears a military uniform.'

'It's not that bad. What about men like Captain Ryan and Captain Jepson? They both like you and are willing to follow your lead.'

'Honey, I think they are few and far between. I mean really, Ari, think about it; what are we doing out here that the military can't do better? This is a war. I served proudly when I was younger, but that was a decade ago. Since then I've become a completely different person. What do I know about battle strategies?'

'Obviously enough, because like I already said, the President trusts you. Heck he handpicked you two years ago to lead the mission that changed everything.'

'I have to tell you, Ari, that I wonder sometimes if we were better off never leaving our solar system. The Agalum weren't at war with us and may have never been.'

'No, they were just infiltrating our governments and replacing key people including General Abruzzi and even President Scaleia. Think about what you're saying.'

'I know, you're right. Sometimes I just feel like I'm not in control of anything anymore, let alone my own life. Things were simpler when I just designed spacecraft and weapons.'

'Someday they'll be like that again,' she replied.

Mark chuckled silently. *'I'm on my way back to the command deck. I'll see you in a minute.'*

'See you then.' She cut the connection and Mark rose from his chair, and ran his hand through his hair.

"Time to get this show on the road," he said aloud, and exited the conference room.

***

Eighteen hours later…

The *Cagliostro* exited hyper-warp into a war zone. Explosions rocked near space around them followed by blindingly brilliant flashes of light.

"Shields at maximum, camouflage on," Mark ordered.

The *Cagliostro* appeared for only a split second, then disappeared just as quickly, its camouflage unit causing it to shimmer and fade from view.

Red turned toward Mark. "The *Triumphant* is in trouble. The Agalum have them separated from the rest of the fleet."

"We can't help them, Red. We have a mission of our own. They'll be okay. I trust those men."

"Mark," Ariel interrupted, "The *Triumphant* is calling for help. We're the closest ship."

Mark sighed, "No, we're not. We're not here, we're on our way to the bigger mission. The big ships have to fend for themselves. Dan, take us down."

Dan looked at Mark and grimaced. He then turned and began accelerating the *Cagliostro* through the battle. Ships on both sides of the conflict fired at each other all about the *Cagliostro*, which invisibly moved through the battlefield in space. Once clear of it the *Cagliostro* arced invisibly down toward Chakix's surface.

The red skinned alien exited the maglovator with Dr. Troiano to watch the *Cagliostro*'s descent.

"I am almost home," the alien said in its strange modulated voice to Mark.

"You are. Now as soon as you are able, contact your people-"

"My children," Chakix corrected.

"Very well, your children then, and prepare them for what they must do."

"They will do as I command them. You will have your aid upon the ground."

"Good." Mark nodded affirmatively. "Because we won't be able to do this alone."

The Chakix possessed alien nodded. "I understand."

"We're entering the atmosphere now, Captain," Red announced.

"Okay, Red. Take us to the coordinates that Chakix gave us."

"You got it, Mark."

The red skinned alien turned to Mark, "I leave you now. Return my child to the ground. He will know where to go."

Without another word the bare chested alien stumbled as if cut loose from invisible strings. It grasped its head as if pained. Then it looked up in shock, as if just realizing where it was.

Mark nodded to the two security officers standing by the maglovator doors. They quickly walked to either side of the alien.

"Come with us," Security Officer Dorn spoke, authoritatively. He was a tall, powerfully built black skinned man.

"We'll take it from here," the female officer named Crosby agreed. She had short blonde hair and a no nonsense demeanor.

"Be careful with our friend there. He's disoriented and means no harm. You can take him to the entry ramp. He's going home as soon as we touch down," Mark ordered.

The *Cagliostro*'s hull glowed with reentry heat, even through the camouflage. It became a glowing outline as it quickly descended.

"We can be detected entering this quickly, you know," Dan reminded Mark.

"Only visually, Danny. I know. But it can't be helped we have to strike quickly. Time is against us."

The *Cagliostro* landed softly, its landing engines switched to a vertical take-off and landing or VTOL configuration. The ship touched down and within instants the native was out the door and running into the thick forest.

Mark directed, "Keep the camouflage unit on, and shields powered up. Anonymity, people. That's what we're looking for. At least until the rest of the ground forces arrive. Red, saddle up. It's time to go."

Mark touched a control on his virtual control panel. "Secondary command crew to the command deck."

The secondary crew entered the command deck less than a minute later. Immediately the primary crew stood and headed toward the maglovator, with Mark and Ariel pausing as Matt Marek walked toward them.

"Mr. Marek, take care of my ship." Mark shook Matt's hand as both men nodded mirthlessly.

"Will do Sir," Marek replied.

Mark turned and headed toward the maglovator with Ariel beside him.

The command crew met in the armory along with seventy other crewmen and women.

"I didn't think I'd be playing wartime medic anytime soon, much less wearing something as ridiculous as this," Dr. Troiano announced. Her diminutive body was suited up in a heavy battle suit. Nearby everyone else save for a handful of others were all in various phases of donning the heavily armored suits. The remaining men and women were putting on jet black skin tight suits with hoods and face masks.

"Are you ready?" One of the black suited crewmen said to another.

"Yes, let's try this out."

Both men touched buttons at the waist of the suits and they instantly disappeared.

"Whoa!" Ariel exclaimed. "I knew what to expect and even I wasn't ready for that."

"Fully functional stealth suits Ari," Mark advised. "They use the same technology as the camouflage unit on the ship. You and I will be wearing them as well as Eddie and Dan. Red will be leading the security men and other crewmen in the field. We, as well as Dorn and Crosby, who are already in their stealth suits and outside the ship, will be infiltrating that base. Hopefully these suits will surprise the Agalum as much as they just did you."

She nodded and smiled. "Knowing you, darling, they'll work just fine." Ariel leaned forward and kissed him on the cheek. Mark smiled and took her in his arms and kissed her full on the lips with passion. The crowd of crewmen began clapping earnestly.

Mark broke the kiss and they both smiled. "All right, everyone, let's get our minds back on the attack. It's time to move."

Mark finished donning his stealth suit as did Dan and Ariel.

"Strike team Alpha, power up," Mark ordered.

The small team of stealth suit wearing men and women turned their suits on and immediately faded from sight.

"Goggles on," Mark ordered again. Everyone placed the goggles they held in their hand or that rested upon their heads over their eyes. Instantly the invisible strike team became visible to them all. A dull yellow glow enveloped everyone wearing a stealth suit. The goggles plugged into a port by the neck of the suit with a thin yet sturdy cable. "Remember, everyone. These goggles must *not* fall into Agalum hands."

"Strike team Beta, power up," Mark commanded. The rest of the crew wearing heavy suits activated their armor. They hummed to life and almost immediately quieted.

"Alpha, begin our assault. Beta, stay back until the predetermined time for your attack. Let's go people we're burning daylight."

They exited the *Cagliostro* and began to step silently into the jungle. '*I wonder how the battle in space is going?*' Ariel asked telepathically.

***

"The battle is going badly," Captain Nagata spoke to his companions.

"I know, Nagata. My ship is already badly damaged," Captain Ryan barked.

"Where are you, Ryan?" Nagata questioned.

"Check your sensors. We're several thousand miles off from you. We got drawn into a battle with a smaller craft that tried to escape us. We followed it and it led us right to a G'Kor planet crusher. We're in trouble."

"We're on our way. I'm continuing to your position, Ryan. Hold on," Captain Carlson replied.

"If you don't hurry, Carlson, this G'Kor that's on my ass is going to chew it up and spit it out."

"Just hold on," Carlson reiterated.

The starscape above Chakix was alive with firepower. Six Earth Protectorate vessels against three times that number of Agalum.

The ships of both fleets spun through space chaotically. Energy blasts and missiles careened through the inky blackness lighting up the sky below brightly.

"I've got the *Triumphant*, Carlson. Help Nagata," Captain Argento of the *Crossbow* cut in.

The *Crossbow* blazed brightly through space arcing down toward the G'Kor class planet destroyer that was about to obliterate the much smaller *Triumphant*.

While not as large as the G'Kor it was still a mile long monster fitted with enough enemy crushing power to raze cities from space. Now all that firepower was unleashed at the G'Kor. Within instants the tide of that battle changed. Where before the G'Kor had been mercilessly hammering the *Triumphant*, now the

Crossbow was doing just that to the larger ship. The *Triumphant* spun back toward the *Crossbow*.

"Fire all forward guns!" roared Ryan. "Double shields to the rear of the ship. Fire full brace of Star Cores, now!"

The *Triumphant*, a much bigger ship than the *Cagliostro* by almost twice, unleashed hell upon the suddenly embattled Agalum G'Kor ship.

"The one problem with a ship as massive as the G'Kor's is that they don't turn all that quickly, and when pinioned between two powerful war ships as ours are, well it's a bit hard for them to draw a bead on us. They're made for planet razing, not really for ship to ship combat," Argento commented. He watched a moment more as the G'Kor split in two and exploded spectacularly above Chakix.

"My crew and I thank you for the save, Captain Argento. Now let's get back to the others," Ryan said.

The two powerful vessels began to turn back toward the area above Chakix where the majority of the battle was taking place when another powerful blast lit up the sky.

"What was that?" shouted Argento. His crew looked at him fearfully across his command deck, looking and waiting for some word of encouragement that it wasn't one of their fellow Earth ships that had just exploded.

For several seconds there was only static, and then Nagata replied, "That was the *Tempest*. Captain Brennan and his crew are gone."

***

274

'How much further?' Ariel asked telepathically.

'Another quarter mile and we're there,' Mark replied.

They continued on in silence, walking the last quarter mile easily, quickly, and invisibly. They came upon a small clearing in the forest and entered it, stopping there.

"This is the place," Mark spoke quietly aloud. He touched the control on the side of his waist and immediately became visible again. The rest of the crew followed suit.

'Now what?' Eddie telepathically asked.

'Now we wait,' Mark replied.

They did not have to wait long. Within minutes the forest about the crew came alive as red skinned natives, roughly hundreds of them, stepped forth brandishing crude spears and knives.

"I see Chakix kept its word," Red muttered as he looked about.

Then the great red ape stepped forth, breathing heavily. It stared down at Dan angrily, actually curling its lip in closely bottled rage.

"Looks like your pal remembers you," Eddie jibed. "Maybe he thinks you're its brother?"

"Shut up, squirt. I don't have time to play games with you now," Dan retorted.

Eddie turned to where Dan was staring and watched. A beautiful red skinned woman stepped out from between the trees closest to them and smiled. She was naked to the waist save for a heavy covering of leaves, which covered her breasts and privates.

Mark gave a smile and a half bow. "Chakix I presume? The real you this time."

The woman smiled and nodded. "Welcome, Captain Johnson. This is my true form, yes, you are correct. You behold the body of a goddess."

Eddie looked to Dan. "She looks pretty goddess-like to me," Eddie snickered quietly.

Chakix shot him a disapproving glance, but returned her gaze to Mark Johnson. "All is in readiness I see?"

"It is, Chakix. We are fully prepared."

She walked up to him and stared up at his face. "I regret to tell you, Captain Johnson, there has been a change of plans."

"What kind of change?" Mark rumbled menacingly.

"I am sorry. Truly I am, Captain. But I must do what is best for my children which live upon myself, my world."

"Chakix..." Mark growled menacingly.

The brush about them split apart as Agalum troops surrounded everyone in the small clearing. All their weapons were aimed directly at the *Cagliostro*'s crew.

"I once again apologize, Captain, but the Agalum invaders left me no choice."

"Be quiet, Chakix," an Agalum officer commanded. He pushed past her and aimed his gun directly at Mark. "Kill all the others. This one is going to spend the rest of his short life on our home world, telling us all of his savage and crude world's secrets."

Chapter 35

Mark locked eyes with the Agalum who faced him. The purple skinned 'lettuce head' stared down the barrel of his gun toward Mark. "You will witness the deaths of your people, then you will come with us to our base where your very long, very painful interrogation will commence."

Mark smiled. It was a slow, deliberate thing, starting at the corners of his mouth and working its way up his face, while his head dipped lower. "I don't think so."

The air around the small clearing seemed to shimmer for an instant. The Agalum and the natives spun in surprise. Even Chakix was taken aback. Surrounding the clearing were at least fifty of the *Cagliostro*'s crew wearing heavy battle suits. They had weapons aimed directly at the Agalum soldiers, the natives, and Chakix herself.

"H-how?" Chakix stammered.

The heavy suited crew began to disarm the Agalum and restrain the natives as well.

"What, Chakix? Did you really think I could make close fitting camouflage suits like we're wearing, but not be able to add that property to my heavy battle suits as well?" Mark continued to smile. "But to answer your first question, very easily, actually. You overrate your position here, Chakix. Now maybe you could make the ground swallow us all up if you wanted to, but I kind of doubt that will happen because your children would get killed or injured in the fracas as well. As to how I knew you were going to try to double cross us, well let's just say I knew what to look for from you. We had your vessel on board the *Cagliostro* long enough that we were able to study you, surreptitiously of course and discern when you were making contact with your world or larger body or whatever the planet really is to you."

"You studied me?" Chakix almost bellowed in humiliation. "As if I was some base creature?"

"Oh it gets better, Princess. We were ready for you in every way shape and form. When you sent your signal to the planet, looking for this Agalum son of a bitch," Mark jerked his thumb at the officer who stared numbly at him, "Red knew immediately and informed me of it on the command deck. You were standing right there, trying to be oh so slick. Letting your Agalum cronies know we were coming back and where we would meet you. Red and I had a code worked out. He called me 'Captain'. Red never calls me 'Captain'. The *Cagliostro* is just not that kind of ship. We're corporate, not military. But anyway, that was the code word we worked out. You sent that signal that the Agalum knew how to process, and we all knew the game was on. End of story. See, Chakix, we really did not trust you, no matter how long we had you aboard the ship. You proved that caution was the right way to go where you were concerned."

"Now what?" the Agalum officer asked.

"Now you shut up and stay put," Red ordered. "No talking, no moving. Sit on the ground, don't say a word. Unlike you Agalum animals, we won't treat you disrespectfully unless you force us to. As of now you're all prisoners of war."

"That includes you too, Princess." Mark nodded toward Chakix.

"I am a prisoner? Upon myself? My own world? I think not." She began to turn to run, but Ariel stepped forward and punched her in the mouth. Chakix dropped like a bag of stones, clutching her bleeding mouth, her eyes wide in abject shock.

One of the heavy suit wearing crew placed a blocking helmet back on her head, but on her true body this time.

Again shock registered upon her face.

"What? Did you think I only had one of those helmets? I can manufacture as many as I need in the *Cagliostro's* fabrication facilities. The one we used in the other dimension was only the first version prototype. This one is version ten. Yeah, we've been updating it since you came aboard," Mark confirmed. "You're not going anywhere unless we let you."

"Now what?" Eddie asked.

"Now we take that base," Mark replied.

"Good," Red interrupted. "There's twenty men up there in camouflaged heavy suits awaiting your word, *Captain*," he added with the faintest of grins.

"Okay, these bastards are all disarmed?" Mark inquired.

"Yes all of them," Red replied.

"Communication devices too?"

"Yes absolutely."

"Good. Leave twenty men to guard them, including her." Mark pointed at Chakix. "The rest of us are going to take that base."

***

Twenty minutes later, the entire camouflaged phalanx stood fifty yards outside the mouth of the Agalum base.

'We're ready, Mark.' Red announced through the telepathic link supplied by Ariel.

'Okay people, as they used to say, it's go time.'

The heavy suited troops moved off silently toward the side of the false volcano, while the stealth suited contingent waited at the edge of the forest.

Telepathically Mark apprised everyone gathered with him of the their next move. *'Red will move the heavy suited troops to the hangar exit we discovered in subsequent scans of this base the camouflaged probe did. When they begin the attack we hope at least that all of their attention will be drawn over there, allowing us to enter through this hangar deck entrance. We should be able to slip in unnoticed. These stealth suits are silent in every way, as well as undetectable, at least through every method I know of. They are faster than the heavy assault suits and as I said already, silent.'*

'When do we move in?' Eddie asked.

'We'll know as soon as we see the signal.'

'I kinda wish Red was with us and not leading that other assault,' Eddie commented.

Dan chuckled, *'What's the matter, squirt? Afraid? Don't worry about it, I'll protect ya.'*

'Get outta here, you freak,' Eddie snapped back. *'I just don't like us going into a battle without everyone here. It doesn't feel right for us to be split up.'*

'That's the way it's got to be for now, Eddie.' Mark replied. *'Just relax, we should be going-'*

'Mark, look at the entrance,' Dan interrupted.

The entire crew stared where Dan indicated, and saw the Agalum guards running toward the back of the hangar and the exit at the opposite end.

'Time to go, move it,' Mark ordered.

Mark, Dan, Ariel, Eddie, and Dr. Troiano along with the two security people, Dorn and Crosby, moved silently and invisibly toward the hangar doors. Surreptitiously they all entered the base. There were only a handful of Agalum troops left guarding the entrance and the group of seven slipped past undetected.

'This is so not in my job description,' Dr. Troiano telepathically muttered.

'Sorry, Ann. For today it is,' Mark replied.

'Stay near me, Ann, I'll watch out for ya,' Dan offered.

She smiled within her stealth suit, *'Thanks, Danny, you're a gentleman.'*

'Yeah but don't let it get around,' he replied with a smirk.

They continued to move deeper into the dark complex. It was lit with low level lighting throughout.

'Look at the engineerin' in this place,' Dan mentally exclaimed.

'I agree, Dan. This is something amazing. Once we get it under our control we can explore it at our leisure. Right now is not the time.'

'You got it, Boss,' Dan replied tersely.

'Mark,' Ariel called. *'I'm sensing something else headed our way. It looks like a large group of troops are*

281

coming right toward us from where we entered. There must have been a passageway we missed. They're going to run right over us if we don't get out of this hangar area. They're heading toward the back and the rest of the crew outside.'

'Can you contact Red?'

'I'll try, but I'm going to have to shut down with the rest of you to do it, to concentrate my accuracy and mental strength.'

'Just do it. Let me know what happened afterward.'

Ariel nodded and closed her eyes. In the dim yellow glow of the goggles they all wore her hazy image seemed to waver while she concentrated her efforts. Mark stopped a moment and watched her intently even though he knew the squad of Agalum were closing from the rear on them all.

He saw something he had never seen before. Somehow the goggles that allowed them to see one another when camouflaged also allowed him to see her telepathic ability. Her head glowed a brighter yellow, followed by a spike of energy reaching out toward the back of the hangar area, where Red and his men were.

"Amazing," he whispered.

The others turned and looked at him quizzically, then first Dan, followed by Eddie realized what he was looking at. Ann Troiano was the last to see what was happening.

Mark looked behind him and saw the squad of Agalum foot soldiers getting closer. Quickly he shook Ariel's arm, breaking her concentration.

She looked up, saw what was happening, and quickly reconnected with them all. *'I see them coming. Where can we go?'*

Mark looked at his sleeve and an image formed on it. Not a stand-up holographic image like it would on his regular tech suit, but rather one on the sleeve itself, which remained invisible to those without the special goggles he had designed.

'This way. Dorn, Crosby, take point,' he telepathically said.

Everyone followed quietly, the two security personnel at the forefront.

'Left turn in twenty feet,' Mark ordered.

Dorn first, and then Crosby stepped around the corner. Crosby almost immediately stuck her head back around and beckoned everyone to follow her and Dorn.

The remaining five people stepped around and flattened against the back wall of the corridor.

Heavy boots began to thud along the hangar deck and an instant later a large contingent of Agalum appeared, passing right by the camouflaged and veritably invisible crew.

Everyone stood silently, not even bothering to breathe. Soon the large group of Agalum had passed them all by noisily.

'What now? Dorn asked of Mark.

'We head to the base commander's office and take him prisoner. He tells his people to stand down, and we win.'

'What if he won't?' Crosby asked.

'Then we make him. I have no issue with that, do you, Crosby?'

'None whatsoever, Sir,' came her terse reply.

Mark nodded. *'Good, let's move out.'*

Dorn and Crosby took point once again, followed by Dan and Eddie. They continued down the same corridor they had stepped into, when the sound of stomping feet came toward them from around the next bend in the corridor.

'Uh-oh,' Ariel mentally cried. *'They're coming right toward us.'*

'There's nowhere to go,' Eddie commented.

'Tell me somethin' I don't know, short stuff,' Dan grumbled. *'Doc, stay behind me,'* he said as an afterthought, *'Cause all hell's about ta break loose.'*

Troiano looked at Mark and thought, *'You owe me a raise when all of this is over.'*

'If we survive this, it's your,.' Mark replied.

'I'm holding you to that,' Troiano nervously countered.

Chapter 36

Outside the base, Red's heavy assault troops fired everything from blaster rifles to Red's favorite weapon, the handheld energy cannon. They took their toll on their enemy's forces, but what the Agalum missed in technical savvy they made up for in numbers.

"Red, we're starting to get overrun," Security officer Malcom Joiner shouted.

"No kidding Joiner. There's fifty of us but there must five hundred of them."

"What are we gonna do?" Joiner practically begged.

"Keep fightin' till the last man drops, if we have to," came Red's guttural reply.

All about the embattled troopers the Agalum forces began to circle and close in upon them. Red fired his cannon repeatedly, almost non-stop, but it seemed like for every five Agalum the *Cagliostro* troops would take down, ten more would take their place. The Agalum came down upon the small fifty man team in waves, firing concentrated energy blasts of their own upon them.

Joiner called Red once again. "These heavy suits are all that're keepin' us alive."

"Why do you think we're wearin' them, Joiner? The boss knows what he's doing," Red shouted above the roar of battle. Then added almost silently, "I hope."

The battle continued to rage. The small group of fifty began to spread out, slowly backing away from their enemies. There was a plan to all of this, but that plan was badly hampered now without the natives joining them.

But then Red Robinski grinned, something he never did. He had an idea…

***

Above the small green world, the two fleets were engaged in an epic battle. The five remaining Earth ships weathered devastating assaults from almost three times their number of Agalum ships.

"Carlson, bring the *Revenant* around to mark zero two zero one five," Captain Nagata ordered. His own ship, the *Coronado,* rocked violently under multiple attacks.

"Shield status?" Nagata barked.

"Forty five percent and holding, but barely," his security officer advised.

"It'll have to do. Helmsman, bring us about to mark seven zero nine four five."

Again the *Coronado* shuddered savagely from multiple attacks.

"Hold together, girl. Hold together," Nagata muttered.

"Captain, that G'Kor is releasing small fliers, dozens of them," the security man informed Nagata.

"My God, here they come," Nagata whispered.

Akin to bees from a hive, a steady stream of the ships those aboard the *Cagliostro* had battled and called 'Predators' were issuing forth in streams from the remaining G'Kor planet crusher.

"Concentrate all heavy weapons fire on the larger ships. Smaller guns can be brought to bear on the 'Predators'," Nagata commanded his fleet.

"Come through for us, Johnson. A lot of lives are depending on you," Nagata muttered.

***

Deep within the mountain base Mark Johnson and crew slowly made their way down winding passages.

'How much further?' Dan asked.

'According to the intel we received from the probe, we'll be at the communications center as soon as we clear this corner up ahead,' Mark replied.

Still camouflaged and invisible, the crew surreptitiously moved through the darkened hallways, avoiding groups of Agalum workers and officers when they had to.

'I still can't believe how empty this base is,' Ariel commented.

'They're all outside battling Red's troops,' Mark replied.

'I know. Still, it's very empty, Mark, don't you think?' Ariel mentioned.

'She's right, Mark.' Dan agreed, *'This is too empty.'*

'What do you all think? A trap?' Mark queried.

'It's possible, and it's definitely not out of the probable,' Dan offered.

The two security personnel had stealthily padded ahead and stopped by an open section of the wall.

Dorn's deep, basso telepathic voice intruded, *'Sir, this room appears to be exactly what you had surmised. It is their communications hub."*

Mark and the others moved forward invisibly, until they were standing near the edge of the huge opening in the wall, which looked upon the communications hub. Inside the room was filled with Agalum techs with only a few officers near the front of the room, surrounded by several guards.

'How do you want to play this?' Dan asked.

'As planned. We're the invaders and we're outmanned here. We bomb this room.' Everyone nodded their silent agreement.

Dorn and Crosby removed several grenades from their packs, and after Mark nodded his approval, they rolled the grenades into the room, then quickly back peddled out into the hallway.

An instant later the floor rumbled like an Earthquake. Flames shot from the opening to the hallway as screams filled the corridor.

The crew backed up and silently ran back toward the main corridor.

'Where to now?' Eddie asked.

'Now we go to the base commander's office. He either walks out on his own or he gets carried out. It's going to be his choice.'

The group moved quickly through the poorly lit corridors, then turned directly into a group of Agalum soldiers, who were thundering down the corridor toward the devastated communications facility.

There was nowhere for them to go. The troops were heading where they had just come from.

'To hell with it!' Mark telepathically roared. *'Open fire!'*

Dorn, Crosby, and Eddie fired immediately and invisibly, Eddie being the first one on the trigger by a hair.

The Agalum soldiers were taken totally by surprise. Blasts seemingly from nowhere tore through them. They scrambled backward under the withering attack of the *Cagliostro*'s crew.

'Fire and move, don't stay in one spot. Move, move, move,' Mark implored.

The crew split about the hallway, separating and leaving large gaps between themselves. Agalum laser bolts splashed against the walls and floor, but hit no one.

"Find them, kill them!" Shouted an Agalum officer, his purple skin turning a deeper shade driven by his anger.

"I don't think so," Mark replied and dropped the Agalum with one blast of his pistol.

Now panic was careening through the Agalum. They fired where the voice came from en masse. But Mark was no longer there. He and the rest of the crew were running backward the way they had come. Mark looked at his suit's display being played out upon his wrist. *'Back two corridors then left. There's a maintenance passage we can cut through.'*

The group quickly disappeared down the maintenance hatch, shutting it silently behind them.

Back in the corridor they had just escaped from, laser blasts seared the air. The Agalum troops knew they obviously had enemies about, but had no idea where to aim.

"Stop firing, you idiots," a salad headed Agalum ordered. The bald headed purple skins ceased immediately at his command. "They are obviously no longer here," he continued. "Find them and bring me their skins."

The Agalum troops spread out and began cautiously searching for the escaped and so far undetectable enemies who were running rampant within their compound.

***

'Where the heck are we?' Eddie asked.

Mark replied through their telepathic link, *'Maintenance shaft that bridges levels, hence this ladder we're climbing down. We get off at the next level and head across. We probably should have done this to begin with instead of meeting those salad heads straight on.'*

'Hindsight an' all that,' Danny rumbled. He turned toward Ann Troiano. *'Are you okay, Ann?'*

'All I can tell you, Dan, is that this is the most excitement I've had in years, and I don't know if that's a good thing or not.'

Dan smirked. *'Just stay near me like ya did back there, Ann. I'll protect ya.'*

She reached up and hugged his arm, *'Thank you, Danny. If I could reach you I'd give you a kiss right now.'*

Dan blushed beneath his goggles, but replied, *'I'll take a rain check on it fer now, okay?'*

Dr. Troiano nodded and smiled.

They continued their climb down, leaving the ladder behind and now invisibly padding down the dimly lit, circular maintenance tunnel.

'Not to look a gift horse in the mouth, but ain't you guys surprised no one else is scourin' these maintenance tubes yet? I mean they gotta think we ducked down here,' Eddie mused.

'Honestly I'm not that concerned. I'm more worried about exiting this tube into a barrage of Agalum laser fire,' Mark replied while staring at his sleeve and reading the information displayed there. *'We should exit here,'* he announced.

Dorn and Crosby once more took point, cautiously opening the panel from within. They looked outside and stepped out.

'Come out it's clear,' Crosby confirmed.

Within an instance they were all standing in the corridor. *'This way,'* Mark ordered. They all followed, pausing at every corner to stare down long corridors either filled with running Agalum troops or surprisingly empty, with no in between.

Mark held up his hand and hissed mentally, *'Hold up something's happening here.'*

Immediately Dorn and Crosby slid before him, protecting him from whatever he was viewing.

Everyone's eyes widened at what they saw coming toward them.

'Oh no...' Ariel squirmed.

Walking toward them alone in the corridor was a creature out of a nightmare. A monstrous, foul smelling horror they had encountered twice before.

'I see it.' Mark hissed, *'It's a 'Quel'. One of those anti-telepath ghouls we encountered a few years back when all of this began.'*

'Mark I have to get out of here, it'll hear our thoughts.'

But it was too late. The horrible eight foot tall creature turned toward the spot Ari was standing, its gaunt physique spinning about seemingly in slow motion, like a creature out of a fantasy vid. It slowly reached forward, its horribly formed hand and multi jointed fingers flexing toward Ariel. She immediately dropped to the ground clutching her head painfully.

Mark did not hesitate. He pulled his blaster and fired. So did Eddie. Both men looked at one another and nodded. The Quel hit the ground even as its head exploded and splattered the ground about it with gore.

Dan helped Ariel to her feet slowly. She still held her head. Dr. Troiano moved to her side and began speaking to her in a whisper. "Are you all right, Ari? Can you talk?"

"This is a bad spot. We must move," Dorn advised in a hiss.

Mark nodded and whispered, "Agreed, Dorn. Keep your head up, all of you. I may have to carry Ari. The last time we met one of these things Ari defeated it, but the time before that it almost killed her."

"Maybe we should abort the mission," Dan suggested.

'No! I-I'm all right,' Ariel interjected telepathically. "Ari, no, you're still recovering from what Chakix did to you. You should never have come on this mission," Troiano breathed.

'Stop it Ann. I'm, okay I can do this. The team needs me. I can rest when we get home to Earth. I'm okay, really I am,' Ariel retorted, again telepathically.

Mark walked up to her and placed both his hands upon her shoulders. *'Are you certain? We can get out of here and back to the ship. I don't want to lose you. That almost happened once already on this trip. I don't know how many lives you have left, kitty.'* He smiled, hugged her. and patted her head.

'Let's get outta here,' Dan grunted. *'We're in this one spot way too long.'*

'You're right, Dan. Move out. Dorn, Crosby back on point. Follow my directions. We're almost at the base leaders office.'

'What if he's not in there?' Eddie queried.

'He has to be. This place is not run like an Earth base where the commander gives orders surrounded by his subordinates from one central command center. These Agalum leaders give their orders from their private quarters linked to others by their comm system. I learned that much from watching the probe's readouts.'

Mark motioned to Dorn and Crosby, and both moved out heading toward their destination that was hidden far beneath the false and inactive volcano.

'This is it.' Mark halted them. He pointed at a dark wood colored door before them.

Dorn raised his gun and fired. The bolt blasted the door to kindling.

Everyone rushed into the office behind him and Crosby. Then all hell broke loose.

Chapter 37

Outside the base, Red's phalanx of heavy suited crewmen continued to move invisibly through the edges of the deep forest. The Agalum had now begun to try to track their movements through trampled brush and disturbed tree limbs.

But it was to no avail, for each time they came near a member of the *Cagliostro*'s invisible crew, a blast would ring out, killing the Agalum soldier where he stood.

"Now we're cooking with fire," Malcom Joiner hissed. He had a smile plastered across his face within his heavy armored suit. The helmets they each wore obscured the wearer's countenance but Red knew it was there just the same.

"Keep your head in the game, Joiner," Red admonished through the armored suit's comm link.

"Will do, chief," Joiner replied immediately.

"Good man," Red added.

The Agalum stood outside the edge of the forest. The heavy suits' sensors depicted them within the helmets.

"What are they doing?" Bennet, one of the other crewmen, asked.

Red didn't answer, but something was wrong and he knew it.

"Back up, all of you. Fast, something's going on here."

The men ran backward, holding their weapons at the ready. What came next they weren't ready for. Over four hundred Agalum troops raised their weapons and fired into the forest, burning it to the ground.

"Run, move!" Red shouted.

En masse the crew retreated back as laser blasts lit up the dense foliage.

"Oh no," Red murmured.

He heard it coming before he had seen it.

The woods about them lit up with laser fire from an Agalum Predator. It swooped down from the heavens and unleashed hell on the *Cagliostro*'s camouflaged troops, decimating the forest. It was reduced to kindling in seconds.

"Damn it," Red growled. He dragged Joiner to his feet from where he had fallen next to him. "Get up, Mister. Shake it off. This armor protected you as much as it did me. Now move out, all of you!"

Moving swiftly through the group, Red grabbed men and shoved them forward, pulling many to their feet. Joiner and Bennet aided him now, as did more and more of the stunned crew. They roused those who received more of the damage from the attack than they did.

"Is everyone okay? This armor should have protected us at least that one time, though I wouldn't count on it a second. If that refractive coating gets burned off we're goners."

The men all nodded or called out their continued existence.

"Okay everyone made it through, which I figured. It's time to back up, maybe draw these bastards back with us. They still don't see us. At least the camouflage is working yet. But I-"

Screams intruded upon Red's speech and without hesitation he ran straight for the sound. To a man his troopers followed him as closely as possible.

But Red Robinski was a unique individual. He was already strong and athletic. The suit he was wearing only added to that. He leaped through the tough, packed woods like an Olympian sprinter, leaving the others almost immediately behind.

"Whoa, look at him go!" Bennet exclaimed over his communicator.

"Keep your head in the mission, Bennet," Red ordered from up ahead.

"You got it, Sir," Bennet replied.

Red pulled up short when he entered a familiar clearing.

"My God," he muttered.

"What is it, Sir?" Joiner queried.

"They killed the natives, all of them. The ones we had restrained here, including Chakix."

"What about the guards we left behind?" Joiner asked.

"Here, but stunned. I think their armor protected them as much as it did us."

"That Predator is circling back around for a second shot," one of the other men shouted.

Red spun and immediately pinpointed the incoming craft.

"Everyone back beyond the tree line now. I want all weapons fully charged and aimed at that thing when it gets into range. You fire on my mark!"

The crewmen scrambled back to the trees on the opposite side of the clearing. They all lay down amongst thick foliage that was left standing and was not a burning disaster.

"We're only going to get one shot at this. If this thing fires on us we're as good as dead." Red propped up his canon and began overloading it, bypassing the safeties and pushing its charge well beyond the safe level, as he had done earlier aboard the *Cagliostro* against the robots that had been left there. "This bastard is too close to the tree tops to be running with his shields on. He's strafing us and the natives. He can't see us yet. Without his shields that ship is vulnerable to a concentrated attack."

Red slung his cannon off of his shoulder and began readjusting the settings on the digital interface. "All of you set your weapons to one hundred and ten percent."

"Aren't they going to explode like that?" Bikowski, a female security trooper, asked.

"Not if we discharge them first. All rifles and blast cannons skyward. We have to hit him before he hits us. That means we can't wait for him to get directly above us. Aim for the belly of this thing. Hold onto your pistols, they're not going to be any good here anyway. Here it comes!"

The Predator circled overhead and then finally began its strafing run.

"Don't fire until I order you. This bastard still can't see us and thinks he's finishing off the natives."

"What about the rest of the enemy soldiers? Are they still heading our way?" Bennet asked.

"Forget them for now. Here he comes, weapons up and hot!"

The Predator swooped low, beginning its strafing run. Before it could attack Red shouted, "Fire!"

298

The fifty men and women from the *Cagliostro* fired their overloaded weapons as one. The energy blasts leaped from their weapons and slammed into the Predator. So powerful was the concentrated blast that it tore the underside of the craft open and sent it careening into the forest tumbling end over end and trailing smoke until it came to an abrupt stop at least a mile away.

"What happened? Why'd that ship attack the prisoners here? Some of their own people were among them," Bikowski asked. She pulled off her helmet and a mane of blonde hair fell out.

"Because the Agalum are animals, Bikowski. Life doesn't mean a damned thing to them, not even their own. Now get your head gear back on. We've got hundreds of Agalum back beyond that ridge line and probably heading our way now that their ship went down."

"Why aren't they here already?" Joiner asked.

Red snapped his gloved fingers. "Of course. Mark took out their communications center. These guys are firing in the dark. They have no idea what to do because they can't get in touch with their superiors."

"That doesn't make them any less dangerous though," Bennet added.

"No, but maybe it's time we used their tactics against them." Red keyed his comm. "Robinski to the *Cagliostro*, do you copy, Marek?"

Instantly Matt Marek replied, "Yes Red, go."

"Matt, we need an airstrike on our position. We've got four hundred and change Agalum thugs heading our way. We just took out a Predator and are down to our hand guns. Can you fulfill the airstrike?"

Without hesitation Marek replied, "We're on our way."

"How long do you think till they get here?" Bikowski asked.

"I'm not sure, Robin. It could be five minutes, it could be less," Red answered.

"I hope it's sooner, because here they come," she added.

Robin Bikowski shook her blonde mane of hair out and dropped her helmet to the grassy forest floor beneath her feet. Red grimaced at that but kept his attention focused on the quickly approaching oncoming horde.

"On my mark," Red ordered.

The Agalum soldiers stepped closer, brandishing their own laser weapons. Red grimaced beneath his helmet and barked, "Now!"

The fifty crewmembers fired in unison, sweeping their blasters from left to right together. The first group of Agalum went down screaming, but there were still over four hundred enemy warriors approaching the mere fifty on the ground.

"Keep firing," Red commanded. "Back up after each wave. Bikowski, get that helmet back on your head now!"

She stooped low to pick it up and was instantly hit in the shoulder by a stray laser bolt.

"Aaagghh!" She shrieked, grasping her smoking shoulder as she fell.

"Her armor's compromised, get her out of here!" Red shouted. Two more troopers picked her up and carried her moaning form out of the line of fire and dragged her deeper into the woods.

"C'mon Matt, where are you?" Red growled.

He reached into a compartment on his armor and retrieved a grenade. Without hesitation he hurled it at the troops in front of him. The resultant explosion knocked a dozen screaming men into the air. Before Red could enjoy his small victory another dozen attackers surged forward and opened fire on his camouflaged position.

"Shit!" he exclaimed and began scrambling backward while laser blasts fell all about him.

The entire fifty man crew was now in full retreat as almost ten times their number was gaining on them and pushing their advantage.

"We're dead if the *Cagliostro* doesn't get here now," Joiner commented.

Red said nothing, but continued to back up and fire his blaster. He reached back into his suit and produced three more grenades, throwing each of them whenever the Agalum got too close.

All too soon he was out. Like an angry pack of wolves the Agalum approached their invisible enemies, firing their weapons indiscriminately.

Many more of Red's people fell, wounded. The refractory coating was clearly burned off their heavy suits by the powerful Predator ship's attack. Still, those able to stand and fight did so.

"We can't back up any further. We'd be leaving people behind and I refuse to do that. Keep fighting. It's do or die!" Red shouted.

The Agalum kept coming toward them, slowly, methodically firing their lasers. Some of the heavy armor suits' camouflage units were beginning to fail from the damage wrought by the Agalum.

Then the sky exploded in fury and thunder from
behind the backed up group. With a blinding blast of
heat and light the *Cagliostro* flew overhead, strafing the
ground and burning the Agalum forces to ash where they
stood. The shadow cast by the thousand foot long ship
stunned both sides of the fray. The *Cag* spun around in
midair and lowered itself until it hovered twenty feet
above the ground. From its bottom a telescoping
maglovator reached down and kissed the ground. "Ten at
a time please," Lily Wallflower's voice advised.

"Hurry it up," Red countered. "We have wounded."
"Everyone else back to back with me surrounding the
maglovator until the wounded are safely onboard."

"I hope the boss and the others are doing okay,"
Joiner thought aloud.

"I'm worried about them too, but they ain't the only
one's I'm concerned about," Red replied.

He turned his eyes skyward and watched as the blue
sky above was lit up by bright explosions in space.

Chapter 38

"Get those forward guns back online!" Nagata shouted.

"Working on it, Sir," came his engineers' static filled reply.

"My God, they're everywhere," The *Coronado*'s comm officer breathed.

On the main view screen dozens of small Predator craft filled space, forcing the five remaining EPIC battle cruisers away from their Agalum counterparts.

"Once we get far enough away from that G'Kor, it can use its big gun on us. Then no matter how tough our shields are we'll be done for," Captain Argento growled from the Tempest's command deck.

"I am aware, Argento," Nagata tersely replied.

"We have to retreat," Carlson advised.

"We can't. We're close to gaining control of this world. We have to see this through!"

"It's no good Nagata. We just lost forward shields," Jepson on the *Eagle's Claw* interrupted. "We're breaking off the attack."

"You fool, they won't let you. Don't turn your back to them," Nagata implored.

But it was too late even as the big battle ship turned to put some distance between it and its attackers, the Agalum ships, Predator attack craft and larger ships alike ,opened fire and concentrated on the *Eagle's Claw*. The explosion was both horrific and spectacular.

"No!" shouted Nagata, while leaping from his chair.

It was too late. The *Eagle's Claw* had joined the *Tempest*. Both were destroyed.

"All remaining ships form up together. We'll strengthen our shields by being in close proximity," Nagata commanded.

"Oh no," Nagata's security officer moaned.

"What is it?" Nagata demanded.

"Captain! That G'Kor, it's turning toward us and its main gun is starting to power up. Even with the ships tightly packed together, our shield strength won't be enough to survive that."

Nagata gritted his teeth while a million possible thoughts ran through his mind trying to find a way to avoid certain death.

***

Mark, Dan, Ariel, Eddie, and Dr. Troiano followed Dorn and Crosby into the headquarters of the head of the Agalum base. The moment they stepped through the doorway laser blasts began burning the air about them. Inside and tightly packed were a score of troops. Even though the *Cagliostro*'s crew was camouflaged and invisible they were in a confined space. Dorn and Crosby each caught laser blasts. While the stealth suits were derived from the standard tech suit Mark had developed to resist energy blasts and afforded its wearer some protection, the repeated blasts that hit Dorn and Crosby were too much, too close together. Both dropped to the floor of the Agalum leader's office, their bodies smoking from multiple laser blasts.

"Back!" shouted Mark. He lobbed another grenade into the office and ran back into the hallway, ducking low and pulling Ariel and Troiano underneath him an instant before the explosion shook the walls and sprayed everyone with debris from its concussion.

Dan was the first one back through the door, followed by Eddie. Inside it was carnage and devastation. Dead Agalum were everywhere. Dorn and Crosby's bodies were buried beneath the detritus.

Mark pushed past Dan to the desk at the back of the room. Atop it were controls built into its surface and it was relatively unscathed.

"What is all of this?" Mark muttered aloud. Ariel joined him while Dan and Troiano stood together near Dorn and Crosby's bodies. Eddie stood just inside the doorway scanning the corridor.

"It looks like monitors and cameras throughout the complex," Ariel replied.

Mark looked up. "Did any of you find the Agalum leader amongst the dead?"

"No, Mark, unless he's one of these guys," Eddie answered from the doorway.

"No, he'd have to be a yellow skin. You know what I'm talking about, with the full black eyes."

Both men and the Doctor looked about at the bodies all around them.

"There's no one here like that," Troiano replied.

Ariel pointed at one of the monitors embedded in the desktop. "Look."

Mark followed where her finger pointed and saw a yellow skinned Agalum running through a storage room.

"Dammit, he had an escape hatch somewhere around here," Mark growled. "Step back, Ari."

He began firing his blaster at the floor behind the desk, then at the walls, burning away the veneer. Within seconds he found the disguised hatchway at his feet. "Stay back," he ordered Ariel. Stepping back himself, he turned his blaster all the way up and fired. The hatchway melted into atoms instantly.

"C'mon," he ordered. Mark jumped through the still smoldering hatch into the hidden corridor below. Ariel followed him. Dan was next, followed by Dr. Troiano and then Eddie, but both men stopped with the Doctor pinned between them before jumping down and stared at the desk with the monitors built into its top. They both looked at the same monitor and the room it showed.

"Are you seein' this, squirt?" Dan asked.

"Hell yes, amigo," Eddie replied.

"What is it?" Ann Troiano asked.

"Hang on Doc," Dan ordered before he touched his sleeve and activated his comm. "Mark, I just saw something up here on this desk top that you better take a look at."

"What is it? Fill me in on the run."

Eddie watched the monitors and the same one that showed the yellow skinned Agalum leader running past a few minutes ago now showed Mark and Ariel passing its camera by.

"Mark, this whole base, the fake volcano. It's all a weapon."

"What? What do you mean?"

"There's a room that's emptying out now. The techs within it are abandoning the base with everyone else. It's a control room for the weapon."

"But what weapon? What are you talking about?" Mark pressed. He was continuing to run, with Ariel doing her best to keep up behind him.

"The top of the volcano, it's a weapon. They must have never fired it, maybe it was never ready, but it looks like it's just been completed recently. The cone of the volcano is no cone. It's the barrel of an energy cannon. They could take ships out of orbit with this thing."

Mark stopped running and stood stock still while what he was just told sank in. He turned around toward Ariel. Her eyes widened in surprise as she shouted, "Mark look out!"

Mark turned but too late. A laser blast rang out from the darkness catching Mark Johnson fully in the back and dropped him agonizingly to the floor.

Chapter 39

Mark writhed in pain on the floor. His stealth suit shorted out and he immediately came into view. Even so, his stealth suit's resistance to weaponry saved him from an instant death.

"So this is the great Mark Johnson of Earth. The Scourge of the Agalum Empire," The yellow skinned alien stepped from behind shelves filled with supplies, still holding his laser.

"I assume you have an accomplice hidden here as well. Someone else I cannot see with the naked eye. It doesn't matter. I can see you now, and I can just as easily blow your head off of your shoulders, no matter what the standing orders from the high command may be."

The yellow skinned Agalum aimed its laser at Mark's head when a blast of energy appeared out of empty space. It caught him square in the chest and blasted him back through a pile of crates. His weapon careened off into the darkness.

Ariel shimmered into view with her gun still aimed toward the direction the Agalum disappeared in.

"I was wondering when you were going to show up," Mark croaked painfully. He pulled himself to his feet. "I have to find this guy. I can't let him get away."

"You can barely walk. Forget him. If he's not dead he's not in good shape, and he lost his weapon. We'll find him later," she implored.

Mark winced and begrudgingly turned back toward the hatch they had dropped though. They cautiously walked down the darkened corridor between two sets of shelves with boxes stacked on either side; all the while searching for the missing Agalum base commander.

While they searched a box abruptly dropped from the top shelf. Mark threw himself between it and Ariel, knocking her aside. His blaster careened out of his grip, disappearing under more shelving. As she fell Ariel hit her head and was instantly unconscious.

"Ari!" Mark shouted.

The box of equipment had caught him squarely on the shoulder. He was pained but still able to move. The Agalum they had been looking for dropped down from above, a malicious smile plastered across his foul bright yellow face.

Chapter 40

Mark slowly stood up to his full height. His back and shoulder ached terribly. The Agalum faced him and smiled a pencil thin grin of evil. Both men were approximately the same height, though the Agalum looked heavier, thicker than Mark.

"So, Mark Johnson, we are both weaponless, and both of us are wounded, but it seems you more so than I. I will make this short and as painless as possible."

The Agalum lunged toward Mark with both his hands outstretched for Mark's throat. Johnson ducked under the two handed grab and chopped his own arms upward, snapping both of his enemies hands ceiling-ward.

Before the enemy could react Mark smashed a right legged Thai kick into his foe's gut.

The Agalum immediately stumbled backward. Then it reversed position. Spinning left he kicked out at Mark's legs sweeping the right out from under him. Mark hit the ground with a thud and a groan, slapping out with both arms to cushion the fall.

The Agalum lunged again at Mark. This time Mark caught him by his shirt and stuck his foot in his opponent's stomach, throwing him overhead. The Agalum landed with a thud behind Mark.

Mark fought his way to his feet but so did his enemy.

"You are a trained fighter, Mark Johnson. Good, good. I would like to see what an enemy can do before I kill them," the yellow skinned fiend drawled.

"Come and find out," Mark growled.

The two enemies circled each other both looking for an opening.

The Agalum lunged again, this time with a right cross. Mark stepped left and parried the blow with his left hand. Grasping it with his right he pulled the fist through, throwing his foe off balance while hammering him with a powerful left.

But Mark did not stop there. He grabbed the Agalum's shirt and pulled him toward himself, slamming his knee into his enemy's stomach. He finished with a strong short chop to the base leader's neck. The leader dropped to the ground at Mark's feet. Mark stumbled backward huffing slightly.

"Th-this is not over, Johnson," the yellow skinned alien groaned. The Agalum leader fought his way to his feet and began to pull his fist back, but Mark was much faster. He stepped forward and unleashed a powerful right cross, smashing his enemy across the left side of the face. His eyes fluttered and the Agalum fell to the ground, unconscious.

"Sure it is, Smiley," Mark quipped.

"Oooh, my head."

Mark spun around and found Ariel grasping her forehead, struggling to her feet.

"Easy there babe. I've got you." He held her tight for a moment, and then relaxed. "Let's get Troiano to look at you before we go anywhere."

"I already called her," Ari replied.

"You did? I didn't see-" Then Mark paused and smiled. Ari was holding two fingers to her forehead smiling.

Mark shrugged. "I suppose sometimes I *do* forget."

Dan's telepathic voice exploded in Marks mind.
'Mark, we've got a situation up here you better take a look at.'

'On my way, Danny, but I need you to come down here and take care of a package that needs restraining.'

'On my way, Boss. We saw the whole thing on the monitors.'

'Oh really? And what? You didn't think to lend a hand?'

'We were on our way but you finished him off before we could get down the hatchway.'

'All right, Danny, just come down here and find something to tie this guy up with. I don't want him getting away.'

Mark put his arm around Ariel and smiled. "I see your telepathy is working fine."

"Yes, I'm okay, just a little banged up. We better get upstairs I'm sensing a lot of urgency from them." She motioned with her thumb toward the floor above.

They hurriedly climbed the short staircase to the leader's quarters, passing Dan as he ran toward the unconscious Agalum commander.

"What is it, Eddie?" Mark asked as they reentered the room.

"Here, Mark look. This is the battle in orbit."

Mark stared silently for a moment watching the embattled Earth ships careening through space, swarmed over by the Predators while trying to avoid the remaining G'Kor. A bright flare exploded across the monitor. Mark punched the top of the desk in anger and despair. "That was the Tempest. Dammit. Can we do anything to help them?"

"I think we can," Eddie replied. "But we have to do it fast."

Eddie ran out into the corridor of the now abandoned base, followed closely by Mark, Ariel, Troiano, and the just returned Dan, who had deposited the still unconscious yellow skinned Agalum leader on the ground. He was now wrapped up in steel shelving material that Dan had found below.

"What's the plan?" Dan asked.

"That weapon control room, it's right here," Eddie replied.

He turned a corner and pulled up short. Twin laser blasts scorched the air mere inches from the top of Eddie's head.

But Eddie had dropped into a crouch, pulling his own blaster at the instant he recognized trouble. He fired two quick blasts and the same number of bodies could be heard smacking lifelessly to the floor.

Eddie twirled his blaster and holstered it smoothly. "C'mon," he urged them.

They raced around the entrance into the weapon control room, past the two dead Agalum.

"The weapon's controlled from here."

"What weapon? What are you talking about?

"We tried to tell you before," Dan continued. "This volcano is an energy cannon of some kind. They must use the thermal energy of the volcano to power it."

"My God, that's insane," Mark exclaimed.

Troiano looked at the men, then helped Ariel into a vacant seat. "Sit a minute, Ari. Let me look at your head." She thumbed up the integrated medical scanner on her stealth suit and ran its beam around Ariel.

"No concussion, I think you're okay."

Mark had one ear on Troiano and Ariel and the other on what was going on with Eddie and Dan. Quickly Dan activated a monitor and pinpointed the battle in space. Mark began priming the weapon itself. "I hope we're doing this right."

"Hey if anyone can figure this out on the fly it's the two of us," Dan replied.

"The G'Kor is coming into range now," Eddie notified them.

"This looks like it's ready," Mark announced. "I hope you two are right about this."

"That ship is building its charge up. It's going to fire on Nagata and the fleet," Dan shouted.

"Fire, Eddie!" Mark ordered.

Eddie hit the alien button with his thumb.

***

The last of the injured had just boarded the *Cagliostro* when the air about the volcano turned bright orange. "What the hell?" Red exclaimed. "Get us outta here, Samuels."

Barton Samuels didn't hesitate. He slammed the throttle forward and the *Cagliostro* darted away from the mountain. A heartbeat later a shaft of energy leapt from the cone of the volcano and streaked spaceward.

***

Even as the G'Kor class ship was powering its weapons, it was torn in half by a quarter mile wide beam of light.

The crews on all the Earth ships covered their eyes as view screens automatically compensated for the sudden, intense blinding brightness.

"What in God's name was that?" Nagata questioned.

His crewmen merely shook their heads dumbfounded.

A moment later he got his answer.

"Captain," the comm officer called, "Captain Johnson of the *Cagliostro* is requesting to speak to you."

Chapter 41

Several hours later, The *Cagliostro* sat quietly cooling in a field near the volcano turned weapon. In its conference room Mark and the remaining Captains compared notes.

"A weapon that size, it boggles the mind," Carlson admitted.

"It wasn't theirs either. Someone designed that for the Agalum. This is more of the same tech we saw already with the Predator ships," Mark commented.

"Those ships are dangerous and deadly. We're going to need a counter measure to them. We can't rely on luck if we're going to win this war," Nagata opined.

Mark agreed. "You're right, Captain. I already have a few things in mind based on what I've seen of their capabilities and the scans I managed to do of the one that fell into our hands."

"Good," Argento nodded. "You keep doing what you're doing out here, Captain Johnson. You're our ultimate secret weapon against these alien creatures."

"I have no intention of stopping, believe me Captains. One other thing to bear in mind, there's a new player in all of this and possibly two. The first one is an unknown. They're supplying the Agalum with weapons and technology that might be a level up from what I'm building. They may have just taken the upper hand in this war."

"You mentioned two. Who's the second?" Ryan asked.

"We had an engine malfunction. You'll all get the report when I get ten minutes to actually write it. We ended up in another dimension. One of purple space and clouds floating within it. It was filled with a race of ghoulish beings that took some of my crew hostage. They were called the Tahir Ga'Warum. We rescued the crew and returned here. We also did a lot of damage along the way. Their starship was organic in a strange way. Almost as if it was grown around its steel frame. They were horrible, grotesque creatures. They looked like old interpretations of ghouls or vampires or some such creature."

Mark paused a moment to gather his thoughts and then continued, "Honestly I hate to admit it, but I'm getting shivers running down my spine just thinking about them now. They actually crawled all over one another when they were coming for us like snakes. If they discover a way to come to our dimension we'll have another major threat on our hands."

The other captains were silent a moment as they mulled over what Johnson had just told them.

"What of...Chakix? Was that her name?" Captain Ryan asked.

"Yes. It seems the Agalum killed her where we had her tied and secured. We had a dampening helmet on her so I doubt she could have left her body. I'd have to say I *believe* she's dead."

"You don't sound convinced?" Nagata noticed.

"There was this...ape. A giant hundred foot tall red furred thing. We haven't found it yet. It disappeared during all the chaos. We think maybe she hitched a ride with it mentally. It's hiding from us somehow. We can't find hide nor hair of it with all of our advanced sensors. It's possible she placed her consciousness within it, but we don't know. We found her body that she claimed was her real form, and we had it mind dampened with that helmet I rigged up. But anything's possible."

Nagata stood. "Indeed it is, Captain Johnson. As we're standing here is proof of that."

The captains all shook hands.

"One last thing?" Mark stopped them. "Call me Mark."

***

Back on the command deck, Mark relieved Matt Marek. "Thanks, Matt. I've got it from here."

"Sure thing, Boss. Call me if you need me," Marek replied. He headed for the maglovator with a nod toward Ariel and the others.

Mark slid into his Captains chair and relaxed.

"So? How'd it all pan out?" Eddie asked.

"The *Triumphant* and the *Crossbow* will stay here until EPIC can place a complete crew in this base. Nagata and the *Coronado* are leaving now to return to Earth. He'll take point on that."

"Carlson and the *Revenant* are going back to Earth also for refits and repairs, which we need to finish once we arrive there as well."

"When do we lift off?" Ariel asked.

Mark turned toward Dan, who was sitting at his pilots/engineers station, "What do you say, Danny?"

Sledge swiveled his seat around. "All systems are a go, Boss man."

"Mark," Ariel began, "After everything we were just through, did we actually make any headway against the Agalum? Did we really win or do anything that matters?"

Without hesitation Mark replied, "Yes Ariel, we won a major victory today, but this war is far from over," Mark observed. "What we did was take a base away from them that was on our celestial doorstep. We have to start striking against the Agalum on their own turf. We have to make inroads to their galaxy and we have to find their home world. They know where we live but in two years of fighting against them we haven't gotten any closer to discovering where they're from. With their mysterious new benefactor they may have gotten the edge on us they needed."

Ariel quickly turned in her seat to stare at Mark, her wavy blonde hair following her. "You can't be serious? No matter what these Agalum throw at us we'll beat them. We have you. That's the one variable they cannot match."

Mark smiled. "That's what I love about you, Ari. You cut right to the point and don't feel bad about letting me know what you think."

"It's the truth, Mister. You are our one best shot at winning this war once and for all, no matter how long it takes."

Mark got out of his seat and leaned forward. He kissed her gently. "Thanks for the vote of confidence."

"Like you needed anymore," she snickered.

"No, not really. I actually do have more than enough in buckets." Mark turned back toward Dan Sledge. "Danny, it's time to go home. Light it up."

"With pleasure, Boss man."

The *Cagliostro* lifted upward vertically then turned on edge and shot toward space,

"Red, how's deep space look? Anything you see coming our way we should be concerned with?"

"Not a thing, Mark. Sensors are reading all clear, for now at least. Tomorrow's another story."

Mark chuckled. "Agreed, Red. Let's get out of here. Mr. Sledge, take us home."

"Gladly Boss, gladly."

Dan engaged the hyper-warp and the *Cagliostro* disappeared in a burst of light.

The Cagliostro Chronicles 2: Conflagration

Epilogue

Days later, in the exact quadrant of space the *Cagliostro* had left its dimension from, static lightning flashed, space rippled and tore. A horrific blood red vessel that seemed more alive than mechanical flew through that tear. It halted its progress for the longest time, as if its crew were looking about. Then in a burst of crimson energy it disappeared. The Tahir Ga'Warum had arrived. Woe be unto us all...

The End...
For Now...

The Cagliostro Chronicles II Appendix

Agalum- Alien race, the enemies
Barton Samuels-A pilot aboard the Cagliostro.
Barukt: Captive alien Tahir Ga'Warum.
Bennet- Another security personnel
Captain Argento of the 'Crossbow'
Captain Brennan of the 'Tempest'
Captain Carlson, Captain of the 'Revenant'
Captain Jepson of the 'Eagle's Claw'
Captain Nagata, Captain of The 'Coronado'
Captain Ryan of the 'Triumphant'
Chakix-Alien intelligence of the planet they are trapped on.
Colm Maxwell: Technician
Dr. Ann Troiano: The Cagliostro's diminutive ships doctor. She stands a mere five feet tall. Has long black hair and looks almost pixie-ish. She's generally a happy person and enjoys her job aboard the Cagliostro. She's thin with rosy cheeks.
EPIC- Earth Protectorate Interstellar Command
G'Kor class ship- Huge alien battle ship approximately a mile and a half long. Shaped like a block of cement and just as stylish. Capable of destroying worlds.
Lilly or Lilac Wallflower- Junior Comm officer
Lori Westin- Junior Comm Officer
Madison Monroe: Exo-Biologist aboard the Cgaliostro
Major Matt Marek: former Major in the space force, and Mark's secondary command crew leader.
Malcom Joiner: A security officer.

Monotriglycine: Special ore that is needed to repair the magno-disc engines.

Robin Bikowski: Female security trooper

Star Core Missiles: Missiles aboard the Cagliostro and the Stargrazer

Security Officer Crosby: Cagliostro female Security Officer. Tough as nails and no nonsense.

Security Officer Dorn: Cagliostro Security Officer. Red's second in command in the security division. A grim faced black man. Very good at his job as well.

Tahir Ga'Warum: Alien race that resembled ghouls or vampires.

Tridar- Advanced scanning and sensor system of Mark's design.

Other books by Ralph L. Angelo Jr

- Redemption of the Sorcerer, The Crystalon Saga, Book One: A mighty sorcerer and ruler of his world is deposed and exiled to a world identical to his own, save for one difference, magic doesn't exist there. Now he must fight against seemingly insurmountable odds to regain his powers in time to save both parallel universes from utter destruction. ISBN# 0615763030
- Torahg the Warrior, Sword of Vengeance: In a land before recorded time, a world of warriors, monsters and wizards, a young prince is framed for the death of his father by his own evil brother and riven to exile. For twenty long years he wanders the world, until finally he is coaxed into returning to his homeland seeking justice for his father and bloody revenge for himself. ISBN# 1490516263
- The Cagliostro Chronicles: In the depths of space awaits danger for all mankind. When man's first faster than light space flight begins, it opens up a whole new universe for mankind. But it is a universe filled hostile enemies as well as a century-long conspiracy against humanity. Will mankind survive? ISBN# 0615854427
- Help! They're All Out to Get Me! The Motorcyclists Guide to Surviving the Everyday World: A Non-fiction motorcycle

safety and instructional manual for the new
and returning riders. A 'Must Read' for those
seeking to better their motorcycling
experience. ISBN# 0615756786

- My Enemy, Myself, The Crystalon Saga,
  Book Two: It has been two years since
  Crystalon defeated the mad warlord Maceyis.
  Much has changed in that time. Crystalon has
  become his adopted world's hidden mystic
  guardian, protecting the Earth from those
  who would threaten it with evil, sorcerous
  intent.
  Until a visitor from his past, one he never
  expected to see again would appear within his
  very home. Now he and his companions must
  travel between worlds to his home dimension,
  a universe where he is hated and feared, to
  face a threat that dwarfs any challenge he has
  ever faced before. The challenge of an enemy
  who wears his very face. The challenge of
  'My Enemy, Myself'. ISBN# 149950523X

If you enjoyed 'The Cagliostro Chronicles II: Conflagration' then be sure to check out the first book in this star spanning, action packed series, available at Amazon.com and other fine book sellers across the galaxy!